RIFT

RIFT

richard cox

BALLANTINE BOOKS • NEW YORK

Rift is a work of fiction. Names, places, and incidents are
the products of the author's imagination or are used fictitiously.
Any resemblance to actual events, locales, or persons, living or
dead, is entirely coincidental.

A Ballantine Book
Published by The Random House Publishing Group

Copyright © 2004 by Richard Cox

All rights reserved under International and Pan-American
Copyright Conventions. Published in the United States by
Ballantine Books, an imprint of The Random House Publishing
Group, a division of Random House, Inc., New York, and
simultaneously in Canada by Random House
of Canada Limited, Toronto.

Ballantine and colophon are registered trademarks of
Random House, Inc.

www.ballantinebooks.com

Library of Congress Cataloging-in-Publication Data is available
from the publisher upon request.

ISBN 0-345-46283-1

Manufactured in the United States of America

2 4 6 8 9 7 5 3 1

First Edition

Book design by Julie Schroeder

For Sue

acknowledgments

As many books do, *Rift* has lived through countless changes, and even a few overhauls. I'd like to thank the friends and associates who helped make it what it is.

I owe Ed Stackler a debt of gratitude for sharpening my vision and my writing, and introducing me to the world of publishing; he is a talented and truly generous man. Matt Bialer, my agent, who believed in the manuscript and whose suggestions vastly improved it. Mark Tavani, my editor, whose enthusiasm for *Rift* surprised and delighted me.

For believing in my lifelong dream, for polishing my rough patches, for enduring the emotional storm that accompanies the compulsion to write fiction, for her love and compassion and understanding, I graciously thank Elaine La Fontaine.

My mom, who early on encouraged me to read, and my dad, who instilled in me the work ethic and persistence to see this through to the end. My sister, Chanda, for her love and encouragement, and my brother, Brandon, for his straightforward support. Eric Romero, for the per diem; you always knew it was for me. Abbie Peraza, whose intelligence and razor-sharp insight helped my writing (and, consequently, me) find another level.

Special thanks to Chera Kimiko for her love and support as the book neared publication.

And last, for suggestions that in one way or another made it into the story: Brian Weir, Jeff and Laurie Keeley, Scott Rubin, Larry Pfaff, Paul Gilmartin, Natalie Matheson, David Warren, Shawna Prather, Jennifer Sternberg, and Chris Logan.

Of course any factual errors in the book are mine.

RIFT

one

▌▐▌

I have this recurring dream. It involves my own death. My funeral, really. The service is held at Hemingford Unity Cemetery, where every so often a body is hidden in the red clay north of Wichita Falls, Texas. I suppose this particular cemetery was chosen because my father lies there, and because I will eventually bury my mother's body beside his. But did Misty really think I belonged with them? I've lived in Houston for nearly twenty years now, and the drive to Wichita Falls is not short.

The first sign of something wrong is the number of attendees. My wife and my mother and two uncles are here. My best friend, Tom Bishop, is here. And a minister, but of course he was hired to come.

The images generated by my subconscious are impressive in detail. A great, ageless oak tree casts a skeleton shadow across the congregation. Rows of headstone soldiers stand guard over long-dead namesakes. And beside my casket stands a mound of dirt covered with a blanket of synthetic grass.

What's missing is the eulogy. The hired minister finishes his prepared words and looks to pass the baton to the next participant. But no one steps forward. I guess Misty thought Tom would say something, and I guess he thought she would do the honors. My mom suffers from Alzheimer's disease, so no one would have mistaken her for the speaker.

Finally the minister asks someone, anyone, to come forward and say a few words for the deceased. Misty and Tom briefly exchange glances and then ignore each other. The uncles watch red dirt ruin their wingtips. My mother just stares into space, probably remembering the time when she was eight and someone in school set her only pair of shoes on fire.

"Very well, then," the minister says and walks away.

After a moment the handful of mourners wander to their cars, fire up engines, and leave the cemetery. I remain with a bearded groundskeeper, who removes the synthetic turf, lowers the casket, and shovels red clay back into the hole from where it came.

Recently I saw a therapist and told him about the dream.

"So," he asked, "do you think this dream might have something to say about you?"

"It seems obvious," I said. "I feel like I'm not doing anything with my life."

"Yet you seem relatively successful to the outside observer—six-figure household income, beautiful wife. What exactly should you be doing?"

My answer was silence. I was either unable or unwilling to think of something.

A couple of days went by, the question still unanswered, and eventually I mentioned my concerns to Misty. She delivered an Ann Landers–esque quote that has increasingly and alarmingly become her standard response to any unpleasant matter she encounters.

"Something will come up," she said. "It always does."

Two days later Batista made me the offer, and I've never seen my wife wish so badly that she had been wrong.

Channel-surfing on our bedroom TV is doing nothing to take the edge off. It's not like I haven't agonized over this decision to the point of absurdity, but today is the day, after all.

Now is the time.

I've already passed by three "talk" shows, and while I've seen a lot of shouting and a fair amount of screaming, I've yet to encounter any talking.

I flip absently, past a baseball game and an infomercial and a *Star Trek* installment, on my way to CNN when I happen upon a televangelist.

". . . lost, just like I was lost, that's right, *just like I was lost.* When I lived in that sin-infested town, that Babel nestled among the hills and jutting into the bay like an angry finger, like a vile *middle finger* thrust hatefully into the air . . ."

I can't remember seeing this particular fellow before, but here in Texas, TV preachers are as common as houseflies. According to the caption in the bottom right corner of the screen, his name is Yale Thayer. He's a thin man with pale skin and fire-red hair.

". . . begins at conception, *not* when some godless scientist says it does. They want to farm *human beings,* my friends. They want to harvest cells from someone who could turn out to be your sister, your best friend, your aunt Ruby who tapes *Wheel of Fortune* every weekday on her VCR. And they hide behind their own corrupt morals, trying to influence public opinion by giving false hope to those unfortunate enough to contract incurable diseases. 'We can *save lives!*' they cry! 'We can help people who are alive!' But to do this they want to steal the life away from innocent babies, each with a soul given to them by God and saved by His Son, Jesus Chr—"

I touch the television remote and end his tirade midsentence. I'm supposed to be packing, so I jack up the volume on CNN and head back into the bathroom, where toothpaste and cologne and grooming implements patiently wait to be dropped into my suitcase. When I happen to look at my reflection in the mirror, the fear apparent in my own eyes unnerves me.

I carry the suitcase back into the bedroom—now ready for underwear briefs and white T-shirts—just in time to catch the beginning of a Breaking News Event brought to me by a striking, articulate brunette.

". . . don't really know exactly how long the group has been missing. Police in neighboring Corpus Christi notified the FBI after numerous missing person reports were filed by concerned friends and relatives who claimed to have lost contact with suspected members over three weeks ago. Authorities expressed skepticism, however, when questioned about sources who estimate the group had swelled to over nine hundred members in recent weeks."

A short, muscle-bound fellow dressed in a navy blue FBI jacket appears on the screen behind the caption: Special Agent Gerald Weir.

"We are currently gathering information on the group, which calls itself Primordial Carbon," he says. "Apparently this group made a pilgrimage into a remote area of the King Ranch and chose a gathering place about sixty miles south of Corpus Christi. As to the allegation that their numbers approach one thousand, we have reason to believe this has been somewhat exaggerated. But I would like to assure the public that any and all leads are being investigated."

The beautiful brunette anchor further explains the significance of this news event, declaring it the largest mass disappearance of humans in recent history, and asks us viewers to tune in to CNN for a special report beginning promptly at—

"Cameron," Misty calls from the kitchen, "did you pack your golf shoes yet?"

"No," I tell her. "I think they're still in the trunk of my car."

"I'll get them."

She's been remarkably calm today, my wife, considering her attitude over the past three weeks. When I first told her she threatened to divorce me. She didn't care about the money, the five million dollars NeuroStor offered for the test. She didn't care when I explained that my job was being eliminated, that our entire company's financial health—and my retirement stock options—might rest on the success of the transmission machine. Instead she said—quite predictably, I might add—*All I need is you, Cameron.* Sure it is. Easy to say when there is plenty of money to go around.

The idea of divorce scares the hell out of me. Maybe, considering our declining intimacy over the past several years, it's something we should have discussed a long time ago. But when you marry young like Misty and I did, and when your relationship stretches on for five, ten, and now fifteen years, it's not easy to give up the comfort, the bedrock upon which your life rests. You want to know the laundry is going to be done every Sunday afternoon. You get used to the daily ritual of cooking familiar meals for two. You lull yourself to sleep every night with the rhythmic pattern of your wife's breathing. Boundaries box you into predictability, and eventually you grow dependent upon the razor-wire walls that form the perimeter of your life.

But something changed in me the day Batista made the five-million-dollar offer, and in the end I realized there was no way I could *not* accept. That recurring dream, the one where I go to my grave with no eulogy? It was trying to tell me something, and I'm going to heed its warning.

I'm going to do something with my life.

Misty looks over at me periodically as she negotiates the Beltway traffic, and while her voice trembles with anger, I read more from her eyes. Like fear. And grief. And uncertainty. The one thing she knows for sure: She doesn't want to let me go.

"You're crazy, Cameron. Do you hear me? I should have you committed."

The overcast sky paints the city in shades of gray, and even the conditioned air in the car feels uncomfortable and sticky. Fifty or so miles from the Gulf, Houston is close enough to draw tropical moisture out of the ocean but too far away to be cooled by any sort of sea breeze effect. That's one benefit of choosing Phoenix as my transmission destination—not a whole lot of humidity in Arizona.

The radio mumbles a conversation I can't quite hear. Misty's speed hovers just below the posted limit of seventy miles per hour, which is interesting when you consider that she drives like a demon most of the time. She's making time to stage one final confrontation, you see.

"Really, Cameron," she says. Her eyes shift but never quite make contact with mine. "Will you please seize this last opportunity to reconsider? I've told you a thousand times that I don't care about the money, and I don't believe the job market in Houston is as bad as you say it is. You could find *some*thing. I could make more money. Don't act like this is the only choice you have."

"Honey, we've gone over this. It's not just the money—"

"You're just bored with accounting, that's all. You need a vacation. That's why I think you should go ahead and visit Tom. Fly out there and stay for a week and play golf every day. I know you'll feel better."

"Misty . . ."

"Please just fly. Just take an airplane." One of her hands leaves the steering wheel and rummages into her purse. She pulls out an envelope and shoves it at me. "I bought this for you. A direct flight to Phoenix. It leaves at five thirty."

"Airplanes go down all the time, Misty. And someone had to try them first. Someone *always* has to be the first."

"It's a first-class ticket, see! I think they serve drinks before the plane even takes off."

"You don't underst—"

"I understand that you might die!" Her eyes have gone red now, and she just glares at me with them.

"Misty, watch the road."

She drops the ticket into my lap.

"The road. Of course. Don't want to be injured on the way to your death."

Misty already knows I've come to terms with the unlikely botched transmission. I think she's trying to find similar ground on which to stand.

"I'm not having this debate with you again, Misty. It's not just the money. It's not about my retirement or even trying to save the company. I want to do something. I want to make a difference, for myself. For everyone."

Now she looks away from me, out the window. I can't see her eyes, but I hear the tears.

"What about *me,* Cameron? Why won't you do something for *me?*"

"Misty . . ."

"Don't think I don't know the real issue here. You're not trying to make a difference. You're just tired of drifting."

"Drifting?"

"You heard me. Sometime after Luke died you lost your way, and now you're a drifter. A lost soul. And I'm the one to blame because I never gave you children."

Now Misty's quiet tears turn to sobs, and I put my arm around her trembling shoulders.

"Please don't cry. We've gone over this a thousand times. It's not your fault."

"Yes it is! I'm the barren one!"

Luke, our first and only child, was born thirteen years ago, two years after we married. He was a beautiful child, but an undeveloped brain killed him after only three weeks. We tried to conceive again, but after two miscarriages and years of fertility specialists we finally gave up.

Misty could have allowed Luke's death to wreak havoc with her mind, but she's a resilient person, much more so than I am. She whipped her body back into shape and found useful ways to spend her time. For several years she wrote freelance magazine articles (her very first submission—a story describing reduced calorie consumption as a way to slow the aging process—was accepted by *Ladies' Home Journal,* paving the way for more than twenty sales to various small- and large-circulation magazines). And later she joined the local theater group, where she acted occasionally and wrote several original plays. Her mother also managed to convince her that God could help ease the pain, and for the first time since we married, she made church a Sunday routine.

I did not fare so well. Golf isn't therapeutic the way writing apparently is, and I haven't found, nor do I care to search for, God.

"What am I supposed to do, Misty? Just call up Batista and tell him I changed my mind? It's too late now. He's counting on me. Everyone is."

"They wouldn't be counting on you if you had listened to me in the first place! If you had respected the opinion of *me,* your *wife,* instead of confiding in your boss, instead of going all buddy-buddy with that slimeball."

"He's not a slimeball. If it wasn't for—"

"Oh, come on, Cameron! Now you're *defending* him? You've done nothing but complain about him for *years*! He's too young, a kid just out of college who has no business trying to direct seasoned workers. Those are your words."

"I know they are."

"And now, just because he chose you to die in this—"

"I'm not going to die."

"You think just because he chose you to try this ridiculous machine, you think he's gone from untested child to brilliant leader in the span of a few weeks."

I look out my own window and watch a short line of cars moving up the freeway entrance ramp from the feeder road. A black BMW, a silver Dodge truck, a red Chevrolet sedan. The accelerating Chevrolet farts a disturbingly large cloud of black smoke as it merges with traffic, adding a little spice to the already polluted, humid Houston air. A little spice, but not really a lot, not when you consider the other three million cars in the area, not when you consider the stinking refineries on the southeast side of town, not when you consider twenty million passengers a year flying in and out of the city's three commercial airports. Houston's air pollution, after all, is among the worst in the United States, often as toxic as perennial favorite Los Angeles.

"It could be a good thing," I tell Misty. "Did you ever think of that? If the technology works—if it becomes popular, I mean—economies of scale could one day make transmission portals as ubiquitous as the automobile. Imagine how much less noise and pollution, how much less time we would spend—"

"Cameron, stop. I know you're frightened and you want to convince yourself that this is the right thing to do, but don't try to sell me. I'm not going to buy it."

I first learned about the "volunteer" program during my midyear performance review. In Batista's office, sitting side by side, leaning over a poorly thought out form designed to pigeonhole my job performance into one of three categories: Below Targets, Above Targets, and Achieved Targets. You'd think a relatively new company—a startup, really—would find a more radical (read: logical) way to measure an employee's work ethic and value. And of course he asked me the question that probably every manager in the world poses to his subjects: *Cameron, if you were me, how would you rate your performance so far this year?* In this situation you are supposed to aim high (to prove your confidence) without aiming *too* high (which reveals arrogance or an inflated self-worth). I rated myself a solid Achieved Targets, the same as last year and every year. After all, I didn't do anything differently. I didn't launch any new initiatives or identify new synergies in the routine expense accounting that comprises the bulk of my daily work. No, I pretty much maintained the status quo, which is what Batista asks of me since I never do anything else.

You could say that Batista and I enjoy a pretty good relationship considering neither of us respects the other professionally. His distaste for my corporate apathy doesn't prohibit him from inviting me to his house every month or two for slow-cooked baby-back ribs and buttered corn on the cob. I ask about his ailing father (prostate cancer) and his athletic sister (she was an alternate for the 2002 Winter Olympics) in spite of the insidious way his artificially upbeat management style infects our office. Batista and I coexist in spite of our differences, and for this I owe him a certain amount of gratitude. He owns the power to terminate my employment at any time, to replace me with a younger accountant who would surely bring a fresh attitude to the work I take for granted, and yet he doesn't. I don't mind admitting that his reasons for this baffle me.

This time, though, something was different. When I predictably uttered "Achieved Targets," Batista replied, *I don't think so.* He pointed out that I had absolutely no interest in NeuroStor other than the paycheck the company issued every two weeks. In fact, as Batista launched into his motivational speaker voice about how NeuroStor was looking for Go-Getters and Forward-Thinkers and teammates who would Walk the Talk and genuinely enjoyed being part of the Corporate Family and blah blah blah—you get the picture—as he droned on about all this I honestly thought he was about to fire me. Perhaps he wanted me to think that. Because when he finally got around to his offer, I was ready to entertain anything. Of course, he didn't just come right out and ask. First he revealed that NeuroStor wasn't just an information-age startup that had learned to mimic the neurological structure of the human brain to develop faster, higher-capacity digital storage devices. No, the company had really been formed to develop another product that required this sort of massively improved storage. He also made clear that this as-yet-unrevealed-to-me product was a secret only a select few NeuroStor team members guarded with their lives. And when I asked what it was, Batista gleamed and explained how they had developed a way to transmit matter from one place to another using a wrinkle in quantum physics.

This was quite a bomb to drop on someone who thought he was overseeing the financial ledgers of a company that made ridiculously expensive flash memory cards. Not that it mattered, I suppose—accounting no matter how you slice it isn't much more than number crunching—but something about possessing this knowledge immediately made working there seem a lot more intriguing. And when he saw he had me (I probably cracked a smile for the first time since he had called me into his office), Batista pounced. *I like you, Cameron,* he said. *But I can't just sit by and watch you drag ass around here. Everyone else works their butt off, and you act like you don't care.*

I remember just looking at him, unable to mount any sort of defense because he was speaking the absolute truth.

And frankly, he continued, *I don't foresee any change in your attitude. Do you?*

I tried to tell him that I could change, that I needed my job and would do whatever it took to keep it, but he just waved his hand at me.

We both know you're not going to do any of that. You don't like working for a corporation and you never will. If I fire you, you'll eventually find a job somewhere else and hate it there just as much. Is that any way to live?

I didn't know how to answer him. I wasn't used to that sort of honesty from a corporate superior. Previous experience had taught me to never tell your boss how you really felt, to never admit that you'd rather play golf every day than sit in front of a computer crunching numbers.

Eventually I tried to point out that no one really liked working for a corporation, that some people were just better at hiding it than others. Why had he chosen to single me out?

Because you are particularly miserable, he explained. *And since I like you, I'm going to make sure you never have to work for another corporation again.*

Rather than drive in silence, Misty reaches forward and turns up the radio. The conversation that had been too low to hear before now blares out of the speakers like a spike into my ears.

". . . on sale for a limited time only. The *definitive* video on the Antichrist and the end of the world as we know it! Everything you should know about the dangers of one world currency, of a secret council of nations governed by a *single man,* of a global network of computers linked together to create a—"

It's the Conrads. Jacob and Rachel. I try to be out of earshot when Misty watches their Christian television program every Saturday and Sunday morning, but somehow I always manage to hear the fundamentalist sales pitch anyway. And yet I never say anything because I don't think it's one person's place (namely mine) to tell another person what to believe. But she doesn't have to listen to it *now,* does she? Now?

"Misty, can we please turn this down?"

She doesn't respond.

"Misty?"

"Do whatever you want," she growls.

Of course, *Do whatever you want* is loaded permission. What she really means is *Turn it down if you like, but you'll pay later*. So I leave it.

We exit just after the US 290 exchange, and now NeuroStor is a little more than three miles away. Holy Shit.

The details of Batista's offer weren't really negotiable. The test would be composed of two trips: an outgoing and a return segment. I could choose among a half-dozen destination cities. A minimum of two days were required to pass between segments, and upon completion of the second segment—my return to Houston—I would be paid five million dollars.

Five million dollars. Enough money, without question, to live comfortably for the rest of my life. One hundred and twenty-five thousand dollars a year for forty years, and that was if I didn't invest a single penny. It was like winning the lottery.

But there was the rub. It *wasn't* winning the lottery, not by a long shot. If Batista was willing to part with five million dollars for the test—and especially considering there would be not one but *five* volunteers participating, which meant a total of *twenty*-five million dollars spent convincing employees to participate—it was plainly obvious that each test subject would be accepting a serious risk. Perhaps the risk of all risks.

After all, what the hell did I know about quantum teleportation? Wasn't there a strong likelihood I would end up on the other end scrambled like eggs? He assured me the machine had been tested and retested. He showed me videos of a German shepherd before the transmission and after. He did the same with Jack, the chimpanzee. But still I wasn't sure. We were talking about my life, after all. And that's when anger began to creep from beneath Batista's collar, a patch of crimson that spread into his face, reddening his already-dark complexion.

Goddammit, Cameron! he yelled at me. *I'm going to fire you either way, and it's not like Houston's economy is exactly kicking ass right now. If you're going to be unemployed, I think you'd enjoy it more with an extra five million dollars in the bank!*

I've always heard Batista could be volatile, but until then I'd never seen the evidence firsthand. The NeuroStor grapevine describes him as a man who parades around the office like the world's nicest CEO and then screams at middle managers behind closed doors. He reportedly once fired two employees for writing funny haikus about him during a market segment meeting. But this was my first experience with his anger, and I found it more than a little unnerving.

I wasn't going to let him bully me, though, so I asked for a couple of days to think about it. He offered one. I left work, headed for my country club, and wandered around the golf course for three hours trying to decide what to do. The next day I drove to work with shaking hands and told a beaming Batista that I would accept his offer. I signed a short document that outlined the test exactly as it had been described to me, a confidentiality agreement, and a waiver that forfeited my right to sue NeuroStor if I was unhappy with the effects of the transmission. Then I spent the next three weeks trying to convince myself that I had made the right decision.

Obviously what I would like is to do something meaningful with my life. But isn't that what everyone wants, at least while youth still provides the energy to care about such things? I hold no illusions about the uniqueness of my desire to be someone, to do something, yet here I am, about to test a teleportation machine that could park my consciousness into some never-ending digital storage limbo. Or, more likely, kill me.

My clammy hands are making fists now, driving fingernails into palms. My heart pounds a rapid beat. On the radio, Jacob Conrad's piercing voice suddenly grows sharper, louder, and I am startled out of my reverie.

"Do you want to DIE?" Jacob asks.

"Oh no they don't," his wife, Rachel, answers.

"Do you want to go to HEAVEN?"

"Yes they do, to join the Father in His almighty glory."

"Well, *understand this.* If you are not *saved* by *Jeeeee-sus* you will be denied entrance to that righteous and almighty kingdom."

"Oh no," Rachel Conrad moans.

"Oh *yes*! Our nation of sinners, in fact the entire human fruit of our great *Earth* is doomed to Hell without the divine benevolence of God's only son, *Jesus Christ.* And if—"

When I reach out to turn down the volume, Misty blocks me.

"You should listen, Cameron."

". . . would devise such subversive technology, my children. The Internet is the Mark of the *Beast* and—"

Despite Misty's wishes, I turn off the radio.

"Cameron!"

"I don't want to listen to that shit."

"That *what*?"

"Those people are crazy, Misty. Either crazy or acting like it to swindle hard-earned money out of people who don't know any better. Some of whom *ought* to know better."

She looks at me with wide eyes, and two shiny fillings blink at me from the darkness of her open mouth. Perhaps I've said too much.

"What are you saying? That you don't believe in God?"

I've always hated to fight, physically or verbally, because such activity reduces rational human beings to children with reasoning power that's primitive at best. Look at us now. Instead of using the last minutes before my transmission to reaffirm our love for each other, we are arguing about religion.

"I'm not saying I don't believe in God, Misty. I'm just not sure."

"I can't believe I'm hearing this. We've been going to church together for thirteen years!"

I don't know how to respond. I'm certainly not going to admit that the only reason I go to church is to please her.

"Cameron, don't you shut me out. I want to know what you mean."

We've stopped at a red light, and just ahead I spot the blue-and-white logo on the side of our two-story brick building: NEUROSTOR—FLASH MEMORY FOR THE NEW MILLENNIUM. A nervous lump lodges in my throat. The car idles, awaiting my answer to Misty's theological question.

"All I meant," I reluctantly say, "is that I have questions. Don't you? Don't you sometimes wonder if life is just a cosmic accident? That we're only here because the universe happened to evolve that way?"

"So this is why you're lost. All along I thought it was me, but I've been beating myself up over nothing. Without God, your life will never have meaning."

The light turns green. Misty moves the car forward at a snail's pace.

"Did it ever occur to you," she says to me, "that your soul might be lost in the transmission? That even if you come out on the other side looking like you, it might not actually *be* you? Spiritually, I mean?"

"No, that never occurred to me."

"Well, it should have. I think it's a real possibility."

I suppose I should have seen this coming. Misty's shift to stronger religious beliefs has been gradual but steady. Luke's death was the beginning, but until three or four years ago, she was mostly a Sunday Christian, much to the chagrin of her fundamentalist mother, I should add. Then she joined the church choir and met a woman, Julia Perry, who also had lost an only child. Julia had turned her life around by giving it over completely to Jesus. She had been Born Again. When I once tried to tell Misty that she had already turned her life around without having to be Born Again, she cried and claimed I didn't understand. I didn't say anything about it after that.

What bothers me the most is that Misty has always been embarrassed by her mother's extreme beliefs. Many times, early in our marriage, she expressed a desire to act in ways that her mother *never* would. And I believed her.

We met at the University of Texas during a rally occasioned by the appearance of *Playboy* on campus. A group of do-gooders materialized to protest the "sexism" and "misogyny" perpetrated by the evil "porno magazine," led by a troupe of women who staged a buff-bare run through campus to show they weren't opposed to nudity but rather the way *Playboy* presented it. These running women were mostly a camera-unfriendly lot, and I've always believed that many of them would have eagerly jumped the proverbial fence had they possessed *Playboy*-caliber bodies. Anyway, I found myself bumping hips and elbows with a girl in the pro-*Playboy* crowd, whose chestnut hair and brown eyes kept distracting me from the cause I was there to support. Finally one of the conservatives challenged the women in our group to apply for the pictorial they were so eager to defend, and when the chestnut girl turned to me and asked if she should do it, I answered the only way a self-respecting college dude could—I told her to go for it. Her picture appeared in *Playboy* six months later, but by then I knew Misty's naked body better than what you could see in that airbrushed photo.

You'd think a relationship borne out of a common desire to defend sexual freedom would have a better chance than most to preserve its own romance. Sadly, this has not proven to be true. Certainly our failure to produce another child did not serve to increase the frequency of our sexual encounters, but it seems to me that Misty's passion for religion may have robbed enthusiasm from other areas of her life. We have not made love, in fact, in more than two years.

I suppose stronger spirituality is often a function of increasing age—the closer you come to death, the more relevant afterlife becomes—but today our differences in belief (or the difference between our *intensity* of belief) divide us like never before. As NeuroStor approaches quickly on our right, this separation grows so strong it's like a third passenger in the car with us. And while it hurts me to consider the possibility that Misty is no longer the woman I married, that I am not the man she fell in love with, what the hell are we supposed to do about it?

Misty steers crookedly into a parking spot and slams on the brakes, her nerves obviously confusing her reflexes. I push open the car door and claw my way out. Is it just me, or do all marriages eventually become more about getting away from your wife than about staying close to her?

I grab my luggage from the trunk and meet Misty as she emerges from the open driver's side door. She takes the suitcase and leaves me with the golf bag. As we reach the sidewalk, a tall, well-built black man dressed in a very expensive Italian suit approaches us. This is our director of security, Stephen Gates. He was drafted as a tight end for the San Francisco 49ers a couple of years ago but (rumor has it) forfeited his signing bonus and initial year of pro eligibility when he tested positive not once but three separate times for a controlled substance. General managers in the National Football League can be remarkably forgiving when it comes to evaluating players who can help their franchise win a Super Bowl, especially when those players come cheap because of past transgressions, so my only guess about Gates is that he lost either his desire or ability to play football, because, well, here he is.

"Mr. and Mrs. Fisher," he says. "We're glad you could make it." He takes the suitcase from my wife and asks us to follow him inside.

I've entered this building innumerable times before, sometimes tired, often bored, but this is the first time I've ever experienced the front lobby of NeuroStor with such a strange combination of scorching fear and nervous excitement. The eggshell-colored walls and thick brown carpet observe our presence in silence, and since today is Saturday, the usual traffic of white-collar professionals and clerical staff is nowhere to be found. Gates leads us past the greeting desk, through a maze of cubicles (there goes my old desk on the right—Misty has never seen it before, but I realize this is not the time for a guided tour) all the way to the rear of the building, where the office narrows to a short hallway with a door on either side. The only people who ever come back here (or so I've always believed) are the maintenance staff and the hard-core IT guys. These two rooms, after all, house orphaned office furniture (left door) and our network servers and data storage facility (right door). I, of course, have never been inside either one.

Gates produces a key chain and unlocks the door to the computer room.

"Nervous?" he asks.

"Should I be?"

"Not if you ask me," Gates says. "I think you're a lucky man. Certainly a very rich one."

Next to me, Misty glares at this man with contempt, a glare that would make anyone squirm.

Gates ushers us into what looks like a large meeting area (not a computer room after all, I see) equipped with a long rectangular table and videoconferencing equipment. At first I wonder if he's going to ask us to sit down, but instead we walk past the table. The fear in my throat rises briefly as I try to figure out why he has led us into the back corner of this empty room, but then I notice we have gathered in front of another door. This door is different from most at NeuroStor in that its surface and frame (and even the knob) have been painted the same eggshell color as the walls, which is why I didn't notice it right away. Someone has made a small effort to conceal the door, at least from the casual observer, and I have to admit that it works better than I would have expected.

Gates flips through his chain to find the correct key and unlocks this door, as well. Aside from posting armed guards throughout the office, it's obvious Batista is taking no chances with security, even when no other NeuroStor employees are present. He motions us through the door, where we find a steep set of concrete stairs descending many feet below the ground floor of what I've always thought was a two-story office building. Misty takes careful steps downward, and I follow her. Behind us, Gates pulls the door shut with authority and locks it.

At the bottom of the stairs stands Batista.

The man is imposing, there's no question about that. He stands at least three inches taller than me, maybe six four, and I'm sure he weighs over two hundred and ten pounds. His skin is the shiny, golden brown of a Hispanic man who has known nothing but the high life since childhood.

"Cameron!" Batista yells cheerfully. His perfectly groomed hair shines black beneath the white fluorescents, and the contrast of remarkable orthodontic work against his dark skin is striking. He's a single man, and I imagine he must make women swoon wherever he goes.

"And you must be Mrs. Fisher," he says to Misty. "I'm Rodrigo Batista. Cameron never told me you were so beautiful."

"Thank you," she deadpans.

Whatever pretense I operated under previously, however I convinced myself to tolerate Batista's personality and behavior before, is gone now. Disappeared into oblivion. There are a number of reasons I dislike this man, but perhaps the most unnerving or disheartening to me is not his Harvard education or the undeserved wealth from which he springs, but that he is barely twenty-six years old. To a lifelong middle-class accountant such as myself, Batista's youthful brashness, his absolute assumption of unquestionable power, is pure evil. What does he know of real work? Of countless hours of meaningless toil for faceless corporations who suck the life out of their slaves and then toss them into the garbage heap of inadequate retirement benefits? He has paid no dues. He has done nothing but talk a bunch of moronic investors into sponsoring this . . . this . . .

He regards us for a moment and then clasps his hands together. "You are right on schedule, and so am I. Why don't we head on back and get started? This is all very exciting."

My hands have begun to sweat. I discreetly wipe them on the cotton fabric of my pants and then take Misty's hand in my own. She squeezes a little too firmly. I wonder if she can feel my pulse, feel the blood in my hand throb as adrenaline turns my heart into a thundering machine.

"Hot out there in Arizona," Gates says as we proceed down another narrow hallway. Ahead, Batista marches to his left and disappears through an open door. Farther down, at the end of the hall, stands a door labeled TERMINAL. That's where it's going to happen, I guess, where I'm going to put my life on the line in the name of—

"This way, Cameron," Batista says. He's standing inside a hospital-white room, motioning for us to follow him inside. A short, solid woman wrapped tightly in a white lab coat stands waiting. Her navy slacks aren't quite long enough to cover a pair of alarmingly thick ankles, but she doesn't seem to mind.

"This is Judy," Batista tells us. "She'll be performing the neurological evaluation."

An examining bed is pushed against the wall on my right, and on the left, beyond a secretarial-style desk, stands a short, androidlike machine that reminds me vaguely of my optometrist's office.

Judy holds out a folded hospital gown. "Please put this on," she says and points to a door behind her. "Change in there, and we'll get started with the exam."

Batista and Gates are discussing something about Arizona when I open the door and step back into the room. The gown is oversized and drafty. My hands feel for the back to make sure everything is secure.

"Did I hear something about Arizona?"

"I was just telling Mr. Batista about the desert climate in Phoenix," Gates says. "And how hot it gets."

"Even in September," Batista adds.

"Yeah, but—"

"But it's a dry heat, right?" Gates laughs.

I respond with an obligatory chuckle, but Misty's serious expression doesn't change at all. Her face might have been cast in plaster.

"Let's get started," Judy barks. She gestures toward the examining bed. "Stand there."

I do so.

"Hold your hands out like this," she says, and extends her arms outward, even with her shoulders, parallel to the floor.

"Great. Now, while keeping your elbow outstretched, bend your arm and touch your nose with your index finger."

This seems easy enough.

"Okay, now close your eyes and do the same thing. Great. Now do the same with your left hand. Great. Now . . ."

She runs through a standard neurological physical examination—measuring my ability to sense pressure, vibration, and temperature; evaluating my gait, balance, and reflexes—and then we move to the android.

"This instrument will evaluate your vision by surveying different areas of the eyeball—the cornea, iris, lens, conjunctiva, et cetera—and then by measuring your response to moving visual stimuli."

She makes a few adjustments to the machine and then instructs me to follow a point of yellow light as it dances through a black void. By my watch, the test lasts less than three minutes, but somehow it seems to drag on for hours.

"That's great, Mr. Fisher. We're almost done here. All I need from you now is a urine sample, and then we'll measure your height and weight. You'll find specimen cups above the sink in the bathroom, which is across the hall. Are you currently taking any medications?"

"No."

"Very well then."

The spectators part as I walk toward them on my way into the hall. Misty's face reads pure exasperation. She doesn't say anything, however, and neither do the two suits. I trudge across the hall and—

"Mr. Fisher?"

It's Judy. She has followed me into the hall.

"I think I can handle this test on my own."

"I know that," she barks. "But I forgot to tell you to save some."

"I'm sorry?"

"For the test afterwards," she explains. "Since your body will interpret the transmission as instantaneous, there won't be any urine left if you completely empty your bladder now."

A genuine smile spreads across my face—the first of its kind since I entered this building—and I nod to Judy.

"So I should save some."

"Yes."

"No problem."

But my humor dissipates quickly. An unfamiliar man looks back at me from the bathroom mirror, a man whose face shimmers with fear. Certainly they must all see it. Surely they must know that my heart now beats in my throat, must know the bitter taste of adrenaline in my mouth. Their machine, after all, is going to disrupt my body at the quantum level and then use the effects of something known as EPR correlation to reassemble me twelve hundred miles away—by far the most complex task modern technology has ever reputed to solve. Shouldn't they have brought me in hours before my transmission instead of just a few minutes? What about blood work, MRIs, or other similarly detailed examinations? Is this really it?

My hands shake as I drain warmth into the specimen cup, and twice my aim squirts off the mark. I finish and then wash my hands thoroughly. Splash a little water onto my face. If Misty detects how truly frightened I am, she'll drag me out of the transmission station by my hair.

Batista waits eagerly for me as I stride back into the examination room.

"Are you ready, Cameron?"

"I think so."

"Then let us proceed." He steps out into the hall and motions for me to follow him. I look back for my clothes and find them in Misty's hands.

"No need to redress," Batista says. "Nothing can accompany you into the transmission portal."

I already knew this, of course—that I would be transmitting nude—but I didn't realize they were going to parade me around the office in this ridiculous gown.

Batista turns right and heads for the end of the hall, where the door marked TERMINAL waits. Like a black hole it waits, an unknown entity, a singularity where perception is stretched like taffy and sucked into an alternate universe. I can avoid that hole simply by turning away. Its gravitational pull can entrap me only if I get too close.

"Welcome to the Houston transmission terminal," Batista announces.

He gestures into the room with a wide, sweeping arc of his hand and steps through the doorway. I turn to Misty—looking for what, I don't know—and then follow Batista into the terminal.

I suppose I was expecting something out of the future: a room full of bright, polished metal decorated by countless flashing lights and computer screens, technicians in full body jumpsuits running to and fro, shouting coordinates and download times and all kinds of other jargon. Of course, the terminal is nothing of the kind. It is a small and comfortable place that closely resembles our offices on the floor above. Several chairs have been placed on this side of the room, and against the far wall stands a row of three tall oak desks, semicircular in shape. Behind each is a set of two doors, labeled PASSENGERS and LUGGAGE, respective. At present only one of the desks is manned—by a thin, middle-aged woman I've never seen here at NeuroStor. She smiles as Batista ushers me toward her.

"Cheryl," he says, "this is Mr. Cameron Fisher."

"Pleased to meet you," she beams. "Thank you so much for coming."

I look like an idiot in this hospital gown. I might as well be wearing pajamas.

"We have fashioned this room to resemble what we think the first transmission terminals will look like," Batista explains. "Of course, when the technology is in wide use, there will be more portals in a single terminal, so this should be considered a scaled-down version of the real thing."

I stand there looking at him as if this tidbit of information actually matters to me.

"Your transmission will begin whenever you are ready," Batista says, and somehow hearing it spoken aloud weakens me further. My knees feel as if they might fail me. "The scan will last approximately ten minutes, transmission between fifteen and twenty. You should arrive at the Phoenix station by four o'clock Mountain Time, where reassimilation will cover another fifteen minutes or so. So we're looking at about forty-five minutes total transmission time."

"Just like you explained to me about three times already," I add.

"Right. We're sure that one of the initial misconceptions about transmission will be that it's instantaneous. After all, it's in our nature as human beings to be drawn to the sensational, confrontational, and romantic. *Star Trek*, I'm sure people will say, because a five-second 'Beam me up, Scotty,' is certainly more fantastic than the forty-five-minute process it actually is."

I'm astonished that he thinks I might have forgotten any of the details he has been hammering into me over the past few weeks.

"Do you have any questions before we get started?" he asks me.

I look around the room, wondering rhetorically just how I came to be in this situation, how I went from being a middle-class pencil pusher to a near-millionaire about to risk his life in the name of corporate science. And just as I am ready to tell him to get on with the test, I spot something on the ceiling that gives me pause.

"What's that camera doing up there?" I ask him. "Who's watching us?"

Batista's nearly imperceptible pause is enough to tell me he's about to lie.

"No one," he answers. "It's been standard procedure to record each transmission test."

This makes perfect sense, of course, but somehow I get the idea that others with vested interest in this test are watching remotely. The board of directors at our home office in Plano, for instance? Or maybe investors? But why wouldn't they want to observe their precious invention in person?

"You sure? If anyone else wants to watch, why don't they just come in here and—"

"Cameron," Batista growls, "may I remind you that we are rewarding you handsomely for this test in part because of your sworn secrecy? I don't think ridiculous questions about possible outside observers solidifies with me your ability to keep your mouth shut."

In seconds, Batista has reminded me of my place in this situation, of how I am no more than a pawn (albeit a soon-to-be-rich one) in his worldly chess game.

"Fine," I tell him. "I'm ready whenever you are."

"Very well, then," he says, and nods to Gates. The security director walks to the door marked LUGGAGE and opens it. From here I don't really notice anything remarkable about the space inside. Looks sort of like a shiny, metal closet.

"We'll send luggage and anything else inanimate through first," Cheryl says to me. "If that's okay with you."

I nod obediently. As if it would make a difference if I disagreed.

"Once inside the portal, you'll have a few moments to remove the gown, undergarments, and any jewelry. There is a small trapdoor marked CLOTHING, and you'll want to place these items inside it. They will be transmitted along with your luggage."

"Okay."

Silence creeps into the room now as I wait for more instructions.

Beside me, Misty stands perfectly still, although inside she must be screaming. Like I am screaming. This is crazy.

"Is there anything else, Cameron?" asks Batista. "Or are you—"

"I'd like a moment alone with my wife, if that's okay."

He clasps his hands together again. "Of course! Of course. Cheryl? Stephen?"

The three of them smile politely and leave the terminal. Misty's hand is on my arm even before they are gone.

"Cameron, I don't like this."

"I know you don't. I'm a little nervous myself."

"No, I don't like *this*. This whole operation. Something isn't right."

"What? What's not right about it?"

"For one thing, where the hell *is* everyone? You'd think they'd have the board of directors or investors or someone else important here to see you off. It's not like they've got a hundred volunteers lined up outside the door."

"I'm sure that's what the video camera is for," I tell her. "You saw how sensitive he was when I asked him about it."

"Still, I don't like this one bit. I know you think you don't have any choice, but will you *please* reconsider, for God's sake? I think your life is in *serious* danger."

"Misty—"

"Look at the examinations they performed on you! Do you think they were thorough enough? Of course they weren't! For what you're about to do, they might as well have just asked you to open up and say 'ahhhh.' Can't you imagine how many different ways this could go wrong?"

"I know something could go wrong! You think I don't know that?"

"Then why—"

"Misty, I'm sick of this. I'm so tired of going over the same damn thing over and over again."

"We go over it so much because you never answer my question! What if something *does* go wrong? You're so worried about yourself, so mixed up in this midlife crisis of yours, that you've forgotten about me. What will *I* do if you don't make it back?"

"It's going to be fine, Misty. We both know that. Tom will be there to pick me up, and we'll be laughing about this an hour from now."

She begins to cry, very softly, and I wrap my arms around her. The smell of her hair is sweet, like strawberry. I regret her fear, her pain, knowing as she does that something could go wrong, just as it went wrong with our only son. Why am I putting her through this? Is deliverance from the daily grind of life really worth the misery inflicted upon my wife?

"Honey," she says, "I know you haven't been happy. I know you think the money will make it all better. But don't you know that we can work through this? Can't you see how much more sense it makes to try therapy again than this foolhardy chance you're taking?"

Could it be that she's right? Should I at least take a little more time to think before I rush into something that owns the potential to end my life?

I let go of her, about to acknowledge her concerns, and that's when the NeuroStor officials burst back into the terminal. I don't know whether to attribute this to coincidence or the video surveillance. Batista doesn't really give me much time to think about it.

"Are you ready, Cameron?"

"Actually, I'd like to speak to you for a moment, as well."

"Certainly. What is it?"

"I mean I'd like to speak to you privately."

It's obvious from the furrowed brow and narrow eyes that Batista isn't pleased with this deviation from his plan. I wonder for a moment if he might just pick me up and toss me into the transmission portal, but then his features relax and he brings out that winning, artificial smile.

"Of course, Cameron. Will your wife be joining us?"

I turn to Misty. "Let me have a word with him, okay? I'll just be a minute."

She nods. I can see in her eyes that she thinks I've changed my mind, and perhaps I have.

Batista leads me out of the terminal and finds a nearby office that isn't locked. He sits down behind a desk and invites me to take the visitor's chair.

"What's on your mind, Cameron?"

"I'm having second thoughts."

"Jesus, did you have to wait until the last minute to tell me?"

"Did you think I was going to just show up here and jump into the portal? I don't know what the hell that thing is going to do to me."

"So you're scared, is that what you're saying?"

"You're goddamn right I'm scared. Wouldn't you be?"

Batista considers this. "Sure, I would be scared. But I'm not in your situation, so I don't have to worry about it."

"What situation is that? You're not talking about my job are you?"

"No."

"Because I can find another job. I'm not doing this because I'm afraid of unemployment."

"Then why *are* you doing this?"

"You never said what situation I'm in. Answer my question."

"The situation you're in, Cameron, is that you don't know what to do with your life. You're a smart man. You don't have the luxury of coasting through life on ignorance like a lot of people. You're acutely aware of your potential, that you have something meaningful to offer society, but you can't really figure out what that 'something' is."

I was expecting some kind of financial or career-related discussion. I had no idea Batista was going to try his hand at psychology.

"You'll just waste away, Cameron. If you don't figure out a way to play the corporate game or get off your ass and open your own firm, if you don't figure out some way to be happy in your work, you'll end up killing yourself. With a heart attack or with a razor blade, it doesn't matter. And if you don't want that, if you don't want to kill yourself, the question you have to ask yourself is this: What *is* going to make me happy?"

Batista smiles as if he has impressed me with his monstrous intellect, but this apparent insight is nothing more than any intelligent human could surmise about the world around him. Most men age quickly, after all, their career and salary arcs flattening around the age of thirty-five, the balance of their days forming a plateau that for better or worse defines their usefulness to society, and any armchair sociologist can recognize this. Anyone with reasonable observation skills can employ the celebrated bell curve to illustrate how the haves and have-nots occupy America's nether regions and leave the vast, flat plain of homogeny for the middle-class majority. This is not what I want from him now.

"We all need something," he continues. "We all have to make a difference somewhere. You don't have any kids. You don't seem to be that much in love with your wife—"

"What the hell are you talking about? You have no idea what—"

"Look, Cameron. I'm not going to order Gates to force you into the portal. If you don't want to do it, then I'll find someone else. But you need to think hard—and quickly—about what you want from life. I know it isn't accounting, that's pretty obvious, so what do you want? I know you're really into golf, so maybe you could be a professional. I don't know. But this opportunity for financial freedom will give you the chance to find out what you want and pursue it. How else are you going to do that if not volunteer for this test? At the very least, if you never figure out what turns you on, at least you'll be able to say you helped test transmission technology. At least you'll have contributed that."

Finally some kernel of adventure, some payoff for my risk besides the money.

"Even if the machine kills you," he adds, "you'll be remembered as a pioneer."

This is what I want to hear, the affirmation I need to solidify my decision.

"Do you think it's going to kill me?"

"Absolutely not."

"Do you think I'm going to come out on the other side scrambled or insane or permanently blind?"

"I've shown you the videotapes. We've perfected this machine. But we need human tests on record if we're going to market this idea to the public, and that's why I'm willing to pay you so much money. Because this company will make a thousand times that if people buy into the technology."

"But you're not willing to test it yourself. You wouldn't have to pay yourself five million dollars if you were a test subject."

"That would be a conflict of interest, for one thing. And yes, of course there is a risk that something could go wrong. But I don't have to accept this risk. I have enough money to pay someone who needs it more than I do. And I think you make the perfect candidate."

Somehow Batista's honesty regarding the machine's risk factor means more than anything he's said since he first offered me the test.

"Okay," I tell him as adrenaline streaks through my body like electricity. "Let's go do it."

"Good, good," he responds, once again rubbing his hands together, as if warming them.

We make our way back to the terminal, where Misty waits with wide eyes and hopeful expectations. The fear returns as I see the transmission portal, and I smile to conceal this from her.

"Well?" she asks.

"I've decided to do it."

"Oh, Cameron . . ."

"It's something I really want, Misty. We've talked about this. I just needed a little reassurance from Rodrigo, that's all, and now I'm ready. Really ready."

"But—"

I bend down and kiss my wife. With my lips pressed against hers I try to make her understand that my love for her is part of what drives my desire to do this. I want to be a better person. A better husband. And if something goes wrong, I want her to remember this. This kiss.

"I love you, Misty, but I have to do this."

She lets go of me.

"Are you wearing contacts?" asks Cheryl, the transmission attendant.

This is part of the drill. During the transmission process, a human body must go through minus anything not permanently attached. Just a protective measure, I've read, but I can't help but think of that little mishap in the Jeff Goldblum version of *The Fly.* Sweat moistens my upper lip.

"No," I tell her. "Had laser surgery."

"And," she smiles reluctantly here, as if to apologize for saying so, "you'll remove anything else attached to your body that is not permanent?"

"Certainly."

"Good," she says, and then looks toward Batista. "I think we're ready?"

"Right this way, Cameron," Batista says, opening the door marked PASSENGERS. The black hole stands before me, door open, shadows concealing whatever may lurk inside. And suddenly the fear returns, unexpected. It begins near my heart, simultaneously hot and cold, and swells rapidly, fluidly, until my entire chest cavity floats with it. Then into my arms, my legs, and now I'm afraid I will simply collapse onto the floor, a boneless, shapeless heap, my insides completely melted.

Melted by this sudden fear of death.

"Cameron?"

Behind me. Misty. Her hand on my shoulder, her voice wavering, and I turn to hug her tightly once more. Without looking into her eyes. Without admitting what she may already have guessed.

"I love you, baby. I'll call you when I get there. Not even an hour away."

She cries openly now. "Oh, please, Cameron. *Please . . .*"

I release her and look only briefly into her eyes. "I'll call. I promise."

"Good-bye, Cameron," she says, and turns away.

"Inside the portal," Cheryl tells me in a soft voice, "we'll communicate via intercom. If you have questions or wish to abort the procedure for any reason before the scan begins, just say so."

I step inside the transmission portal. This time it is just how I imagined—a square of seven by seven feet with a sturdy-looking metal seat positioned two-thirds of the way to the back wall. The starkness of this room somehow resembles my impression of the electric chair.

I turn around and look out into the terminal. Misty stands there, watching me. I wave and mouth the words *I love you* to her. She nods and then looks away. The sum of our fear is overwhelming.

Painted on the closed door is a short list of instructions, including a bold reminder to REMOVE ALL JEWELRY OR OTHER NONPERMANENT BODY ATTACHMENTS.

"Cameron?" Cheryl calls over the intercom. "Doing okay in there?"

"Fine," I say.

"We'll send your luggage as soon as you place your personal effects in the other portal."

My hands, slick with sweat, tremble as I remove the gown, my watch, and underwear.

A few moments later I stand buck-naked, having placed everything through the trapdoor. I fight off the urge to cover my privates and quickly sit down in the chair. It's made from titanium or stainless steel or some kind of effortless alloy, and damn, is it cold. Gooseflesh marbles my skin.

"Cameron? Are you ready?"

My heart climbs into my throat. I'm shivering where I sit. Couldn't they heat the chair?

"Yes," I say, and fear it's a lie. As surely as I have convinced myself that this is the right thing, I think I've changed my mind again. Death is not the answer. I have no desire to die.

"Your luggage and clothes are gone, Cameron," Cheryl says. "Your scan will begin in less than a minute."

Oh God. Oh, my God. This is crazy.

"Everything all right in there?"

"I'm fine," I say, not bothering to hide the fear now. They all know. Probably they're placing bets on how long it will be before I cry out in terror. But I won't. I've made it this far. I'm—

"Cameron?"

"I'm fine!"

"Someone here wants to talk to you."

I don't respond. Shortly I'll be reduced to nothing more than entangled quantum particles. I'm not thinking clearly.

"Cameron, honey? It's me."

"Misty?"

"Yes, honey. I love you. I'm . . . oh, Cameron . . ."

"I love you, too, Misty."

"Be careful."

"I will, baby. I will."

A pause. Rattling as the intercom changes hands.

"Cameron?" It's Cheryl again. "Fifteen seconds."

"Thank you."

After listening to Batista drone on about it over the past few weeks, I've formed a pretty good idea about what will happen when my transmission begins: nothing. The scanning procedure will render me unconscious almost instantly, and the next click of my mental works should take place in Phoenix. Everything in between will, in effect, become lost time. I should experience instantaneous transmission.

As I try to pass the last few seconds, I become aware of something different, some new sensation, something unexpected. Something else in the room with me.

A smell. A sweet—and oddly enough, familiar—smell. When have I experienced it before? Should I say something to Cheryl? Is some-thing wr—

"Begin scan."

Now I feel a little light-headed. And drowsy. Is this normal? Did something just bite me? A n—

two

⦚⦚⦚

I can't believe how goddamn cold this chair is. Couldn't they have mounted a cushion on it? Or at least put a heating element beneath the surface? It seems needlessly uncomfortable.

"Cameron," a female voice says, "you may open the 'clothes' door and put on the gown."

I'm still waiting for the scan. For the transmission to begin.

Or perhaps I've already done it.

And I'm not dead. Not dead *not dead NOT DEAD*!

And suddenly I am seized with such an exquisite delight that I nearly stand up and scream *Hallelujah!* at the top of my lungs. I've done it! I've transmitted from Houston to Phoenix by means of quantum teleportation. Beamed myself across the country like some hero from *Star Trek*. Unbelievable. I've done it! And I'm alive!

From the chair I move to the door marked CLOTHES. My belongings are here just as I left them. I struggle with my watch and ring because my hands are shaking. Shaking with joy. I grab the gown, hold it up to my face, and smell it. I can easily discern the scent of my deodorant, and to a lesser extent the fragrance of my aftershave. A few of my chest hairs cling to the cotton fabric inside the gown. When I put it on, it fits as badly as before.

I can't wait to go out there. By God, I've—

"Cameron, are you dressed?"

"I am!"

The door opens a moment later. Standing before me are a female transmission attendant and two familiar-looking suited men. All watch me rather quizzically, as if I'm some sort of special exhibit at the zoo.

One of the men, the older of the two at perhaps sixty, steps toward me. His navy suit is obviously tailored and probably set him back five thousand dollars. He is taller than I am, larger, and even his smile and extended hand strike me as imposing.

"Mr. Fisher," he says as we shake firmly, "I'm Stanley King, vice president of research and development for NeuroStor. Behind me is Ted Lloyd, Arizona district manager. On behalf of NeuroStor, we'd like to welcome you to Phoenix."

"Thank you," I answer. Behind them stands the transmission attendant, a short young woman who this Mr. King apparently did not find worthy of an introduction.

"How do you feel?" he asks.

"Great. I didn't even realize it was over until she spoke to me over the intercom." I nod in the direction of the attendant.

"Wonderful," King says in a commanding baritone. "This test seems to be a success. We are most pleased."

"I should thank you for the opportunity to volunteer," I say to him. "I think this will turn out to be one of the more important experiences of my life."

"May I ask why?"

"Because if the technology proves to be economically feasible, I think it will revolutionize human culture. I think it has been an honor to contribute to the project in some small way."

"Good," he says. "Very well."

"I guess it's time to run your tests?"

"Of course," King says. "Let's get started so you can be on your way. Mr. Lloyd, will you escort Mr. Fisher into the examination room?"

I follow him out of the terminal and into a hallway identical to its counterpart in Houston. Now gathered in the small examination room: the two suits, the nurse (older this time, but also much thinner), and me.

This is it, I suppose. The tests. Did I make a mistake? Will I pass, or did the transmission alter me in some way? I know I should be nervous, that everyone in this room probably expects me to be awash with fear, but again I get the feeling that something inside me has changed. Confidence has replaced doubt. Confidence that I am a man who can face the world the way I see fit, and if I choose to believe the transmission procedure sent me through intact, that is my prerogative.

"How do you feel?" the nurse asks.

"Fine. No different."

"Dizziness, nausea, numbness or tingling in your hands or feet?"

"No."

"Taste or smell anything funny?"

"No. At least not now."

"What do you mean by 'not now'?"

"Well, in the transmission portal—when the scan began, I guess—I smelled something a little strange. It was kind of a sweet smell, like air freshener for your car."

King looks up as I mention this, and then glances at Lloyd, the district manager.

"Do you smell it now?"

"No."

"I'll make a note of it in the report."

"Is that something you expected?"

The nurse shakes her head. "You're the first volunteer I've examined. I wouldn't know."

I look wordlessly to King for an answer. He offers nothing, but the look he gave Lloyd certainly didn't appear to be nothing.

We work through the physical exam, and vindication surges through me as the results appear to be the same as before. My balance is still fine, my tactile sensations, and all the rest. She runs through the vision examination next, and again I don't notice any change compared to before the transmission.

"What do you think?" I ask. "Any change?"

"You certainly seem fine to me," she says. "But I don't have anything from the nurse in Houston yet. We'll be comparing results later. Now, if you'll just go across there and provide the urine sample, we'll be finished."

The crowd parts for me as I head out the door.

"I hope you saved some," King says.

"Of course."

I complete my assignment in the bathroom and then rejoin the others. The hospital gown doesn't feel so awkward now that the exams are almost over. My hands are quiet as I dress, not shaking the way they did in Houston.

When I emerge from the changing room, King is looking at me expectantly. He opens his mouth to speak, and for an instant it occurs to me that they have found something wrong, that the test results from Houston have come in and they need to examine me further. An instant, and then I banish the thought, unwilling to give in to the unforgiving fear that has colored me for longer than I can remember.

"You have a telephone call, Mr. Fisher. From Houston."

King leads me into a large, executive-style office with cherry furniture and walls adorned with large, framed paintings of famous golf holes from Pebble Beach and Augusta National. He pushes a button on the telephone and offers the handset to me.

"Hello?"

"Oh, Cameron. Thank God you're there."

"Hi, baby. Yeah, I guess I made it over in one piece. I told you it would be okay."

"I was so worried, Cameron. I kept thinking that someone there would call and . . . and . . ."

She begins to cry softly, and her tears turn my own eyes wet.

"I'm just so glad you're all right," she says.

We talk for a little while about the transmission, and I explain everything to her. She apologizes for being so difficult on the way to the station, and I express regret for being so one-minded.

"Be careful out there," she says.

"I will."

"I guess I need to hand the phone over to your boss. He wants to talk to you, also."

"Oh." I didn't realize she was still at the station.

"I'll see you the day after tomorrow," she says. "I love you, Cameron."

"I love you, too, Misty."

A second passes as she hands over the telephone, and then Batista bursts onto the line.

"Cameron!" he says. "I take it you're happy with the results of this test. All you have left is the return trip and you'll be a rich man."

"Just like we agreed already."

"Of course," Batista tells me. "You're such a literal man, do you know that, Cameron? You'll be on your own the day after tomorrow, of course, but could I give you one more piece of advice as you begin your new life?"

"Sure."

"You could stand to lighten up. Life's too short to take everything so seriously."

"Thanks, Rodrigo," I answer. "I'll see you in a few days."

King takes the telephone handset from me, replaces it in its cradle, and then escorts me toward the lobby. Mr. Lloyd is waiting near the doorway, and just to his right stands the man I came here to see in the first place.

My good friend, Tom Bishop.

I see him just before he sees me, and the tension on his face tells me just how worried he was about this test. But all anxiety seems to melt away when I smile and march into the lobby where he stands.

"Tom!"

"Cam," he says. We hug briefly, and during the embrace I feel his chest heaving, hear rapid breaths against my ear. "You made it. Holy shit, you made it."

"What did you think I was going to do?"

"This test, man. God, I was worried about you."

"I told you everything would be fine."

"I know you did," he says. "But still . . . Jesus. It's good to see you."

I try to play off his concern, because seeing him this way makes me realize again just how much of a risk this was. "You won't be saying that when I kick your ass on the golf course."

"In your dreams," he chuckles.

We step forward, moving past a desk and toward the exit. I'm trying to think of something to say, a sentence or two that can summarize my appreciation for this opportunity and the reality of my importance in their—

Suddenly I'm falling. My feet have caught on the carpet and I'm falling. Involuntarily, I throw my arms out for balance. Stumble forward. Slam my head against the desk on the way down. Hit the ground with a thud.

Tom kneels to help me. "Jesus, Cam. Are you all right?"

"Yeah, I'm fine."

He extends his hand and pulls me to my feet. Thirty-five-year-old bones aren't rubbery and resilient like a child's are. I haven't taken a spill like that in years.

"Mr. Fisher," King says. "I am so very sorry."

But I'm already up, brushing myself off and feeling like an idiot. Everything looked fine during the exam, and now I go and trip over myself in front of everyone. What a fool. They're going to think my sense of balance has been altered in some way. They'll probably take me back to the nurse for more tests.

"No problem," I tell him. "Just tripped over myself. I'm fine."

"Are you sure, Cameron?" Tom says. He's looking at me like I was just hit by a car. "That must've hurt like hell."

"I'm telling you, you're going to wish something was wrong with me when we're on the course tomorrow."

"You keep saying that," he says, but without a smile.

"Before you go," King says, "I would like to take this opportunity to thank you for volunteering, Mr. Fisher. You were right when you said our machine has the potential to revolutionize human culture. And you're playing a big part in that."

"Thank you for asking me to volunteer."

"And for the money," Tom says over my shoulder. "Don't forget to thank 'em for that, Cam."

I want to turn around and punch him, but it's too late now, anyway. King only laughs.

"Have a good stay in Phoenix," he says as we grab my luggage.

"Thank you. I will."

"That was bizarre," Tom says as he weaves his Acura into traffic. Tom is not a well-to-do man, not by any means, but that doesn't stop him from finding the money to purchase showy toys like this car. He bought it used, I'm sure, a twenty-four-month-old model with forty thousand miles on her. His clothes are pricey, but he owns few. The expensive watch is probably ten years old. He's a man trying desperately to halt the inevitable process of aging, but he's also my best friend. I guess I wouldn't know what to do if he decided to grow up.

"When you came out of that damn door," he continues, "I wasn't sure what you were going to look like. I had these pictures in my head of seeing you all mangled and shit. Like you'd have a new eye on your pecker or something."

I give Tom a sour look. He's smarter than he sounds. This Stephen King bullshit is just a ploy to piss me off.

"Or you'd come out all crazy, speaking in tongues or walking in circles."

"Whatever."

"So is it what you thought?"

"I guess so."

"What was it like?"

"Hard to describe. On one hand, it was the most amazing thing I've ever done. I mean, one second I was in Houston, and the next . . . the next second she's telling me to get dressed. If I wasn't looking at you right now— I don't know. It's easy to imagine that maybe it didn't happen."

"So it's like when you go to sleep. Out like a light when your head hits the pillow, and you wake up eight hours later as if no time has passed."

He's right. That's exactly what it felt like. But . . .

"But it's *not* really like that," I say. "I mean, I remember everything to the last second before the scan began. When you fall asleep there's a sort of twilight time, a few moments before you go unconscious that you can't remember in the morning. That's why you can never tell the exact moment when you fall asleep. But there aren't any holes or gray spots in my memory. It's like a scene cut in a movie. Abrupt and seamless."

"Do you have any regrets?"

"No. I just wish Misty wasn't so hurt by this. It's something I really wanted, that I needed really, and yet she—"

Tom is grinning impishly at me.

"What?"

"This conversation is getting too deep for me," he says.

"Every conversation is too deep for you."

"Fuck you."

"Where the hell are we going?"

"You need some beer," he tells me. "I know the transmission is a big deal, and you're going to have plenty of time to worry about the return trip later. But right now you need to relax a little."

"Okay, but maybe I should call Misty again and make sure she's okay. I talked to her earlier, before I saw you in the lobby, and she sounded pretty upset."

"Call her from your cell phone."

I reach for my back pocket but realize before my hand arrives that it's not there.

"Goddammit."

"What?"

"I knew I'd forget something. I plugged my damn phone in last night to charge and never even thought about it today."

He makes an abrupt right turn, and we pull into the parking lot of a small building that proclaims itself to be The Wildcat. About ten cars are parked here. The building doesn't have any windows.

"A strip club? You've got to be kidding me. I just risked my goddamn life for—"

"Come on, Cam. It's time you lived a little. Married life has made you soft."

"Give me your cell phone. She was pretty upset at the station. I want to make sure she made it home okay."

Tom reaches into his pocket and pulls out a slab of gray plastic that resembles a cigarette lighter.

"Is that a phone?"

"Just got it last week. Smallest one you can buy."

"Of course it is."

The buttons are so small that I'm forced to start over three times before finally keying the number correctly.

"Hi, this is Captain Kirk. Misty and I can't beam to the phone right now—"

Answering machine. I'm one of those geeks who thinks it's funny to make jokes on the outgoing announcement.

"She must not be home yet," I tell Tom. "Let me try her cell."

I key in her cell number and listen as the phone rings, but this time her voice mail answers. I leave a short message to let her know everything is okay, and that I'll call her later.

"Okay," Tom says. "Can't say you didn't try. Now can we please go have a good time?"

Today I boldly stepped forward and became one of the first humans in history to be transmitted from one location to another via quantum teleportation. Such is the stuff of heroes, right? Scratch me into the history books right beside Columbus and Armstrong. And when they ask what Cameron Fisher did upon arriving safely at his destination, what will be the answer? Did he make a speech? Nope. Did he record on paper his memories of the trip for posterity? No way. What he preferred to do was drink alcohol and watch topless women shake their breasts in exchange for dollar bills.

At least The Wildcat is more upscale than I anticipated. The lights are dim, of course, but the fixtures shine, the carpet seems clean, and the air is ripe with a pleasant cinnamon fragrance. We find a table several feet away from the main stage and order a pitcher. I sip on my beer for ten minutes, watching the slow procession of women as they take turns dancing for the small audience. There are fifteen or so customers besides Tom and myself. Two are women at a table together. Several men are here alone.

Tom quickly guns down half the pitcher. He wants to go sit at "pervert row," where the women will dance especially for you and put their barely concealed privates within inches of your eyes. I can stall him for only so long. Finally, when a stunning blonde takes the stage, he takes my arm and pushes me toward her.

The music is louder beside the stage. A layered orchestra of guitars and screaming, multitracked vocals melts my ears, imploring me to pour some sugar on someone. I place my beer on the table in front of me and reach for my wallet.

The present dancer is perhaps the most beautiful woman I've ever seen. Her eyes are bright blue and her tanned skin is velvety perfect. Contoured muscles and breasts the size of large melons are unmarked by discernible tan lines. She is probably twenty-five years old.

Tom pulls out a dollar bill, and the girl smiles as she dances, moving toward him, striking poses along the way that would make most women blush. He returns the smile and leans forward to improve his view. I watch as she throws herself toward him, then onto the stage, where she lies on her back and begins to thrust her pelvis up and down in a rhythmic motion that follows the music's simple beat. A few seconds later she scoots forward and pulls the G-string out a little, high on the hip, so Tom can insert his dollar. He clearly wishes she would dance for him a little longer, but the song has reached its closing chorus, and if she doesn't move on to me it means one less dollar this time around.

So now it's my turn. Unlike Tom, I don't just stare between her legs the entire time. A live dancer is not a two-dimensional picture, after all, but a human being with feelings and emotions who will observe my arousal. And I don't flash my money right away. I look into her eyes first, as if to establish personal contact, and then gradually gaze over her entire body, drinking in that flawless figure. She lies on the stage, never taking her eyes off me, and slides her hand over her skin, moving as my eyes move. I arrive at the G-string, red and tiny, and she glides her hand there, not touching herself but creating an effective illusion. Next she turns over, showing me her smooth backside, and then the song comes to its conclusion. The dance is over. My muscles relax.

She turns around, scoots toward me, and pushes her breasts together. I grab a five from my pocket and place it between them. Her teeth are gleaming white, perfectly capped.

"Thank you," I say.

"You're welcome," she says. "You're cute."

"I bet you say that to all the men."

"Not on your life," she returns. "We get a lot of creeps in here."

"How much for a table dance?"

"It's normally twenty dollars, but for you," she pretends to think, "ten."

"I'll tip you more than that."

"I know."

For each new song another woman comes out, and it's time for our dancer to leave. She gets to her feet and winks at me, then waves at Tom. We head back to our table.

"Look at the stud," Tom says as we take our seats. "I think she likes you."

"It helps if you're nice. And loose with the cash."

"Say what you want, but I think she'd come back to the apartment with us if you asked her."

I shake my head at that and gulp down the remaining beer in my glass. I may have seemed confident when she was dancing for me, but that was spontaneous, something I didn't have time to think about. Now that I know she's coming over here, I'll need a stronger buzz to relax. I order another pitcher. Tom is in heaven.

"I knew you'd come out of that shell if I gave you a chance!" he yells over the beginning of the next song.

"Go to hell," I laugh.

We drink for a few more minutes. When our dancer doesn't join us right away, Tom heads back to pervert row. I let him go alone this time. Don't want to stand up my new friend.

I don't know why I asked for a table dance. I don't visit strip bars very often, mostly because the whole idea seems like an incomplete transaction to me. When gorgeous women gyrate their nude bodies just inches from your eyes, there is no immediate way to relieve the tension. At home you can sneak a magazine into the guest bathroom or watch pornographic movies when your wife isn't around, but in a strip bar you are forced to keep a lid on your excitement. And it *is* exciting. No healthy heterosexual man can deny such a claim.

Her dress is black, almost elegant, with the obligatory low-cut neckline and short skirt that falls nine inches above her knee. She stops at my table and sits beside me. I know in my mind that attraction between men and women is more than physical, that without a chemistry of personality there can be no real relationship, but that doesn't stop me from imagining myself with her. In this setting all pretense to civility is gone anyway. And while many argue that bringing sex out of the bedroom and into a public place goes against what is considered "proper" or "civilized," I disagree. People who try to hide their desire by speaking about sexuality in hushed tones, who feel guilty about this most basic human instinct, are the truly uncivilized.

"I'm Crystal," she says.

"Sure you are. My name is Cameron. Nice to meet you."

"It sounds like a stage name, I know, but it's not."

"It's a beautiful name, then."

"Thanks."

For a moment we just sit there. She stares at me closely, and I wonder what she sees. Is there something on my face? A lump or bruise forming where I hit my head earlier? What she finally says startles me.

"Are you bi?"

"What?"

"Are you bisexual?"

"Of course not. Why do you ask?"

"Because that man over there is staring at you." She nods over my shoulder.

"With all due respect, Crystal, if he's staring at anyone at this table, I'm sure it's you."

"Thank you, but he was looking at you before I ever got here."

"How do you know?"

"Because he never looked at me when I was onstage. He just kept staring at you."

Despite her explanation, I find it difficult to believe that I am the object of this mystery man's fascination.

"I was joking about the bisexual thing, of course. But I wonder why he would be so interested in you?"

"I have no idea."

"Are you wanted by the police? Hiding from your bookie?"

"Really, Crystal, do I strike you as—"

"No," she says. "But that doesn't change the fact that he's still staring at you."

I want to turn around and look at the guy, but I don't want him to see me do it. Instead, I change the subject.

"You're a very good dancer," I say, my tongue looser now because of the beer.

"Thank you again," she says.

"But maybe you'd rather just hang out for a while. Save the act for your next stage performance. Can I buy you a drink instead?"

"Sure. You seem like a nice enough guy. But it's expensive."

"How much?"

"Nineteen dollars."

"Wow."

"Yeah. And I usually don't like to do it all that much. Most guys who just want to talk are lonely geeks. It gets creepy sometimes."

"I don't want to make you uncomfortable."

"No, it's fine. Like I said, you seem like a pretty cool guy." She turns around and signals someone at the bar. "So where's your wife?"

"In Houston."

"Oh. What kind of work do you do?"

"Financial. I work for a company called NeuroStor."

"Ah. 'Flash memory for the new millennium.' "

"You know the company?"

"I know lots of things. Are you here on business? I know NeuroStor has an office in Phoenix."

"Vacation, actually. My wife doesn't like to spend time with my buddy Tom, so I came alone. Just got in a few minutes ago. This is the first place he brought me."

"I can see why she stayed home. How long a flight is it from Houston? Three hours?"

The beer, it's really working on me now. Must be the empty stomach. Before I can stop myself, my mouth utters something I wish it hadn't.

"I didn't fly."

A waitress appears at our table, places a strawberry daiquiri in front of Crystal, and then is gone.

"It's my usual," she explains. "But there's not much alcohol in it. Gotta be sharp to dance my best."

"Hope it tastes good. For twenty dollars."

"Nineteen," she says. "You don't think I'm worth it?"

This woman is a genuine knockout and seems unexpectedly intelligent. Flirting with her makes me feel like a real man. A real *married* man, but a real man nonetheless.

"Of course you're worth it," I admit. I try not to notice how full and long her blond hair is, how it falls over her shoulders like strands of goldenrod. Why did Tom have to bring me here?

"So you didn't fly. What was it, like a twenty-hour drive? Or did you transmit?"

I nearly choke on my beer.

"What did you say?"

"I asked if you drove or if you transmitted."

Because of the confidentiality agreement, I want to ask *What does transmit mean?*, but why the hell say something stupid like that? Anyone who bothers to use the word in that context knows what it means.

"How in the hell do you know about transmission?"

"How do people know anything these days? The Internet, of course."

"The *Internet?*"

"You know, a bunch of computers interconnected—"

"I know what the Internet *is*. I just don't understand how you would have learned anything about transmission by clicking around Web pages."

"Well, the Internet isn't just Web pages. It's newsgroups and bulletin boards and e-mail and . . . what difference does it make? I was just joking. You guys are a couple of years away from announcing it anyway, right?"

I'm stunned.

"I worked at NeuroStor for six years monitoring expense accounts, and I didn't know anything about transmission until three weeks ago, when they asked me to help them test it. And you found out about it on the Internet."

"Test it?"

"That's how I came to Phoenix. I transmitted."

"No shit?" She chokes down a swallow of the red liquor and then says again, "No *shit?*"

"No shit."

"I can't believe that. You went through the machine? What was it like?"

"Actually, it was okay. I was nervous about it, but to be honest you don't feel much. You just get naked and sit down in a cold metal chair. Then you're here."

"So how do you feel now? Did it screw you up at all?"

"Of course not."

"I've heard rumors," she says. "Like some animals they sent came through pretty fucked up."

"Rumors, huh? I don't know how much stock I would put in rumors you heard on the Internet."

"Hey, at least I knew about it. And I don't even work there."

Crystal is smiling, but I detect sharpness in her voice that wasn't there before.

"Now you're picking on me."

She pats my hand. "I'm sorry, Cameron. Ever since I heard about your machine I've thought it would be cool to try it. I guess I'm a little jealous of you."

"Even though you read rumors about animals coming through scrambled?"

"Ah, who knows if that's true? You read all kinds of garbage. In fact, according to some of the posts to alt.transmit.conspiracy, mystery man over there is a covert agent watching to see if you go berserk."

" 'Alt.transmit.conspiracy'?"

"You bet. Of course, it's hard to know what to believe."

"I don't understand. If this is common knowledge on the underground Internet, you'd think *60 Minutes* or something like that would be all over it."

"You think they would let the news media ruin their precious little invention?"

"They? Who is they?"

"Whoever is paying to develop the technology."

"How could 'they' conceal bad transmissions from the press? That sounds a little hard to believe."

"Not really. Guys with power—I mean *real* power—can do whatever they want. It's like a network—government leaders, corporate chairmen, televangelists—they're society's demigods, only instead of Mount Olympus they have Aspen. Or Switzerland. Or the Caym—"

"Sounds like you've thought about this before."

"Sure I have. I mean, a lot of people would say, 'She's just an erotic dancer. What does she know?' And maybe they have a right to, because my line of work isn't exactly the noblest vocation in the world. But that's what those big shots do to guys like you. Maybe you make a hundred thousand dollars a year, have a four-bedroom house, and say, 'Hey, I've made it. I'm living the American dream.' But still, the *really* big shots rule the food chain. You eat me for lunch, but they eat you."

"Being an erotic dancer doesn't mean anything when it comes to brains," I say. "Sounds like you're smarter than I am."

Her smile makes me feel like a pubescent boy. I could fall in love with those teeth, let alone the rest of her bodily wonders. But at the same time I can't get past the fact that she's familiar with NeuroStor and their transmission technology. I mean, how unlikely is that? How many others have the same information she does?

"I just can't believe you know about this. Imagine how much of a moron it makes me that *you* knew but *I* didn't. I work there, for Christ's sake!"

"I wouldn't beat yourself up over it, Cameron. I read all kinds of conspiracy shit. Usually it's alien abduction and JFK assassination trivia and stuff like that. I didn't even know for sure that the transmission thing was true until you verified it for me with that poker face of yours."

Crystal smiles at me as she finishes the strawberry daiquiri. She has beaten me and she knows it. I didn't even know there was a contest.

"Before I forget," she says, "why don't you drop me a line when you get back to Houston? I'd really like to know how the return trip goes. You *are* going back the same way you came, right?"

"I am."

"How long are you going to be in Phoenix?"

"A couple of days."

"Anyway, my e-mail address is easy to remember: crystal@two-peaks.com. Spell the word *two*, don't use the number."

"Two peaks?"

"It's a play on words. Sounds like my breasts, but actually I moved here from Flagstaff. The San Francisco Mountains are north of town, and we call the biggest one 'The Peaks.' It's a private joke."

"The San Francisco Mountains are in Arizona?"

"Yep. A couple hours north of here. It's actually very beautiful. Mountains and trees and everything."

"All right," I tell her. "I'll let you know how it went when I get back to Houston."

"Great," she says. "Looks like your friend is on his way back."

Tom is talking to a brunette onstage. He points toward our table, and she nods. Then he strides over to us, smiling ear to ear.

"Looks like you two have hit it off," he says, as if this is a singles bar instead of a strip club. "Michelle told me you guys work on the side. Private dances. At home."

That Crystal would dance privately surprises me. She seems too proud to take her show out of this semiprofessional arena.

"Sometimes," she says. "And always with a chaperone. But not tonight."

"Why not?" Tom pleads. "Michelle said—"

"Michelle's not me, is she? She doesn't know my schedule. I have things to do tonight."

Crystal abruptly stands up.

"Cameron, thanks for the drink. It was very nice to meet you. Come see me again sometime."

She glares at Tom as she leaves the table, and soon disappears behind a curtain near the stage. Gone in a flash.

"Thanks, Tom," I say. Only half seriously, though, because I don't really feel like spending all night here. And I'm curious to see if Mystery Man follows me out the—

Wait a minute. Crystal never pointed him out to me. How am I supposed to watch for the guy if I don't know what he looks like?

"That one's kind of new," Tom says. "Michelle, she's been around for a while. Does private dances all the time. And I thought maybe . . . well, since you guys seemed to have built a little rapport and all . . ."

"Tom, you embarrassed her. If she's new here, then private dancing is probably a little too extreme."

"Why? She makes good money doing it here. What's the difference?"

It wouldn't do any good to explain to Tom what Crystal and I were talking about. The food chain thing. He wouldn't understand that we had found a common ground and were communicating outside this topless arena. Instead he would just laugh and accuse me of having a crush on her.

"It's no big deal," I say. "But do you mind if we leave? I'd like to try Misty again."

This disappoints Tom, but he knows when to cut his losses.

We call a waitress to the table and settle the bill. I ask her if there is any way she could call Crystal back out for just a moment.

"No can do, honey-pie," she answers. "These are working girls. If they're not on the floor, it means they're on break. Off-limits to you."

"But—"

"There are plenty of butts for you to look at out here. Crystal's is off duty."

And then she walks away.

Tom looks at me as if he knows something I don't, which kind of pisses me off. He thinks I have a crush on her. I could tell him that Crystal knew about transmitting, but for some reason I don't think he would give a shit. He doesn't care how I got here or that I risked my life to test new technology. He just wants to play golf. That's the kind of nuts-and-bolts guy Tom is. A man whose life is devoid of subplots. He works, he plays, he sleeps. Everything else is clutter.

For the first time since Crystal mentioned Mystery Man, I turn around. There are more customers now, perhaps thirty sitting between our table and the door. All of them are men except for the occasional dancer. I scan this smallish crowd nonchalantly, spending just fractions of a second on any one person. They are blue-collar men, white-collar men, and greasy men wearing slick hair and synthetic shirts. None of them stand out. None of them look at me any longer than I look at them. In a moment, we walk out the door and into the warm, dry air.

The sun is still high in the sky. My watch tells me it's seven fifteen, but here in Mountain Time it is actually one hour earlier. The parking lot is mostly full now.

"So how often do you come here?" I ask him.

"About twice a month."

"Do you come alone?"

"Sometimes alone, sometimes a couple of us go. Why?"

I'm trying to stall him, of course, to see if Mystery Man will burst out the front door looking for me. We get into the car.

"Just curious. I kind of like this place."

Tom starts the ignition.

"You like that girl," he says.

He's about to put the car into gear. No sign of Mystery Man.

"Tom, look at me for a second."

This finally stops him. "What?"

"Do I look any different to you?"

"Different how?"

"You tell me."

"I haven't seen you in a year and a half, Cam. How am I supposed to remember what you looked like then? Maybe you're a little heavier."

"Heavier?"

"Yeah, a little in the face, I think. Hell, I don't know. Why do you ask?"

"That girl in there, she knew about transmitting. Can you believe that? A corporate secret so obscure that I didn't have a clue about it, and *she* knew."

He looks at me strangely. Like he has something to say but isn't sure how to begin.

"How?" he asks finally.

"Read about it on the Internet."

"The *Internet*?"

"That's what she said."

He just looks at me again.

"Well, I have to admit that's kind of weird. Still, what does it have to do with how you look?"

"Crystal said that she's heard weird stuff about the transmission machine. Like some of the animal test subjects came through pretty fucked up."

"I think she was playing games with you," he says. "What would a stripper know about transmitting?"

I'm about to answer him when the front door opens. A tall, sturdy man with a black goatee steps out. His eyes appear to scan the parking lot, and I try not to stare as his gaze heads our way. After a moment, he turns around and goes back into the building.

Was that him?

"You're right," I say to Tom. "She wouldn't know anything about transmitting. I guess she just got me curious."

He puts the car in gear and heads for the street.

"She's a beautiful woman, Cameron. We should come back tomorrow. She invited you, after all."

I look back at the door again, watching for the man with the goatee.

"Yeah," I answer. "We should definitely come back."

When I call Misty from Tom's house, she is surprised to hear from me a second time. When I ask why, she gives me a one-word answer.

"Tom."

"You know him well," I say.

Everyone says total honesty is the key to a successful relationship, but I don't want my paranoia to needlessly worry Misty, so I don't tell her about Mystery Man. Instead we talk about everything else, which is to say nothing at all. It started raining an hour or so after I left Houston. Her mom is coming a week early this Thanksgiving. She saw another roach in the house again, so we better hire a different exterminator. The building blocks of life.

Our conversation winds down, and I promise to call her again tomorrow.

"And don't worry about me," I tell her. "I'll be back so soon, it'll be like I was never gone."

When we were younger, Tom and I both wanted to be professional golfers. He played a year in college and then quit because of a personality conflict with the coach. I didn't even make the team.

You have to work your ass off to be good at anything, but you really have to work your ass off to be good at golf. After college we spent our weekends competing in local tournaments, won a few, and drew the attention of club pros around town. Tom made a hole-in-one in a local fund-raising event and the next day found his picture in the paper.

And when Barton Creek, one of the finest golf facilities in Texas, invited us to play in a qualifying tournament for their annual PGA event, Tom and I couldn't wait. I was already dreaming about who my playing partner might be—Greg Norman, Nick Faldo, or maybe even Jack Nicklaus. I couldn't believe it. I was twenty-two and about to stand on the tee with real professional golfers.

What I did instead was learn a bitter lesson. See, there are a lot of talented people in the world. Not just in golf, but in every arena where talent can be measured. Maybe you're the best football player on your high school team, but when you get to college you go straight to the bench. Or maybe you turn out to be the starting quarterback on that same college team but don't get drafted by the NFL. It happens all the time, because when you round up all the people who are good at something, you realize just how ordinary you are.

"I'm thinking of trying out for the U.S. Open," Tom tells me now as he addresses the ball. We're playing this morning at Sandy Canyon Golf Club, standing on the number two tee box. Par three. The sky is dark with clouds, and rain is expected by noon. This is why, even though we stayed up half the night drinking beer, Tom and I are roaming the course at six thirty AM.

"The U.S. Open? You've already tried three times. Haven't you had enough?"

He strikes the ball. It flies high, straight, and lands only a few feet behind the pin.

"Look at that shot, Cameron. I play nearly every day now. I hit five hundred balls a week at the range."

"Five hundred is nothing. And even if you hit five *thousand* balls at the range, all perfect, it doesn't matter if you can't produce on the course."

"But I do produce," he says. "I shot sixty-four here last week."

"Against who? Your grandma?"

He doesn't say anything at first. Perhaps he remembers the disaster at Barton Creek when neither of us broke eighty. We played like fools.

I step forward and prepare to tee off. The hole is 185 yards away, and any good golfer can hit the green nearly every time. The challenge is to land it close like Tom just did. Easy enough in a mundane setting like this, but add a little pressure—like grandstands, corporate tents, thousands of spectators—and suddenly golf becomes a whole new game. A game where Tiger Woods is king and at best you're a jester.

The thing with Tom is that he doesn't want a regular job. It's not enough that he makes seventy thousand dollars a year selling cars at the local Honda dealership. He wants the money to be glamorous. And I can respect that. What I can't understand is why he has forgone a serious relationship and abandoned the idea of having a family to pursue his dream. I would do anything to have children, and he chooses not to.

When I swing the club, I realize right away that it's all wrong. The ball pulls left, drops into tall grass beside the green, and disappears.

"Terrible shot," I say and shake my head.

"You can get up and down from there," Tom offers.

We walk back to the cart and drive toward the green. Wind sweeps across my face. I close my eyes. Golf just doesn't excite me the way it once did.

"What's the problem, Cam? You've been in the dumps since you got here. Is everything okay at home?"

"Fine, I guess."

"You guess?"

"We're doing as well as any couple after fifteen years of marriage."

"Then what is it? This is your celebratory golf game. You *transmitted* yesterday, man. You're supposed to be having fun."

Instead of answering him, I grab my wedge and putter and head for my ball. How am I supposed to enjoy playing golf today when all I can think about is my encounter with Crystal? Was she right? Could the transmission really have screwed me up?

From the rough I chip the ball, and it rolls to within a few feet of the pin.

"Good shot!" Tom says. "I knew you could save par from there."

Why can Tom smile so easily? How can he go through each day and not ask the questions that for me never cease? Doesn't it bother him that life seems to be nothing more than a series of random events between birth and death? I suppose it doesn't. Tom has never let go of his dream to be a professional golfer, and maybe that's the secret. His finest days are always in the future.

"Maybe you don't want to talk about what's bothering you," he says and then smoothly makes the putt. "That's okay. But you've got to leave it off the course if we're going to have fun. Agreed?"

"Agreed."

The next hole is a long par five, 540 yards or so. A small rock outcropping separates us from the fairway ahead, something that could prove dangerous for a person of questionable skill. A low tee shot, after all, could hit the rocks and create an unpredictable and dangerous ricochet. For golfers of our caliber, however, it's not really a concern.

Tom hits first, and his shot lands ahead of a giant boulder in the middle of the fairway. Just about perfect. Now it's my turn, and this time I take an extra moment to concentrate on my swing. I can score almost as well as Tom if I pay close attention to my game. Just a slow, smooth backswing and—

Something happens as I start back down. I don't know what causes it, but my feet sway and my hands wobble. Not a lot—it's really just a tiny loss of coordination—but in golf the slightest error can be catastrophic. I hit the top third of the ball, driving it low and to the left. There is a *smack*! as the ball caroms off a rock and heads back our way. It narrowly misses Tom and slams into the cart.

For a moment I just stand there, afraid to look back at Tom. I can't believe I just did that.

"Holy shit, Cam," he says finally. "When did you play last?"

"Two weeks ago. Shot a seventy at Wedgewood. Tied my course record."

"You must be tired. We were up pretty late last night. Or maybe it's transmission lag."

Transmission lag. You don't get lag when you cross only one time zone. And tired or not, I *never* hit shots like that.

"I don't know what happened. I'm going to count that as out-of-bounds and hit another one."

When I line up again, Tom hides behind the cart. What a confidence booster. I stand there for several seconds, smell rain on the freshening wind, and imagine the next ricochet slamming into my forehead. Knocking me unconscious.

I bring the club back and cringe, but this time my shot flies straight. I'm in the fairway.

"Much better," Tom says. "We all hit bad shots every now and then."

I nod my head but say nothing. All I can think about is my conversation yesterday with Crystal.

So how do you feel now? Did it screw you up at all? Some of the animal test subjects came through pretty fucked up.

Like how? I wonder.

We drive to our tee shots. Tom hits first and knocks a three-wood onto the green.

"Good shot," I exclaim. "You're on for eagle."

"Bring on the U.S. Open," he says.

I address my shot next, and already the golf demons are playing with my mind. *You're gonna screw up again. You nearly took Tom's head off a minute ago. Do you even remember how to hit the ball?* Sure enough, I lose control of my swing, and the ball scoots across the ground.

"Shit! I'm playing like a goddamn beginner."

"What's the matter with your balance? You're moving all over the—"

"I don't know what's wrong!"

"This is stupid. I know you're worried about what that stripper said yesterday."

I start walking toward my ball with my three-wood in hand. I don't care if it's the wrong club. I'll hit it anyway.

"Cameron!"

I strike the ball perfectly this time and a wind gust carries it thirty yards over the green. I should've used a different club.

Tom drives up beside me. "What the hell was that?"

"A good shot. Didn't you see it?"

I start walking toward the green. I'm not the most upbeat person in the world, but I generally don't get very angry. In fact, I can't remember the last time I was this mad. Maybe it's the weather. The air feels electric.

Tom rolls along beside me. "Get in the cart, Cameron."

"Forget it. I don't deserve to ride."

"We're holding up the group behind us."

I turn around and look back down the fairway. A cart is already waiting on us.

"I'll go tell them to slow down."

"They're not moving that fast, Cameron. We're going kind of slow."

"Because of me, right?"

"Well, if you'd ride in the cart . . ."

I'm still staring at the cart behind us. My anger now has something else on which to focus. I feel like storming back there, confronting them. God knows I'm angry enough. And—

One of the men just got out of the cart. The other, the guy on the passenger side, is still sitting there. And damned if he doesn't look like—

"Hey," I say.

"What?"

"That guy back there. In the cart. I saw him at The Wildcat last night."

"What? Are you sure?"

"Yes. He's got that goatee. I remember the goatee."

"Cameron," Tom insists, "there are fifty thousand men in Phoenix who have goatees."

"I remember this guy. He came outside after us and looked around the parking lot. Crystal said there was a man staring at me last night. She thought he might have been someone from NeuroStor."

"Come on, Cam. That girl was just fucking around. Why would someone from NeuroStor be watching you?"

Something in Tom's eyes tells me his question was rhetorical, but I answer it anyway.

"To see if I came through messed up."

"Oh, shit. That's insane. They already did their tests."

"So? You see how I'm playing golf today. I haven't done anything like this in twenty years."

"You're just upset," he says, almost pleading. "And tired."

"You think that's it? What about yesterday, at the transmission station? I fell and hit my head like a clown. And that was after you thought I'd come out all crazy, speaking in tongues or walking in circles."

Tom's eyebrows shrink toward each other. He seems distressed. Did I just speak what is on his mind? Does he think I'm nuts? Does he not think I'm the Cameron Fisher who stepped into the portal in Houston?

"We should leave," he says.

"What?"

Still with that concerned look in his eyes. "We have to get the hell out of here."

"Why?"

"I don't know. Because you're being followed. Get in the cart, Cameron."

At the very least we need to clear the fairway so the group behind us can hit their shots. I get in the cart as instructed, and Tom takes off toward the green.

"Tom," I tell him. "My boss, Rodrigo Batista, he's not exactly the most trusting guy in the world. It wouldn't be surprising to know he's having me followed. I'm one of his prize volunteers, after all."

"You're in danger."

We reach the green. My ball is on the other side, and I watch for it as I wait for Tom to slow down. But he doesn't. He keeps driving as if we have completed the hole.

"Where the hell are you going?" I demand. "We're not leaving. I came out here to play golf, and even if I'm playing like shit, I'm not going to let Batista ruin our time together."

"And I'm not going to let you get caught," Tom says, distractedly, almost as if he is talking to someone else.

The distance between the green of this hole and the tee of the next one is considerable. Thirty or forty seconds pass as the golf cart's whining engine pushes us down the concrete path. I'm trying to forget what happened to my golf swing, hoping that my lack of coordination was simply a mental lapse, that Crystal's fears have no basis whatsoever in reality. And here Tom is making it worse.

We reach the next hole, where the group ahead of us is teeing off. One of the foursome glares at us, and Tom stops. We can't drive by during someone's swing.

"Hey," I whisper to Tom.

"What?"

"Isn't that Troy Aikman?"

"Cameron," he hisses. "Will you stop fucking around? We shouldn't be waiting here. They're probably on their way right now."

"Look," I say. "Tell me it's not him."

But Tom's eyes are instead trained on the path behind us. Because of the topography, the rolling, sandy terrain, he can only see about a hundred yards or so in that direction. I pray that the man with the goatee doesn't appear back there. Because if he does, Tom will no doubt drive forward, past these men in front of us, which will not only be an insulting breach of golf etiquette but also confirmation that I am indeed being followed. And while I said I wasn't surprised by that—because really, I'm not—it makes me wonder just how confident Batista is in the accuracy of his machine.

The man who may or may not be Troy Aikman is the last to hit, and Tom looks up as he addresses his ball. At the same time a cart appears on the path behind us. The passenger is without question the man with the goatee. Then Tom turns, sees them approaching, and I quickly remove the cart's ignition key. So when he slams his foot on the accelerator, nothing happens.

"What the fuck?" he cries.

The golfer on the tee is just beginning his backswing. He stops and glares at us again.

"Excuse me," he says. "Do you mind?"

"Cameron, the cart won't go. Why won't the fucking cart go?"

"I'm sorry," I say to the man on the tee. I'm pretty sure it's Troy, but it's kind of hard to see considering the early morning clouds.

Tom grabs my arm. "Where did the key go?"

"I took it."

"Why?"

"Ex*cuse* me," the golfer says again. "I'd like to go ahead and hit if you don't mind."

The cart behind us is thirty yards away.

"Cameron, give me the key."

"Stop it, Tom. I don't want to run. They're too close for us to run now, anyway."

Tom is unconvinced. I cannot understand why he's so worried about Batista's surveillance.

"Listen," I whisper. "They're right behind us now. Let this guy hit before he comes over here and swats us with his driver."

"It's not him I'm concerned about."

The golfer hits. His shot is low but long and straight. He glares at us again as he walks back to his cart, and then the entire foursome drives away.

And now our pursuers have arrived.

I jump out of the cart at once, and Tom reluctantly does the same. This is my first close look at the man who might be a NeuroStor spy. His goatee and obsidian eyes are joined by a tall, imposing frame. The other fellow is even more muscular, but stands shorter and appears to be cursed with some sort of pigmentation problem. His skin is sallow and pink, his hair a shade of blond that resembles white. The two men step out of the cart as we approach.

"We're playing a little slow today," I explain.

"That's okay," the blond man says. "We're in no rush."

"Still," Tom says. "We're going to take our time today and enjoy the round. Why don't you play through?"

Now the goatee man answers. His voice is more direct. "Don't worry about us. We'll slow down so we don't bother you."

I am trying to think of what to say next when another cart swings around the hill. It's a course marshal.

"We got people who want to play golf around here," he says, stopping beside our two carts. He is an older gentleman, and his accent is southern. "You boys gonna tee off or just stand there all day?"

"We were just inviting these fellows to play through," Tom explains.

"No can do," the marshal says, and spits something brown into the nearby grass. "You four boys are going to play together from here on out. I can't have you slowin' down everyone behind you."

Then he looks at the other two men and adds, "You two could stand to watch a couple of real golfers, anyhow. I seen you hit back there and it wasn't pretty."

Golfers can be a cliquish bunch, especially old men who play the game, so this insult is not much of a shock to me. Goatee man doesn't seem to take it very well, however. He wants to shoot something back at the marshal, but his partner speaks first and is surprisingly cordial.

"We'll go ahead and play with them," he says. "We don't want to impede play."

"Good choice," the old man agrees. Already he is driving away. "And I'd hurry if I was you. There's a storm coming."

We are left standing together with these two men, and it is awkward to say the least.

"We should get started," I say. "Maybe we can at least finish the front nine before it rains."

Tom agrees. We grab our clubs and step onto the tee. The two men follow suit, and soon we are all standing there together. Tom will hit first.

"I'm Tom," he says. "This is Cameron."

Goatee man introduces himself as Ivan and his blond buddy as Ed.

"So what do you guys do?" Tom asks, and the slight waver in his voice tells me just how uncomfortable he is. "What line of work are you in?"

Ivan says, "Security. How about you?"

"I sell cars. He works in accounting."

And then Tom hits. His ball flies nearly three hundred yards down the right side of the fairway.

It's my turn next, and my hand shakes slightly as I tee the ball. If these men were sent to watch me after all, I have just given them a front-row seat. And so I become nervous, tournament-nervous, because now it seems obvious to me that everyone here is watching to see if I can still hit the ball. To see if the transmission has altered me in some way. And I don't know what I'm going to do if that is indeed true.

I try to calm myself and use all the stress-management techniques I've learned over the years to keep my golf game in control, but something fundamental is slipping away. No longer can I picture what it's like to make contact with the ball. When I think about the backswing, the rotation of my shoulders and my grip on the club, it comes across as an unseemly system that has no chance for success. Still, I address the ball the same way I have for the past twenty years and focus all my concentration on this shot. I have done it successfully thousands of times. Surely, I can do so again.

I pull back, swing forward, but somewhere along the way the signal gets scrambled. I am distraught even as the club makes contact with the ball because I know this shot is going to be a poor one. The ball flies into the air, barely ten feet off the ground, and heads to the right, flying along the cart path. It hits the concrete at maybe one hundred yards out and rolls along for another thirty or forty, finally coming to rest near the backyard of someone's house.

"Tough shot," Ivan says as he walks forward. He's up next.

I step away to give him room and trip as I walk backwards. Tom catches me with his hand before I fall to the ground, but Ivan sees this out of the corner of his eye—I know he does—and Ed does, too.

My body thrums with fear. Not just because these men are here to witness my coordination breakdown, but because I am beginning to believe that something is significantly wrong with me.

My mind reels further as I watch Ivan address his tee shot. This man is no golfer. He hunches over the ball like a football lineman, and his swing is something painful to watch. Ed is only marginally better. His shot disappears into the left rough about 120 yards away.

"We're all over the place," Tom says. He laughs nervously.

A droplet of moisture streaks across my face as we head for our cart. Ivan steers left, in search of Ed's ball. I insert the key into the ignition, and we begin toward ours as well.

"Can you feel it?" Tom asks me. "Can you feel what's wrong?"

A difficult question to answer. Consciously, no. But something beneath thought, something more fundamental, signals me. Maybe it's just my imagination, but I feel different somehow, changed. Like I'm not the same person I was, at least not physically.

"I feel something. I don't know what it is."

"We have to get you out of here. And then, well, at some point I guess you should see a doctor."

"But what in the world would a doctor look for? And if he found something, how would he fix it?"

"Those guys aren't playing golf," Tom points out. "Ed pretended to hit, but then he just picked up his ball. At least one of them is always watching us."

"So what do we do?"

"I still think we should try to get away from them," Tom says. "I don't like it at all that they're so close. But to have a chance to get away, we'll need to put some distance between them and us, so for now we should continue to play like normal."

"Why are you so worried about them following me? Don't you think it makes sense that Batista would have me followed?"

"Just hit, Cameron. Give me a chance to think."

My ball sits just where the rough ends and someone's lawn begins. The house is a stucco mansion. A large glass door opens to a backyard concrete porch, and standing inside this door is a young child, perhaps five years old. He waves as I get out of the cart. When I wave back, he smiles.

My ball is half-buried in the grass, and I know it will not be easy to make solid contact. I use my six-iron and attempt to punch it out into the fairway again. Instead, I miss the ball completely, whiffing like a batter going after a breaking ball. I look up at the kid. He is dressed in Superman pajamas. He's giggling at me.

"Keep your head down, Cam," Tom says, signaling the precipitous drop my golf skills have undergone today. *Keep your head down* is a tip normally reserved for beginners.

I try again, and this time my ball flies about fifty yards away in the center of the fairway, still far behind Tom's first shot. He starts to say something to me as I climb back into the cart, but just then Ivan and Ed drive up.

"Having fun?" Ed asks.

"Of course," I answer.

Tom drives up a little and then walks out to the ball with me. He recites a few bogus instructions about my swing and moves his hands around as if he's a real golf instructor.

"Next time they're far away from us," he says, lower now, still pretending to swing, "we're going to drive away. Wherever they are, we're going in the opposite direction. And if we can't get far enough away, we'll hide behind a rock."

"Hide on a golf course in the desert?"

"There are hundreds of rock formations on this course. Big ones. Those two guys can't check them all. Besides, the marshal will chase them off the course when he realizes they're not playing golf."

"And then what? They could just go wait at your car."

"In the parking lot, other people will be around. Witnesses."

"Tom, we have no idea what they want or why they're here. I'm a whole lot more worried about what's wrong with me than I am about those two goons."

We've been standing here too long, so I hit the ball and this time land in a sand trap beside the green.

"That was better," Ed says as we drive back to the cart path. "Just a little off target."

"Thanks."

When I look at Ivan, I begin to share some of Tom's concern. He hasn't said a word since our tee shots, and doesn't look like a guy who wants to ask questions about the nuances of my post-transmission behavior. Besides, when you think about it, if all NeuroStor wanted was to observe me, they probably wouldn't have sent a couple of thugs.

Tom and I don't talk as we drive toward his ball. He gets out of the cart, uses only seconds to prepare his stance, and then hits a spectacular shot. The ball travels nearly two hundred yards and stops ten feet in front of the hole.

"I think you *are* ready for the U.S. Open," I say, and Tom smiles. This is as much pressure as any golf tournament, and he's still hitting like a pro.

Things are tense on the green. Neither of the men are talking to us now, and Tom and I make only short, vain attempts at conversation. Surely they must know we've figured them out, but we move on to the next tee—hole number five—without incident. Tom's shot flies straight down the middle again, and the rest of us spray errant shots around, but not on, the fairway. It begins to rain. Sprinkles first, and then more steadily.

Soon we find ourselves a hundred yards or so away from Ivan and Ed. They are parked on the cart path. Tom and I drive into the left rough, at the top of a hill. My ball is buried here, and Tom's sits beyond the hill, another hundred yards ahead and to our right. I am about to get out of the cart when Tom grabs my arm.

"Your ball isn't here," he says. "It rolled farther, beyond the hill."

"No, it—"

"Yes, it did." He drives over the hill until we can no longer see Ivan and Ed.

"Let's get out here," Tom says.

He runs toward the rocks that border the left rough, motioning for me to follow. In just a few moments, we have moved beyond the rocks and are jogging beside them.

"Where are we going?" I ask.

"These rocks run all the way to the green and even go behind it. We might get to the next hole without them seeing us."

"But won't they naturally go in that direction? That's right where the cart path will take them."

"Yeah, but we'll have a head start. Depending on what they do, maybe we can double back. Look, I'm making this up as we go along."

The rain intensifies as we make our way toward the green. It splatters around our feet, turning desert dust into mud. It smacks against the rocks on our right. Several times I slip and once almost slide into a thick, saguaro cactus.

Tom watches the fairway as we run, hoping to catch a glimpse of Ivan and Ed. If he sees them, he doesn't say so. Finally we come to a stop just beyond the green, behind a round boulder that is perhaps fifteen feet across.

My heart is hammering. Sweat and rain moisten my clothes. I struggle to speak between heavy breaths. "Now we wait?"

"We wait," Tom gasps. We are no longer the young fellows of our college days.

Around us, the storm deepens. For the first time, I hear the distant bass signature of thunder. Wind angles the pounding rain, which grows stronger still.

"This is silly," I say, raising my voice so Tom can hear me. "We're not going anywhere out here."

"Then neither are they."

"But what next? Even if we get off this course without them, what's to stop them from finding me again? What if they know where you live?"

"At least that would be on my property. I could deal with these assholes on my own property."

I still am not clear on why we are attempting to get away from these guys. Besides Ivan's threatening demeanor, there is no clear evidence to suggest that they want anything more than to observe me. And no matter what happens today, a bigger problem lies ahead: my entire post-transmission existence. Am I not the man who entered the departing portal back in Houston? My declining dexterity suggests that something indeed went wrong between Texas and Arizona, and it makes me sick to think what exactly the error might have been. Is something permanently wrong with me? And what the hell is it?

I turn to Tom just as his eyes widen, and then see what has surprised him: Ivan. He is walking toward us, but instead of coming from the putting green, he has been slinking around the rocks on our right. It seems as though the one place we forgot to watch is the exact direction from which we came.

Tom grabs my arm. "I knew it! He's got a gun. Come on!"

We scamper between the rocks, onto the green, feet slipping on the wet grass. Our present course would take us across the cart path toward a row of houses, but Ed has foreseen this predictable response and stands directly in our path. Through the driving rain I see a gun held chest high and pointed directly at us. We come to a stop just as lightning stabs out of the sky, branching in several directions as it blazes toward the ground. Thunder booms from nowhere. Rivers of rain pour off the bill of my cap.

I turn around again, looking for Ivan, and find him walking toward us. His gun is now trained on us as well.

"What the hell do we do now?" I ask Tom.

About forty yards separates each of the men from us. If we're going to do anything other than surrender, it better be now.

"I'm telling you, Cameron. We can't let these guys catch us."

"What do you—"

"Just come on!"

Tom takes off, back across the green again, splitting the distance between the two men. I don't know what else to do, so I follow him. We are no longer headed toward the houses, but instead run perpendicular to our former course. They could shoot us now—from behind, shoot us in our backs—but something tells me this is not going to happen. Why would they kill us? What have we done? So I run behind Tom, my legs raw now, feet sloshing inside wet shoes, until we reach the cart path. A small stucco structure stands just ahead. Perhaps a snack bar or bathrooms. The path will also take us back to the clubhouse if we follow it long enough.

The sky is dark now, the color of a bruise. Clouds are lower, rolling near the ground, even obscuring a nearby butte. The rain pelts our backs and the ground without mercy. I can't believe this is happening in southern Arizona. We're supposed to be in a desert.

And then, as if from nowhere, another man leaps into view. Another! There are three of them! Tom veers to his left, his feet slip, and he spills toward the ground in a heap. The man jumps on him at once. Beneath them, the muddy ground slopes away from the cart path—apparently paved at the crest of a small hill—and they slide down perhaps twenty feet.

"Keep running!" Tom screams at me. "Don't stop!"

But I can't keep running. I can't leave Tom behind. I turn around, intending to go after him, when I see Ivan barreling toward me on the cart path.

"Find Crystal, Cam! Get the fuck out of here and find—"

His words are cut off by a gunshot.

"*Tom!*" I scream.

I think I hear him answer. It sounds like the word *run*. But the rain is so loud now I can't be sure. My mind screams at me to go down there, to go help him, but already his pursuer is standing up, gun in hand. Ivan will be upon me in a few seconds.

Tom, please forgive me.

I take off running again.

three

┇┇┇

I t's the end of the world.

The cart path veers this way and that as it circles the small hills that provide the golf course with its impressive relief. My feet, barely able to maintain traction against the slick asphalt, pound along as fast as my adrenaline-enhanced legs will drive them. I don't know if it's fast enough.

Ivan is still behind me.

My father was once a Little League football coach, and he taught me never to turn around when I was running unimpeded for the end zone. *It will only slow you down,* he said, *and that might be the difference between a touchdown and getting tackled from behind.* Sound advice, I suppose, but the survival instinct encoded in my animal brain always overpowered even this simple logic. You want to know who is chasing you, you want to know how close he is, you want to know how much harder you have to run. Or maybe you just want to know when to expect the end.

When I left Tom, Ivan was thirty or forty yards behind me. Since then I have not been able to widen the distance between us. This is disturbing, because I get the feeling Ivan is just biding his time, waiting until I run out of gas. Let the runner tire out, after all, and he'll be in no shape to put up a fight.

Why would Tom tell me to find Crystal? Because she already knew about the transmission machine?

The rain slackens somewhat. It's still a downpour, but at least a person running for his life can now see where he's going. I'm moving alongside hole six, about halfway to the green, and I'm losing energy fast. There are no structures immediately in sight—the last was a restroom stall—and thus there is no one to help me and no place to hide.

I don't know where I'm going, but I'm pretty sure I'm never going to outrun this man. Maybe I should stop right now and try to reason with him. Maybe I should just give up.

My legs pump, my chest heaves. My heart is going to explode at any moment. I haven't run this much since a 10K charity event last summer, and that fiasco laid me up in bed for two days. I honestly don't know how I've made it this far. Adrenaline and emotion, I suppose—two wells of energy that are going to run dry any moment. The only way to avoid capture by Ivan is to use the only tissue in my body not currently exhausted: my brain.

The first thing I do is veer off the cart path. Any idiot knows you don't run straight ahead when your pursuer is faster than you, and yet this is exactly what I've been doing. The cart path still follows the top edge of a small hill, but the drop away from the pavement is less severe now. My feet slide immediately into mud. I nearly fall twice, but somehow maintain my balance all the way to the bottom of the hill. Ivan is not so lucky. As I change directions, I see him slip in the mud about halfway down. His butt hits the ground first, and then he slides for a few feet before slamming into a rock. He flips over and tumbles the rest of the way down in a series of clumsy somersaults. The gun flies out of his hand. It lands about ten feet from his outstretched arms and buries itself halfway into the mud.

I could make a play for the gun, because for a second or two Ivan doesn't move. But as I stand there, his arms and legs dig at the muddy ground, and he manages to bring himself to a wobbly stance. Fuck the gun. I could have run fifty yards while I stood here watching. I turn around and take off once again, paralleling the foot of this hill. My side hurts as if I've been punched in the kidneys. My legs are gelatin. When I finally look back for him again, I am shocked to find him less than thirty yards behind me.

I'm in decent shape for a thirty-five-year-old man, but only Superman could keep up this pace forever. Any moment my legs are simply going to stop moving. I was dumb to leave the cart path, where at least the possibility of encountering other people existed, and now I don't have the strength to get back there, not with that hill to climb.

I look behind me and find Ivan closer still. He no longer carries the gun, but this provides little consolation, since I could surely mount no physical defense against him. I am caught. There is no escape. I am—

My feet slip out from under me while my head is still turned, and I fall headfirst into the ground. Searing pain sweeps across my cheek as my face strikes a rock embedded in the mud. I slide forward, my arms and exhausted legs scrambling against the grime, instinctively trying to resume my flight from danger. With great effort I gather my feet close and struggle to stand. Then arms grasp me from behind in a powerful bear hug. Ivan pulls me backwards briefly and then throws me against the ground, pinning me there. When I try to look at him, mud oozes into my eyes. Stinging me. Blinding me.

"Why did you run?" he screams.

My mind, whirling and nauseous, doesn't comprehend the question. My eyes scream in pain. My ears roar. I think I must have suffered some sort of brain trauma when my face hit the rock.

"What do you know? Tell me or I'll drown you in that river."

River?

"Talk to me, goddammit!"

The roaring is louder now. Not brain damage, but the sound of rushing water. I must have been running directly toward it.

He seizes my shoulders and slings me closer to the roaring sound. I land on my back, solidly, and the impact induces a jagged fit of coughing that I fear will yield blood.

"Your friend back there knew something. He told you to call Crystal. Was this a setup?"

I would like to know the answer to that question myself.

Ivan seizes my shoulders again. This time, instead of throwing me, he straddles my body and drags me forward until the ground beneath my head falls away. Adrenaline pours into me, pooling as terror in my fingers and toes.

I have landed on the bank of a surging current of mud and water.

Even from this compromised position I can see the river tugging at its bank, eroding the rain-softened earth at an alarming rate. Our position so close to the edge is obviously not safe. Already the mud beneath me is moving, pulled toward the river and sinking at the same time. If I go into that water, I will likely die.

Ivan leans forward. Pulls my head close. Tobacco and garlic foul his breath.

"Tell me, motherfucker, or I'll throw you in. Tell me what you know and how you know it."

"Did the transmission do something to me? Am I going to die?"

He doesn't answer.

"Are you going to kill me?"

"I didn't come out here to kill you," he says. "You shouldn't have run."

The ground is still moving, down and away, but now *I* am moving as well. Sinking. My body is two, maybe three inches below the surface of the mud. Ivan seems to notice this the same time I do, because he lets go of me and tries to step away. But his feet are stuck. He loses balance and falls backwards, onto my ankles.

My head fell when he let go and now hangs over the soft edge of the bank, pulling my neck deeper into the mud. Ivan manages to suck his feet out and stumbles away from me, but I can barely move. This mud is like quicksand. My arms and legs are almost completely immobilized. If anything, struggling seems to be pulling me down more quickly.

Fear floods me now, a claustrophobic terror with which I am utterly unfamiliar. This is what it must feel like to die.

"Help me!" I yell.

Ivan stands and seems to come closer. I can't see him, not with my head hanging so far over the bank, but I imagine that he's grinning.

"Fuck off. You're the one who ran."

"Please! I'm sinking!"

"No way, Cameron. Batista will never know I didn't save you. That asshole should have told me you knew something. That lying prick."

Mud closes in over my arms and squeezes my neck until I can hardly breathe. The claustrophobia is like fire inside me, burning me, killing me. Rain splatters on my face. I am about to sink into a muddy grave.

"Oh God PLEASE!"

"Believe it or not, it's better for you this way. If you knew what the experiments were like, you'd be glad to drown."

He moves forward and steps on me. Pushes me deeper. Now my entire torso is enclosed, and my neck goes next. I suck oxygen into my lungs like a machine, inhaling and exhaling with great effort, ignoring the burning, friction pain. I cannot move. I cannot hear. All I can do is scream.

I am screaming.

I am dying.

The smell is raw. Earthen. Mud completely covers my ears and now begins to seep into the corners of my eyes. My lungs inhale and exhale automatically, violently, as involuntary systems struggle to keep me alive.

I don't know if my attacker is still around. I can no longer detect stimuli other than rain and the smell of mud closing around my face. Erosion is going to bury me. A fold of mud closes over my face, covering my mouth and partially blocking my nasal openings. Panic drives the spike of terror farther into my brain. It seems as if I am sucking air through pinholes. Not enough. The air is not enough. Water around me. Pulling me. Down.

Into my grave.

No eulogy.

Water around me. Cool water, eroding the riverbank.

Still sucking for air. Keep drawing in flecks of mud that stick to the hairs in my nose, further constricting the pipes through which I cling to life. Can't see anything at all now. From above I must appear to be almost fully buried.

Water scours away the mud around me, under me, gurgling, gushing, spurting. My breathing comes fast and shallow. I swallow driblets of muddy water.

My God, I am going to die.

Misty gone to me forever. Tom perhaps dead already. My mother, my deceased father, everyone I know and have known. What is death? Is it sleep? Surely I will awake on the other side and laugh away this apprehension and fear. I have no concept of eternal darkness.

I struggle to hold my breath, command my body not to suck in another gulp of water. But desperate for oxygen, my chest shakes and heaves. My mouth opens. Muddy water rushes toward my throat. My lungs sense the danger and attempt to choke out the alien liquid, then greedily inhale more. The machine sputters. Muscles struggle against each other; straining, thrumming, dying.

The soft earth behind me rumbles, shakes, and a great flood of water flows through my grave and washes me out of it. The river is destroying the bank on which I was thrown, carrying the dissolved silt away in a rush, and me with it. I am tumbling, performing involuntary somersaults in the fast-moving current. Water runs up my nose and into my throat again, drowning my burgeoning sense of hope.

Then I break the water's surface. It happens quickly—wind across my face, rain pattering my cheeks—and fleetingly. I barely have time to cough out some of the water in my lungs before going under once again. The river pulls me forward at what feels like extraordinary speed, but the tumbling has stopped, and it appears I am only a few feet below the surface. With a little effort I am able to propel myself upward, and soon my head pops out of the water once again. I gasp for air this time and force my eyes open in spite of the grit that poisons them. I don't know how far I've traveled, but judging from this limited vantage point, the golf course is already long gone. Along with my pursuers, I suppose.

Without warning, I'm pulled underwater again. I begin to roll, tumbling, sinking deeper into this rushing current. After a few of these spins, I cannot tell up from down. My stomach pumps once, twice, and then vomit bubbles out of my mouth, along with most of the air in my lungs.

Something strikes me from behind, something both substantial and yielding. After a moment, I realize it is the riverbed. I slide forward across its soft surface, grasping in vain at anything that might slow my progress. But why do such a thing? I am out of usable oxygen. There is only one direction to go.

I allow myself to tumble over again, so that when I come around this time my feet strike the riverbed. Then I push forward with my legs and attempt to swim. But it is no use. I am so very tired. At this moment sleep seems like such an escape—the only way to retreat from the overpowering fury of the river, in fact—and my mind begins to drift into dreams.

Misty on the deck in our backyard. Sun shining bright overhead.

Birds in the trees. She is young again—a fresh, twentysomething woman.

Let's take a swim, she says, strolling to our kidney-shaped swimming pool. *Come on. Get in.*

I can't, I say. *I'm too tired.*

You must, she says, and dives into the pool. I watch her dark form glide beneath the brilliant ripples of chlorinated water. Then she rises and beckons me. *Swim, Cameron,* she implores. *Swim now if you ever want to see me again.*

And then I am in the pool. The water is brown, muddy. What the hell? I gasp for air, coughing and choking, and look around for Misty. She's disappeared. I jumped into the pool to be with her and now—

Something is scraping my back. I force my eyes open and find myself against the riverbank, out of the river's main throughput. I've come to rest against a thick root of some kind. I notice that the rain has slackened to sprinkles.

I cough, ejecting a soggy mixture of vomit and river water, and then suck in several deep breaths. Muscles all over my body ache miserably. My head spins. I feel like I've been in an automobile accident.

But I'm not dead. Not yet.

This place appears to be the outside corner of a severe bend in the river's path. The current must have swept me wide and pushed me into a tiny inlet protected from the main body of water. The top of the riverbank is several feet above my head and looks newly formed—a sure sign the river is either at its crest or still on the way up. I see nothing solid up there to grasp except for thin roots and grass.

Grass? Grass can't grow naturally in this part of Arizona, can it?

"Help!"

Pain like sharp glass slices my throat.

"Help!" I yell again. Then rest.

No one comes. I should have guessed. Maybe the grass really is some sort of hardy stock indigenous to this area, or maybe I'm near the edge of a sod farm.

After a few uneventful minutes pass, I try again. I scream *"Help"* and *"Somebody?"* and *"Is anyone there?"*

Nothing.

The water in my inlet is moving around somewhat. A little

whirlpool goes by, and then another. The earthen smell makes me want to vomit again.

"*Help!*" I scream again. "*Is anyone there? Please!*"

And this time I think I hear something. Voices.

"Over here!" I yell. "Please help me!"

I hear the voices again, but I don't know if they hear me. I scream another time. So close.

So close, but no one comes.

They must be real, the voices. I didn't make them up. I heard them with my own two ears.

So why isn't anyone coming?

"*Somebody help me! For God's sake!*"

The riverbank rises at least four feet above me, a vertical cliff of dark, damp, crumbling earth. Besides this root, which juts out of the bank below the surface of the water, there is nothing at all to grab. Nothing I can use to propel myself toward the solid ground above. If no one comes to save me, I will be trapped in this tiny inlet—at least until the river erodes it. And I don't know if I can face the current of that river again.

I shift against the root to get comfortable. A few sore spots and bruises have blossomed on my arms, but really I feel pretty good considering what just happened to me in that river. Considering I nearly drowned in it. But let's be honest—the river saved me. Saved me from that fucking goon, Ivan, who was sent to follow me because . . .

Because why?

It was easy to forget about the consequences of my transmission while running from Ivan, when the river was trying to drown me, but now the reality of it can't be ignored. I try to comprehend what could possibly be wrong—like fused cells or missing proteins or a fold of my brain turned backwards—but somehow I can't quite get my mind around the idea that these things might actually have happened to me. I don't want to believe something like that. I want to believe that I will continue to live a long, healthy life like everyone else. I mean, I'm thirty-five years old. People don't get sick when they're thirty-five.

But how selfish is that? Christ, I haven't even thought about Tom since I washed up here. He was shot. My best friend. Did they kill him? Take him out into the desert and bury him? Surely not. Surely he isn't dead. Maybe they left him on the golf course where someone might find him and call an ambulance.

And what about Misty? I can see her now, writing an article or researching one on the Internet, slender fingers clicking across the keyboard, eyes reflecting the silvery shine of the computer screen. And she is alone. Alone. I know I shouldn't worry so much—my wife is an intelligent, capable woman who can take care of herself—but though I know how strong she is, I still see her as a fragile creature. I think I learned this from my dad, who called my mom every night when he was out of town, who always held the door open for her, who jogged with her every night for nine months when she decided, at age forty-three, to lose twenty-five pounds. God, how he hated that. How he hated to run! But he wasn't about to let my mom jog through the neighborhood alone after sundown, so he ran. And lost fifteen pounds of his own in the process.

He died when I was sixteen, my dad. He was fishing on Choke Canyon Lake north of Corpus Christi when a yacht loaded with twenty-five-year-old drunken assholes broadsided his bass boat. Rather than be killed instantly, though, the tough old bird hung on for three days before finally succumbing to massive internal bleeding. He was a petroleum engineer for Shell Oil. I loved him a lot and wanted to be like him, even when I was supposed to be a rebellious teenager. At fifteen, he told me that I was "at that age where kids think their parents are idiots," but that was never true with me. I respected my dad more than anyone else on earth.

The river chugs by me, deceptively quiet, its main current only a few feet away. A man could drown effortlessly out there. Almost unconsciously, I wedge my arm farther behind the root upon which I am anchored and try to flatten myself against the riverbank.

My dad made no secret of his desire for me to become an engineer. He wanted me to make a difference not in petroleum but electronics or some other industry that wasn't killing the environment. I always told him I would, and that's why I was almost glad he wasn't there to see me graduate with a degree in business. After the ceremony, I held the parchment in my hands and cried.

I've made decent money, and my wife has made even more, so we're not hurting financially. But does such a thing really matter? When you're poor, you think lots of money will make your worries go away. When you're lonely, you never stop looking for that special someone who will make your life worth living. But where does it stop? What fills the vacuum? When do you stop searching for happiness and start living it?

But something feels different now, something that makes me think all the self-doubt and the existential questions aren't so important after all. Today I ran like prey from that man, Ivan. I was faced with my own death. And not only did I survive, but I *wanted* to survive. I fought for my life and won it.

Now *that* is something. *That* makes me feel alive.

I don't know what it means when my life must be threatened before I am able to appreciate it—perhaps it is only the survival instinct chiseled into my brain by a billion years of evolution—but right now I don't really care. It's something. It's a start.

Or is it? After all, my life wouldn't have been threatened at all if something hadn't gone severely wrong with my transmission. Those men came to the golf course to keep an eye on me and evaluate my condition. Was Ivan telling the truth when he said they wanted to take me somewhere for "experiments"? What does that mean? What the hell did Batista do to me?

What did they do to Tom?

I can't let myself think about that now. Terror will paralyze me if I sit here and worry about what may have happened to him. Or if I dream up hideous possibilities induced by the transmission machine. I have to *do* something. I have to confront Batista and demand that he tell me what the hell is going on. But how? By talking to Crystal? Just because she found out about transmission on the Internet doesn't mean she's going to be able to help resolve this situation.

The first thing to do is get out of this water. And in order to do that, I'll have to leave this inlet. There must be another place in the river where I might be able to climb out. A place where the riverbank is lower, or perhaps near civilization where someone might spot and rescue me.

Still, the inlet is safe. I'm alive in here. In that raging current I could die.

But Jesus, if I can't gather the nerve to go out there and try to rescue myself, then I'm already dead. Dead inside. And that's the story of my life, isn't it? A lifetime of taking the known path, the safe path, has doomed me to mediocrity. Fantasies unfulfilled. Dreams unrealized.

Ecstasy unknown. Love . . . do I even know what love is? My wife, the most important person in the world to me, begged me not to transmit. And yet here I am, struggling to survive, and for what? Because I was looking for some kind of transformation I thought the transmission machine could provide?

This is not who I should be—looking outward for direction, looking elsewhere for happiness, for something or someone to show me the way to salvation. It has to stop. I have to save myself. Deliverance from within.

I extract my arm from beneath the root and swim out into the river.

four

☰

Surprisingly, the current, while still strong, has lessened to a degree. And I'm not nearly as tired as before, when I fell into the river after a half-mile sprint over rough terrain. It seems easy to tread water and ride the current.

The rain has ended completely now, the overcast sky dissolving into stripes of blue. I float through the afternoon, bobbing like a jet-propelled fishing cork as wind dances across my face. The river is a living organism around me, its liquid sound muted by the muddy banks that contain it. This is my world, my universe. Everything I know and see is defined by these sensations and boundaries. And I think, for now, that kind of simplicity is something I need. It brings focus to a man who has long allowed himself to be paralyzed by the necessary complexity of life.

When Luke died, I couldn't stop asking questions. Why Luke? Why someone so young? I even asked selfish questions like, Why me? But the one I could not get past, the one for which I found no answer, was Why live at all? If you're not a religious person, if you don't believe that death is a portal through which you travel to spiritual immortality, what is the point of existence? What are the consequences?

Why live?

That's one hell of a question, something a person asks right before he goes after his wrists with a razor. Or after his coworkers with a military-issue machine gun. And this point of view—coming from me, anyway—must seem unjustified to the outside observer, who would be quick to point out that my existence on this planet isn't miserable. There are people in the world who struggle to obtain luxuries I take for granted, people with whom I would never trade places. And yet . . .

Is the curse of man his ability to question the instincts that drive him? A cat or a shark or an ant doesn't ask these questions. Animals just go about their business, eating, sleeping, and procreating until *great danger* comes for them, a situation to which they must react. Maybe they fight, maybe they run. But they never question the need to survive. It's an instinct, honed by evolution, never disputed.

But this curse of man, of course, is also his greatest gift. The very engine that allows him to question his own existence also provides the horsepower for unlimited potential. We hope. We dream. We love.

And for many people—I wonder if I may now tentatively count myself among them—something more comes with the gift of the human mind: purpose. Not necessarily a noble fate bestowed upon us by a higher power; it might be something learned or a genetic predisposition. You might be interested in physics, in raising horses, in leading people to a common goal. Your purpose could even be something as simple and fulfilling as running a healthy, well-adjusted household. But without purpose, what? When the basic needs of food and shelter have been met, what else drives a person to keep on living?

What I want . . . what I *think* I want . . . is to admit to Misty what I have been doing for longer than I care to remember: treading water. I want to come clean with her, bare my soul to her, apologize to her. Perhaps learn to love her again, or set her free to find someone who will.

But I can't possibly visit her, or even contact her, really, until I make my story public. Because I cannot go directly to Batista, not after he sent a couple of goons to catch me. What I must do is force him and NeuroStor itself to acknowledge me, to diagnose what is wrong with me . . . and correct it. Because it would be a tragedy to steal life away from a man who may have just found it.

It doesn't really make sense to remain in the middle of the river. If I happen to see something that will help me climb out, I have to be able to reach it. Moving laterally through such a strong current, though, is no easy task, and my swim toward the riverbank is gradual. Hours, it seems. And when I finally make it, my hands just slither along the muddy slope.

I wish I could see the ground above me. Am I in the middle of the desert, or is there a chance that someone up there might see me? All I can see from here is blue sky shining through the clouds.

My arms and legs are tiring. My clothes seem to weigh a hundred pounds. But I can't take them off, because I'll need something to wear when I finally get out of the river.

My hands slap at the bank, fingers closing against the mud, clawing their way into nothing. This is not going the way I hoped it would. The damn river is thwarting my grand entrance back into the realm of the living.

Perhaps I should try to float on my back. Maybe that would require less effort. Maybe if I rest long enough I can try again to climb up the—

Something scrapes against my hands and arms, grinding away flesh. Pain pours into me, and I push myself backwards, away from the bank. But not far enough, apparently, because I bounce into the bank again. This time skin disappears from my elbows, abraded as if by sandpaper.

The riverbank has become concrete.

I must be close to civilization now, because a concrete riverbank means someone is worried about erosion. After what happened back near the golf course, I don't blame them. The river has also narrowed—it's more like a canal now—and the water runs both faster and higher. I'm only a few feet below the top of the concrete bank and bobbing along at quite a clip.

I've got to figure out a way to pull myself out of this river. From here I can see the concrete wall is not completely vertical, more like a seventy-degree angle, but I'll shred my skin if I try to scale it. Fleeting hope quickly dissipates. What did I expect, a flight of stairs?

I guess I could scream, but would it do any good? There are still no signs of homes or businesses above me. So I continue to float, allowing the river to pull me along at its rapid pace. Five minutes go by. Ten. Water begins to lap against my neck, my chin; sometimes it splashes into my eyes. Treading water isn't very easy when you're fully clothed.

It's a race against time now. Surely something or someone will come along. All I have to do is hold out a little longer. Just a little longer.

And then, as if answering my prayer, salvation emerges ahead in the form of a steel pipe sticking out of the concrete wall near the top of the bank. It juts out twenty inches or so, bends ninety degrees, and disappears into the water below. I suppose it's a drainpipe, but to me it looks like a giant handle put there to help drowning people pull themselves from the flooding current.

My arms and legs pound the water, exhausting all remaining energy in those muscles as I move toward the river's edge once again. Just a few feet away, that's all it is. Half the width of a neighborhood street. Any day of the week I could swim this distance in mere seconds, but progress across the current is painfully slow. I appear to be swimming in place. The river pulls me downstream as I struggle toward its edge. The pipe rushes forward. So close. At the last second I extend my arms, lunging forward with fingers outstretched, and touch the pipe. It is coated with a rough layer of rust and scrapes painfully against the tips of my fingers. Then it is gone.

I scream until it feels like my lungs are bleeding. I thrust a clenched fist up at the sky and curse a God in whom I do not believe. How can this happen? How can I come so far and then miss by mere inches my chance to be saved. How? Why?

And because I am looking at the sky and not the river, I am nearly killed by what might be a second chance for salvation.

A bridge. I have reached a place where the river passes beneath a bridge.

The passageway is divided into two canals separated by a rectangular concrete column. The water level is so high it nearly touches the bottom of the bridge, and had I seen it just a few seconds later, the horizontal concrete beam might have split my head open. Instead, I thrust my hands upwards and drop the rest of me underwater. The momentum of the river jerks my arms violently against the concrete bridge, ripping the skin there, but I manage to hold on.

It won't be for long. Water rushes by my ears, through my hair, and I have to suppress the urge to breathe. I am so tired that I can barely think of what to do next.

With no other options, I try to move toward the column. By walking with my hands, I approach it by inches. My heart slams hard in my chest. My hot lungs beg for air. It can't be that far away. Just a few feet.

The rushing water pulls on my legs. It rushes into the waist of my pants as if trying to undress me. My arms strain against its relentless strength. Am I going to make it? I can't hold my breath much longer while exerting so much effort.

My left elbow bangs into concrete, tearing skin again. I made it!

The column is not vertical. It rises toward the bridge at about a forty-five-degree angle. I scoot a little closer until the side of my body rests against the column and then throw my left arm over it. My fingers just barely reach the other edge. I'll need that grip for leverage. My right arm, still plastered against the concrete above me, now must let go and grab onto the column. But the rushing water keeps trying to pull me under the bridge. I'm completely out of air. My torso and legs bob up and down, rippling like a flag in the wind. This dynamic motion is already loosening the grip of my left hand on the column. If it fails, I'll be dragged under.

With a grunt, I slide my right arm away from the bridge and twist my body toward the column. The river pulls like gravity, and I just hang there with one arm, surely dead now. I knew this was my last chance.

But I heave again, and this time my right arm goes over the column. Both hands now have a firm grip. I pull with my arms, and my legs scramble against the concrete. Somehow I've lost my golf shoes, which I didn't even notice until now, and the pads of my toes are being stripped away. The pain barely registers.

Gradually, my hold on the column improves, and after ten or fifteen seconds of intense exertion, I land on top of it.

I lay there on my stomach, heaving great breaths into the air. Below me, the rushing river is torn in two by the column, and the sound of it makes me want to vomit. I don't think I'll ever be able to get into a bathtub again. From now on it's nothing but disposable wet naps for me.

I push with my hands and knees into a crawling position and then start upwards.

And that's when I lose my balance and nearly teeter off the column.

Immediately I collapse to my stomach again and hug the concrete. My waterlogged torso rises and falls with each breath. Mental note: Do *not* fall into the river again.

I summon the courage to try once more. My feet are bleeding, I think, and my arms are for sure. Weird how selective the mind is about pain. In the kitchen a cut brings curses and throbbing agony, but bloody concrete abrasions mean nothing when you're fighting for your life in a flooded Arizona canal.

A steel railing stands at the top of the bridge. I reach out with one arm and grab it. Do the same with the other arm. After dragging myself out of the river, climbing over this short barrier is child's play.

I collapse onto the shoulder of the road like a marathon runner who's just completed his course twice. I shouldn't stay here long, I know—a distracted motorist could veer out of his lane and run over me—but I need a little rest. Like when my rechargeable razor dies, and I keep putting it back on the charger to eke out a little more shaving time. Five minutes, I decide. Five minutes of rest, then get moving again. I close my eyes.

When I open them again, everything is dark.

Adrenaline pours into my body, sending an electric shock wave to my fingers and toes. An urge to get up and run comes over me. Why the hell is it dark? Where am I?

Actually, only one of my eyes is open. Something is holding the other lid closed.

I reach with my hand and rub away something that feels like sand. The shirt on my back crackles as I move. Something is pulling the hairs on my arms. I'm no longer wet.

Now the other eye opens. My whole body is caked with a thin film of dirt. My tongue is thick and dry. How in the hell . . . ?

I look down at the river and am startled to find the water level half of what it was when I climbed out. Nearly tranquil. It's hard to believe I almost lost my life down there, but even more difficult to understand how an unknown number of hours passed by in an instant.

Then I remember—I'm wearing a watch. But when I look down at it, I realize the gears must have stopped turning, because the hands tell me it's 5:13. That's impossible. If I went into the river at—what? Eight in the morning?—then I probably washed up in the inlet at . . . nine o'clock, maybe? Probably sooner. If I stayed there an hour and found the bridge in another hour, that would mean I climbed out of the water at eleven. In the morning.

Five thirteen PM would tell me I had slept for over six hours. But it's too dark to be late afternoon, isn't it? And yet 5:13 AM . . . that would mean . . .

The air around me is cool, much more so than if the sun had just gone down. The dry desert night acts as a magnifying lens against the clear sky, bringing visible stars closer and revealing others I never see through the humid haze that passes for breathable air in Houston. The desert is quiet and I am alone.

Did I really sleep at the side of this road for more than eighteen hours? Surely many cars must have driven past me by now. And not only would their engines and rolling tires have woken me, but someone— everyone, really—would have stopped to check on me. There is no way I could have slept on this bridge for eighteen hours.

The road is four lanes wide and bordered on both sides by a wide shoulder. I turn my head first to the left and then to the right, as if I was going to cross to the other side. It's obvious which way I need to go. Everything on the left is dark, while the amber lights of civilization light the opposite sky. It's hard to tell how far away they are, but I suppose that doesn't really matter. I need to find someone who can help me. I need a drink of water.

I start walking.

Ten minutes into this journey and already my feet are killing me. When the pitted surface of the asphalt becomes too much, I try walking on the sandy soil that borders the road, but uncountable pebbles and sharp little rocks turn that choice into a poor one. So I go back to the road again, hoping I'll get somewhere before my feet are shredded into hamburger.

How did I sleep for so long? I don't remember anything at all after collapsing on the asphalt. In a way, it reminds me of the transmission, only instead of traveling across distance, I skipped through time.

It's like I lost the time.

Sleeping is always like that, I guess—eight hours in bed passes a lot more quickly than the same period of time at work—but something about this seems different. I can almost swear that I simply closed my eyes and then opened them again. And why didn't I wake up when cars passed me? They would have sounded like jets blazing by from where I was lying. Why didn't anyone stop?

I suppose I'm worried that the transmission has somehow changed my sleep pattern. I'm worried about all kinds of things that could be wrong with me. Maybe it's pointless to speculate on what possible phys-iological problems I have now or will develop later, but that doesn't stop me from doing it anyway. I just want my body back the way it was. I want everything to be how it was before any of this happened.

The lights ahead don't appear to be getting any closer. Either I'm miles away from them, or I'm making really poor time. On my left, the sky has turned from black to violet, which tells me dawn isn't far off.

Other than soft footsteps against the asphalt, the desert is quiet around me, at least until a gunshot splits the silence. But it isn't a real gun that makes the sound; it's my mind reliving what happened yesterday. The chase on the golf course. The third man coming out of nowhere. The gunshot—

I met Tom in college. We lived next door to each other in one-bedroom apartments for a semester before deciding that our standard of living would improve if we shared the rent on a two-bedroom unit and divided the utilities. But Tom met a girl before the ink on our one-year lease had dried, and for the next six months I saw less of him than when we had lived in separate apartments. Finally, he asked me to move out so the girl could move in. I hated him for that.

But in the end we became better friends for it. I can only take Tom in small doses, but I have more fun with him than I do with anyone else. I guess it's because I get to be a kid when I'm around him. Because that's all he is—a grown child. Still, I probably wouldn't have gotten away from those men, Ivan and Ed, if it hadn't been for Tom. He convinced me to run and then took a bullet while I went on without him. And now he might be dead. My God. I know I shouldn't . . . I can't. . . .

I walk on. The road in front of me lengthens as the sky becomes brighter. My feet throb and sting.

The sun breaks across the horizon just after six o'clock. Jagged brown mountains stand in silhouette against the battle zone between fiery sun-light and cool blue sky. I realize that it's no longer quiet. Instead, the me-chanical sound of engines and rolling tires floats across the desert from the town in front of me. I see what looks like a row of houses, as well as tall signs lit up against the morning sky, and my footsteps quicken. Civilization isn't far away.

Moments later I notice something in the road ahead. It's rectangular in shape and stationary. My progress brings the object steadily closer, and soon I'm able to guess what it is: an answer to one of my questions about the eighteen-hour nap. This thing in the road is a barrier, one that says, as I pass by and look at it from the other side, ROAD CLOSED. Which means the city, surely a suburb of Phoenix, is expanding so quickly north that someone decided to lengthen the road ahead of time. Because as I turn around, it's plainly obvious from here that these four lanes of asphalt stretch a few miles into the open desert and then simply end. Which is why no one found me on the bridge.

Closer, and now I can see houses on both sides of the road, several rows of them and then an intersection governed by a traffic signal. There is a Texaco gas station and a Taco Bell. My mouth floods with the taste of seasoned ground beef and lettuce and the toasted corn of a taco shell. Cheese and tomatoes and spicy taco sauce. Refried beans. Sour cream.

When did I eat last? More than twenty-four hours ago for sure.

I slip my hands into my front and back pockets, but of course the money clip and wallet are long gone. Last year Misty and I reported more than one hundred and thirty thousand dollars on our federal tax return, and today I don't have enough money to buy a single taco.

I'm just a man stumbling into town after being lost in the desert.

My slow progress eventually brings me to the intersection of a residential street, where I meet the eyes of a middle-aged woman driving an ink-black Lexus. The point in time when my presence fully registers is obvious—her eyes stretch wide under a hurricane of blond hair, and her mouth drops open.

I can almost hear her unspoken dismay.

She turns right and speeds away in the direction I'm walking. The engine of her car growls like a lion. Maybe we'll meet again at the Texaco station. I could beg for a dollar.

This is a ridiculous situation I've created for myself. What the hell was I thinking when I climbed into that transmission portal? Is this what I wanted? To be wandering around with no money and no food and no idea what the hell is wrong with me?

I used to play golf twice a month with an information systems specialist whom I had known since college. His name was Pete. Last spring, just as courses in Houston were reaching full bloom, Pete abruptly stopped playing golf with me. The change was so sudden that I was sure I had said or done something to offend him without knowing it, but two months later he showed up on my doorstep sickly pale and about ten pounds lighter. He said he'd been experiencing weakness and tingling in his left arm and leg for about six months. I asked if he had seen a doctor. *Last week*, Pete told me. *He sent me to a neurologist, who ordered an MRI. And yesterday they discovered a grape-size tumor in my brain.*

Then he cried, right there in my living room.

The tumor proved operable. Pete is still recuperating, and only time will tell if all traces of the cancer were completely removed. I asked him recently why he waited so long to see a doctor. *I didn't want to believe anything was wrong,* he told me. *I kept hoping I had a pinched nerve or something. And all I kept thinking when he told me about the tumor was* Why? Why me? *I didn't want to believe it.*

In Pete's case, finding an answer is beyond the scope of current medical science. My situation, however, is considerably different. I know exactly why. Because Rodrigo Batista and the rest of his corporate demigods are trying to make a buck, and because I thought I could use the transmission test as a way to jump-start my humdrum life. There's no question about the jump start. I just wish I knew where I was going.

I step onto the concrete property of the Texaco station. The Taco Bell stands across the street. Cars pass intermittently through the intersection, and one pulls into the Texaco parking lot. Only three cars are filling with gasoline. Two others are parked in front of the Star Mart.

I shuffle across the parking lot, past a machine marked AIR/WATER and then past a brushless car wash advertising a NEW IMPROVED SPOT-FREE RINSE.

A tall twentyish woman bursts out of the Star Mart just as I reach the front sidewalk. She's wearing an expensive casual suit with shorts instead of a skirt. Her legs are tanned and bare, her auburn hair swept away from her face. She's eating a doughnut wrapped in wax paper, and a covered cup of coffee occupies her other hand.

When the woman sees me, her indigo eyes fly open like window shades. Judging by the frozen, horrified look in her eyes, I must look even worse than I imagined. An urge to explain my appearance to this stranger grips me—you would think such concerns would seem trivial in a time of crisis—but instead I decide to keep my mouth shut and walk past her.

That's when the coffee slips out of her fingers and explodes on the ground in a brown gush. Next goes the doughnut. Her hands fly to her neck and her mouth flies open, revealing a mouthful of white, half-chewed batter.

Instead of just standing there, watching her choke, I move forward quickly. Concern flares in her eyes, as if she thinks I'm going to kill her before the lodged piece of doughnut can, but before she can get away, I grab her midsection and spin her around. My right hand tightens into a fist and finds that special place below her breastbone. Her body is slim and toned against mine. The blouse beneath her coat is smooth silk.

Three sharp thrusts of my fist do the trick. The half-chewed dough-nut batter pops out of her mouth and lands with a *splat!* on top of a red trash can. I don't even have time to let go of the woman before she begins to scream.

I possess no experience in matters such as this. It doesn't occur to me to run away because I've done nothing wrong. But only a second passes before a heavyset man in a red Texaco polo shirt bursts out of the Star Mart and rushes at me. I freeze like a frightened animal, too tired and wary to do anything else, and then he slams into me, his overweight body soft but powerful. We tumble hard onto the sidewalk. I hit the ground on my right side and pain threads into me like burning oil. My body is worn and broken. I have no energy with which to fight and can barely defend myself when he punches me in the stomach.

"Stop it!" the woman cries.

The heavyset man continues as if he doesn't hear, raining blows onto my body as patches of sweat form beneath his heavy breasts.

"Stop that!" she yells again. "You're hurting him!"

The pain fades a little as he punches me twice more. I might be going into shock.

"He was hurting you," my attacker says in a thick, slow voice.

"No, he wasn't!" she screams. "I was choking!"

These words seem to reach the man, because he doesn't hit me again. We lay there for a second or two as he metamorphoses back into a Texaco employee. The vigilante role is over. He rolls off me and climbs to his feet.

"I'm sorry," he says. "You were screaming."

"I was scared," the woman answers. "I thought I was dying."

Neither of them move to help me, so I roll onto my stomach and push myself up. Nothing feels out of place, but the entire midsection of my body throbs. As badly as it hurts now, I can't imagine what this will feel like in a few hours.

There aren't enough people here to form a crowd, but the few patrons who had converged on our little scene drift back to what they were doing. I stand still to get my balance—head throbbing now, also—and realize the woman wants to say something. The vigilante looks away, as if embarrassed, but doesn't leave.

"I'm sorry," I say, which seems appropriate. After all, the sight of me induced her choking fit.

Before she can respond, I begin to cough. My whole body shakes. I put my hand over my mouth and cringe. Each hack is like being stabbed with knives, and warm, sticky liquid collects in my hand. When the coughing finally stops, I am left with a handful of phlegm and blood and nowhere to put it.

"Don't be sorry," the woman says. She can't help but look at my hand.

The glop tries to seep between my fingers when I close my hand to hide it.

"I think you saved my life," she adds. "Thank you."

"Don't worry about it," I say to the woman. "You'd have done the same for me, right?"

She doesn't answer this unfair question.

"I should go." I begin to walk away, rubbing the phlegm into the frayed cotton fabric of my golf pants.

"Hold on," the woman says.

I turn around, and she is holding a bill of some denomination in her hand. It looks like a twenty. She walks in my direction, and I begin walking again myself. Away from her.

"Take this," she says as she catches up with me. We walk by a set of gasoline pumps. One is being used by a heavyset woman refueling her Dodge Stratus.

"I don't want your money."

I try to walk faster, leave her behind, but it's no use. I'm hurt and she knows it. We reach the road.

"Why not?"

"Because I didn't help you to get paid. I did it because it was the right thing to do."

She looks down at the money in her hand and stuffs it back into her purse, as if it has grown suddenly hot. The Dodge Stratus drives by us and turns onto the street. The heavyset woman glares at us.

"I didn't . . . I didn't know how to thank you," she says. "I meant to be gracious."

"I appreciate that. But instead you insulted me."

"I'm sorry. I thought maybe you could use the money."

She's right. That twenty-dollar bill would buy me a whole box of tacos, and an ice-cold Coke to wash them down. But I'm not homeless, and I'm not unemployed.

"I don't want it."

"Are you hungry, then?"

I intend to answer no, but instead say nothing. She correctly interprets my silence.

"What about something to eat instead of money?"

"Really, I appreciate your help, but . . ."

"A meal and a hot bath? Come on. What do you say?"

Nothing. I say nothing. Pride mutes me.

"I just live a few blocks away."

The river on me stinks. A film of dried mud cakes much of my exposed skin. I can't even begin to imagine how good a hot bath would feel right now.

"Are you serious?"

"There's a guest room above the garage," she says. "You can bathe there, and I'll bring you something to eat."

I look back at the Star Mart. The vigilante has gone back inside. Right now the only car parked in front of the store is a silver Nissan Maxima, which I assume to be hers. It's a slow morning at Texaco.

"You don't even know me."

"I'll be fine," she says. "My father was a policeman. He taught me how to defend myself, and we have a gun in the house."

I don't know what to make of that, but how can I refuse such an offer?

"Okay," I say.

A Chevrolet sedan pulls into the parking lot as we head back toward her car, and a brief shot of electricity zips through my body. From this angle the driver bears a striking resemblance to my pursuer, Ivan. I stare at its windows, transfixed, until a traveling salesman type gets out and dispels the illusion.

"Someone looking for you?"

"No," I lie. "A friend of mine drives a car like that."

"Oh." A pause. "What's your name, by the way?"

"Cameron," I tell her. "Cameron Fisher."

She walks to the driver's side of the car, and I head for the passenger side.

"I'm Nicole Shepherd."

We are about to get in the car when the vigilante bursts out of the Star Mart.

"Ma'am?" he says. "Is everything okay?"

"Yes."

He looks at me, the distrust in his eyes plainly visible, then back to Nicole.

"I don't think you should let that man get in your car. He might be dangerous."

"I think someone who tackles and punches a decent man is the dangerous one."

"I'm sorry about that. But he—"

"Please leave us alone. Unless you'd like me to call the police and have you arrested for battery."

The vigilante looks at me again and sneers. Not that it matters, but I've made an enemy of this man.

"Fine," he says. "I hope you're not sorry."

Nicole doesn't answer. She gets into the car, and I follow her lead.

"What a moron," she says.

"He's just looking out for you."

"I can take care of myself."

Nicole's house is typical desert luxury fare and appropriately large. A long driveway curls around to the backyard garage. The rectangular swimming pool is framed by a wooden deck, several covered tables, and a built-in charcoal grill.

"That's the guest room," Nicole says, pointing toward a door above the garage. She shuts off the Maxima and pulls a key from her ring. "This will get you inside. There are plenty of towels and soap. Please take as long as you like."

I take the key from her and open the passenger door.

"What would you like to eat?" she asks.

"Anything will be fine."

"My husband and I ate Chinese takeout last night. We ordered way too much. What do you think about broccoli beef and a couple of egg rolls?"

"My stomach is already growling."

"Good. I'll heat it up in the microwave and bring the whole works to you in a few minutes."

She opens the garage with the remote and hurries inside. For the first time, I notice dirt on the back of her suit jacket. I suppose she wants to change clothes and take a bath herself. Wash away the smell of me.

They've set the place up like a hotel room. Less sterile, of course—the phone isn't marked with written instructions and nothing is bolted down—but the accommodations include one queen bed, an end table, and a television. A vanity stands at the end of the room, beyond that a separate small room for the toilet and shower. I suppose they put guests like the rebellious brother or the unseemly cousin in here. Safely away from the rest of the house.

I draw a hot bath and strip off my grimy clothes. Carefully, I lower myself into the tub and sigh as my feet, my legs, as my everything is enveloped by the heavenly liquid heat. The steaming water dissolves grime from my skin like an alchemist's elixir, expanding pores, replacing dirt with sweet, fragrant soap. The sensation is orgasmic. I guess this is better than bathing with wet naps after all.

So now that I've reached civilization, now that I have access to a telephone, what exactly am I going to do? Obviously, what I would like most is to call Misty and let her know I'm okay. But I have to assume NeuroStor has bugged my telephone line, which means any contact could put her in danger and also help NeuroStor pinpoint my own location.

Besides, I'm not due back in Houston until noon today. She won't miss me before then.

So if I can't talk to Misty, what? Probably I should call all the hospitals in the area to find out if Tom has been admitted anywhere. Or I guess I could try his cell phone. I have to believe he is alive, because I just can't imagine those goons murdering my best friend.

But after that, what am I going to do about me? The most obvious thing I can think of, because this always happens in the movies when a big company slights the little guy, is to contact the media. Unfavorable press is surely the last thing in the world Batista wants, reports that his fantastic invention is flawed. But how exactly am I supposed to do that? Just pick up the phone and call NBC? Assuming I get through to someone—and that's a big assumption—what's the first thing they're going to want? Proof, of course. First that this transmission machine actually exists and then details of the way it has adversely affected me. Of course I have no evidence whatsoever of the machine itself, unless Crystal could help by showing me the way to her Internet information. This must be why Tom wanted me to call her. But even if I could somehow provide details about the machine, what proof can I provide regarding my personal experience? All I have at the moment is a faulty golf game and bruises from my swim in the river. If I go to the news media with that, they'll laugh in my face.

Normal people would contact the police. That's who you call when you're in trouble, right? When people are endangering your life? I suppose I should call the police. But aren't they going to want the same sort of information, the same sort of proof that the news media would want?

What, then? What do I do? I can't call home. I can't go home. I can't go back to Tom's house, and I certainly can't stay here.

I carefully scrub my filthy body, turning the water more and more brown. Before long the tub begins to resemble the river, only here the current has been reduced to a shallow, tepid pool of stagnant water. This image convinces me to drain the tub, rinse the bottom, and start again.

A knock at the front door startles me just as I begin to shampoo my hair.

"Come in!" I yell.

"Sorry it took so long," Nicole says. "Had a quick shower myself."

The aroma of Chinese food drifts into my little room. My second bath is going to be a short one.

"I brought you something to wear," she says. "There's no sense in taking a bath if you're just going to put dirty clothes on again. But unfortunately I think my husband may be a little taller than you."

"I really appreciate your help, Nicole. I'll be glad to send you money for the clothes when I get home again."

She knocks lightly on the door and pushes through a clean, neatly folded Polo shirt and khakis.

"Thank you," I tell her.

"Don't forget these."

Next she hands me a pair of laced boat shoes with beige crew socks stuffed into them.

"Really, Nicole, this is too much."

"You can't go around barefoot," she says.

I towel dry and put the clothes on. They fit well, though the pants are indeed long. I roll up the ends and revel in my cleanliness.

When I emerge from the bathroom, Nicole is sitting on the bed in front of a TV tray. Mine is beside hers, holding a plate piled high with beef and broccoli over rice. She's also poured me a tall glass of soda and filled another with cold milk.

"Wow," I say.

"Sit down. Your food will get cold."

Her clothes are different, of course. She's now wearing a white Arizona Cardinals T-shirt and a pair of red shorts. Her feet are in sandals and her toenails match her shorts. Her hair is damp from the shower.

"I don't want you to think I'm ungrateful," I tell her, "but I'm not exactly sure why you invited me here. If my wife invited a dirty stranger into our home, I'd think she'd gone nuts."

She washes down a mouthful of food with a swallow of soda.

"It wouldn't exactly make sense for you to steal from me," Nicole says. "At least not after that guy in the convenience store stared you down. And your clothes tell me you aren't as destitute as you look."

This is an invitation to talk about my situation. Curiosity, in part, drives her kindness.

"I know you were in the canal at some point. I could tell by the smell."

"I nearly drowned in it last night. I climbed onto a bridge down the road yesterday and somehow slept until this morning."

"Did you fall in?"

Nicole knows I'm weighing my answer carefully when I don't answer right away.

"If you're going to lie to me," she says, "just don't bother." She drops the fork onto her plate and starts to get up from the bed.

"Don't leave. You've been so nice to me."

Nicole pretends not to hear. "You deserve this much for helping me when you did. Please keep the clothes. Matt doesn't wear them anymore."

"I didn't fall into the river. I was sort of pushed in."

"Why?"

I pause again, and this time she folds the legs under the TV tray and heads for the door.

"Nicole, wait."

Out the door she goes. I stuff my mouth full of rice and then follow her.

"Nicole!"

She turns into the garage, but by the time I reach the bottom of the stairs she has disappeared through a door into the house. There are no other cars in the garage. The door is not all the way shut. Does this mean she wants me to follow her? I push the door farther open.

"Nicole!"

If she answers, I don't hear it. Through this door is the utility room, home to a washer, dryer, and a large, industrial-type sink. Another door ahead also stands open, and beyond it I see cabinetry and a stove. The kitchen.

"Nicole!"

The house is pin-drop quiet.

For a moment I consider going back upstairs to finish the Chinese food, but then something unexpected occurs to me: What to do about NeuroStor.

Crystal, I remember, gave me her e-mail address. Twin peaks something . . . no, two peaks. That's it: crystal@twopeaks.com. What if I send her a message and explain in detail exactly what happened? The golf and the river and that I'm in a house somewhere near that river. If she could write back with some directions on how to get the Internet information, that would at least give me somewhere to start. And, conspiracy theorist that she claims to be, perhaps she could come up with other ideas on how to proceed as well.

I push the door all the way open and step through. Past the washer and dryer to the next doorway. The kitchen is empty, and there are two directions to go: through another doorway into what looks like a formal dining room, or through a large archway that connects the kitchen to a great room.

"Nicole?" I call again. "Where are—"

"I'm here," she says from the great room. The overhead light isn't on, and she stands in shadows. Pointing something at me, I think.

"Look, I'm sorry I was hesitant back there."

"I don't like it when people lie to me. Especially a total stranger who I let into my house."

"I didn't lie."

"Saying nothing is the same as lying. If you can't tell me what's going on, then I want you the hell out of my house."

So now I'm supposed to tell her about the transmission, about Ivan and Ed, about the gunshots fired at Tom. I wonder how long it will take her to kick me out when I try to explain "transmission."

"Do you have a computer?"

"We have two. Why?"

"Do you use America Online?"

"My husband does. Why? What does that have to do with any-thing?"

"I'll tell you what happened, why I jumped into the river and every-thing, if you'll let me send an e-mail with your computer."

She thinks about this for a moment. "Forget it. Either you tell me what's going on right now, or I call the cops."

I just stare at her. I'm pretty sure that's a gun she's pointing at me.

"I'm not kidding," she says.

"I don't even know where to start."

"Why don't you tell me about yourself," she suggests. "Where do you live? What do you do?"

"I'm an accountant for a company in Houston called NeuroStor."

"How in the world did you end up in a canal in Phoenix?"

"My boss in the Houston office, who through some strange corporate hierarchy also happens to be NeuroStor's president, tells me that he doesn't need me to work there anymore. Only he doesn't want to just fire me. Instead he would like me to perform one last . . . task, I guess you could say, before I leave. And I will be paid well for it, enough that I can pretty much retire if I want."

"What's the task?"

"Well, NeuroStor is supposed to be in the business of developing new forms of flash memory technology, but it turns out that isn't the entire truth."

"Where is this going?" Nicole asks me. "I still don't even know why you're in Arizona."

"I know. I'm not sure what you're going to think about this, really. The reason why I'm here is sort of hard to believe."

"Try me."

"Well, the real product we're developing is based on a peculiarity of quantum physics that allows for what is commonly thought of as teleportation. NeuroStor calls it transmission, I guess because they scan an object and then transmit the properties of that object to another location, where it is reproduced. I'm no scientist, so I don't know much about how it works, but that's how I traveled to Arizona. They transmitted me."

Nicole spends a few moments digesting this information. "You're right, that is sort of hard to believe."

"The way it worked was this guy, Rodrigo Batista, the president of NeuroStor I told you about, picked me because he thought I would be willing to try it. Because I wasn't happy with my job and because I really don't enjoy the corporate world in general. He offered a lot of money and convinced me the test wasn't much more than a formality. But right now it looks like there was more risk than I thought."

"So I suppose something went wrong, and you're running from them now."

I nod.

"Why would you agree to test a machine like that? Did you have a death wish?"

"Supposedly they did extensive animal testing, but I guess they needed human transmissions on record to convince anyone outside the company to do it."

"Still, that seems crazy."

"It was. I don't know how to explain it, really. I've just been so bored most of my life. Nothing really excites me, and I thought this was something that I could . . . I don't know . . . something that would make me different. Something unique I could contribute to the world, something I might be remembered for. And then there was the five million dollars Batista offered. In the end it sort of seemed like I was meant to do it. Not that I believe in fate or anything like that. I guess I just wanted an adventure."

Nicole steps a little closer to me, but not close enough for her face to completely emerge from the shadows. I don't know if she thinks I'm brave or stupid or lying.

"I can't believe I'm asking this," she finally says, "but what went wrong? Why are you running now?"

"It seems like there is something neurologically wrong with me. Hell, I don't know. I'm not a doctor. But I've had a little problem with balance and coordination."

"Okay. And you ended up in the river how?"

"I was with a friend of mine. We noticed two guys following us, and we ran from them. Tom was shot, I think, but I got away. The river swept me away."

"Really," she says.

"Really."

"Where's your friend now?"

For some reason her question brings Tom's face into my mind, and remorse streams into me like cold water.

"I don't know."

Nicole approaches me. The gun (no question about it now) is lowered, but not so far that she couldn't shoot me with it.

"I'm sorry. I guess I'm not being very considerate. I suppose it doesn't matter whether I believe you or not, so you can use my computer if you think it will help."

"Thank you."

"Follow me," she says.

The house is enormous and immaculate. She leads me down a wide hallway, around a corner, and past a few doors. Now we walk into a large study. Thick, important-looking books cover three walls. A heavy, mahogany desk stands in the middle of the room.

"My husband is a lawyer," she explains as she places the gun on a bookshelf. "This is his office."

There are two chairs, an expensive leather high-back at the desk and a guest chair near the doorway. She pulls the latter toward the desk and motions for me to sit.

"How did you notice those men following you?"

"Tom and I were playing golf. The two guys were following us around on the course. There was that terrible rainstorm. I fell in the mud and slipped into the river. That was after they caught Tom and shot him."

She powers on the computer and monitor. Their internal works whir and beep.

"But you didn't actually see them shoot him?"

"No, but he was yelling at me to run and then . . . and then he wasn't yelling anymore."

"So you fell into the river at the golf course."

"Actually I was sort of pushed in, and when the river turned into this canal, I saw a bridge and used it to crawl out of the water. Then I walked into town."

The computer has completed its boot sequence and awaits a command.

"I know you don't believe me. I appreciate that you're helping anyway."

"It sounds like you know what you're talking about. I don't know why I shouldn't believe you."

"Because you choked when you saw me. Because I don't have any identification or any proof about what's going on."

"I'm not going to lie to you," Nicole says. "What you're telling me sounds like every idiotic conspiracy theory I've ever heard. I don't go along with alien abductions or guns on the grassy knoll. And that's what this sounds like."

I don't know what to say to that.

"So is there any more to the story?"

I tell her the rest, about Crystal and alt.transmission.conspiracy and Tom's desperate instruction.

"I guess you could go ahead and send the e-mail," Nicole says. "What could it hurt?"

"Thanks," I tell her. "I really appreciate this."

We switch chairs so I can direct the mouse. I open the AOL program and select "Guest" as my sign-on name, wait as the modem shrieks, key in my real screen name and password until the screen says:

Welcome, Cam5217!

"What are you going to say to her?"

"I'm going to tell her what's happened to me, I guess, and then ask her what she thinks I should do."

"And you think she's going to know better than you what to do because she's a conspiracy buff? Did it ever occur to you that maybe she was on crack? I mean, she *is* a stripper."

"Stripper or not, she seemed to know more about this than I did."

"What about the police? We have them here in Arizona, you know. They drive cars and wear uniforms and everything."

"I know, I know. And if Crystal doesn't respond to my e-mail, that's what I'll do. But how are they going to help me? It's not like I have any proof to show them."

"I think the police would have some idea how to handle the situation. They'd know better than you or me, at least."

"Yeah, or maybe the police would lead me right to NeuroStor."

"So it really is a big conspiracy, huh? Your company is so important they even control the police?"

"Of course not. But once they start asking questions, especially if they call NeuroStor, how do I know those two men won't show up at the station looking for me? Hell, Crystal thinks NeuroStor manipulates the media, so why couldn't they influence the police, too?"

Nicole rolls her eyes.

"Well, it wouldn't hurt to send the message, would it?" I ask.

"By all means," Nicole agrees.

"Probably she won't get it in time, anyway. Then I can call the police."

"I hope she responds right away. I'm curious to see what sort of advice she gives you."

So now I have to type the message with the skeptic looking over my shoulder. And I don't even know where to begin.

Perhaps with the basics:

> Crystal,
>
> This is Cameron Fisher. I met you at The Wildcat the night before last. I'm the one who transmitted, remember?
>
> I desperately need your help. This is not a joke. I promise this is not a joke. Please read this message carefully and help me if you can.

"Now what?"

"Tell her what happened to you," Nicole says. "Just like you told me."

I nod and press on.

> Tom and I played golf at a place called Sandy Canyon yesterday. It's outside of Phoenix, north of Fountain Hills, I think.

"Fountain Hills?" Nicole says. "That's at least fifteen miles from here! You swam fifteen miles in a raging canal?"

"I wouldn't say 'swam.' More like survived. By the way, where am I? What city is this?"

"Scottsdale."

> You know that guy who was staring at me the other night? He was there. At the golf course. He and two other guys were following me. When it started raining, Tom and I ran, and they chased us. They shot Tom. He might be dead. I kept running and the guy from the bar continued to chase me. He pushed me into a ditch or river that was flooded and the water swept me away. I washed up in Scottsdale and found someone here to help me. She's letting me use her computer to send this message.

I know it must seem ridiculous, sending this to you, but I honestly don't know what to do. I thought of going to the media, but what proof would I have? What I should do is call the police. If I don't hear from you soon, that's what I'll do.

But you seemed to know a lot about NeuroStor the other night, so I thought you might have some other ideas. If so, please reply immediately. I don't know how long I'll be able to wait here for your message.

Please help me. This is not a joke.

—Cameron

"What do you think?"

Nicole looks at me and smiles. "It is what it is. I don't think you could say it any better."

I click on the SEND button and the message disappears.

We sit there in silence. Suddenly it seems like a ridiculous idea, sending this e-mail to a woman I barely know. A *topless dancer* I barely know. How often does the average person check their personal e-mail? Once a day? At the most?

"What if she doesn't respond?" Nicole says.

"I'm sure she will. There's just no telling how long it'll be before she gets my message."

"But you said that if she didn't get it right away . . . I mean, you can't really stay here all day waiting."

"I know."

"Cameron," she says. "The way I see it, there are two possibilities here. One, everything you've told me is true. In this case, I may have put my husband and myself at great risk by bringing you here. What if the men following you somehow figure out where you climbed out of the canal? All they have to do is ask around, and someone will tell them I took you in."

"What's the other possibility?"

"That you're crazy, and all this is a lie."

"Does this mean you're about to kick me out?"

"No, but I think you should call the police. It's really your only option. Even if this girl has some advice about your transmission problem, you're still going to have to get the authorities involved. The police first, and then maybe the FBI. It's not like you're going to be able to do anything by your—"

A short, musical tone from the computer interrupts her, and we both turn toward the monitor. There is another window on the screen. INSTANT MESSAGE, it says, and below:

> TWOPEAKS: Are you bisexual?

I just stare at the screen for a moment, afraid to hope, afraid to believe the person sending this message is who I think it is. Because sometimes when your hope turns out to be false, it hurts worse than if you never hoped at all.

"Why are you smiling?" Nicole asks.

"Am I?"

"Is this your friend, the one from the dance club?"

"I hope so."

My fingers dart across the keyboard.

> Cam5217:   I thought we went over this already.

"What are you talking about?" Nicole asks.

"A little joke we shared at the bar."

> TWOPEAKS: I can't talk long. Don't say anything except
> answer my questions.
> Cam5217:   OK.
> TWOPEAKS: Good. Turns out I was right—you ARE
> bisexual. And suddenly I'm out of the closet,
> too, which is why I left town. You remember
> what I told you in the club? You'll find me at
> the highest point in San Francisco.
> Cam5217:   Got it.
> TWOPEAKS: I'll be watching for you, then. Good-bye.

"You're not kidding," Nicole says. "She is paranoid. How could someone intercept your instant messages?"

"I'm sure AOL can access anything they want. And if they can, then someone with the right contacts could do the same."

"Okay. But how in the hell are you supposed to get to San Francisco? And how are you going to find her there?"

"San Francisco doesn't necessarily mean California," I tell her. "Crystal is originally from Flagstaff, and the mountain range—"

"The San Francisco *Mountains*," Nicole finishes. "She's in Flagstaff."

"I hope so."

"That's only a few hours away. Straight up I-17."

But she trails off as she says this, knowing as I do that it's more than a few hours away if you don't have a car to drive.

"Nicole, I know you're not sure what to think about this, and I feel awkward asking you for help. But—"

The computer chimes again, surprising me. Crystal should've been long gone by now. I turn back to the computer and see another instant message window open. It's not from her.

> BATIROD: Give yourself up or your wife is dead.

"Cameron, who the hell is that?"

I sit there and stare at the screen. Nicole sits next to me, agitated, waiting for me to act. But BATIROD doesn't wait.

> BATIROD: I know where you are. Wait there for us or
> Misty will be killed. I am not fucking
> around, Cameron.

Nicole's hands begin to shake. Her indigo eyes bulge out of their sockets.

"Is it them? The men who were chasing you?"

"It's Batista."

"How can they know where you are? What if they come here? They can't come here!"

"Nicole—"

"You have to get out of here!"

"Nicole, please! They're talking about my wife!"

Her feet drive hard against the floor, pushing her chair away from mine, and she lurches toward the bookcase. I can't pry my eyes away from the monitor, from the instant message window from BATIROD.

"Log off now," Nicole says from behind me.

When I turn around, Nicole is holding the gun in her hand. She is more or less pointing it at me.

"Cameron, please *log off*!"

The command makes sense—if they are somehow tracing the call back to this house, we shouldn't help them by keeping the line open—so I reach forward with the mouse and disconnect.

"I'm sorry about this, Cameron, I really am. But I am not a saint. I feel badly for you and want to help, but I can't let myself get involved in your problem."

"So you could care less if they kill my wife and me? What about the other volunteers?"

"It's not my problem!" she screams. Her face has gone an angry shade of red, but her eyes are not as convinced. They dart from side to side, wide open with fear, but something else, maybe? Compassion, perhaps?

I must stall her long enough to think of something. Even if Batista really knows where I am, there must be a way to remove her from this situation. That's the only way I'll convince her to help me further.

"I'm sorry, Cameron," Nicole says and begins walking toward me. More confident with the gun now, which she's pointing directly at my head. I walk backwards and make it to the doorway.

"I'm sorry," she says again. Moisture leaks from the corners of her eyes. "I can't let something random like this ruin my life. Please leave."

We're in the hallway now. I move slowly, feeling my way along the wall with my hands. Nicole doesn't seem to realize that if Batista is telling the truth, it already *is* her problem, whether she asked for it or not. But I'm not going to win her support if I just come out and tell her this. I've got to think of something, some way to extricate myself from her life and use that to my own advantage. But how? How do we erase this random event from—

"Hold on a minute."

"What now?"

"I know how to get you out of this."

"I'm getting out of this by showing you the door."

"But if they really know where I am, don't you think they're going to come here? Even if I leave, this is where they'll show up."

"No! I won't let them in. I'll call the police right now. They're not coming here."

"They *are,* Nicole. If they traced the computer call somehow, they're coming here. And if I'm gone, they might force you to tell them where I went."

"I'll tell them. I don't care. I'm not going to put my family or myself in danger to protect you. I'm sorry."

"Even so, do you think they'll tip their hats and say 'Thank you, ma'am'? They already shot my friend."

"You don't know that."

"I heard the gunshot."

"Then I'll just leave," she says. "Go pick up my husband and check into a motel."

"You might as well post a sign on the door that says 'I left because Cameron told me you'd be coming.' If their intent is to clean up loose ends, do you think they won't watch the house until you come back? Or figure out where you're staying and go after you there?"

Nicole just stares at me, and the contempt in her eyes is obvious.

"What the hell do you want me to do?"

Relief surges through me. "We have to make it look like I came in here and forced my will on you. It's the only way to convince them you know nothing. If I tie you up, maybe lock you in a closet, you'll look more like a victim."

"Which I am," she moans.

"Which you are. And if they show up here, you can scream for help, play it up. Act like you don't know a thing."

"And what do you do?"

"I leave right now for Flagstaff."

"How are you going to get there?"

"I'll take your car."

"My car! Are you crazy? I'm not going to let you take my car!"

"Of course you won't let me take it. I'm going to steal it, and you're going to let the insurance company work out the claim. If you want, I'll wire you the sticker price when I get home."

"You're crazy!"

"Think about it. This is better than just sending me off on foot. If they get here and you're not subdued somehow, they'll know you voluntarily helped me. And if I *don't* steal your car, they may not buy the story at all. What kind of fugitive would walk out of here when he could ride?"

When she doesn't immediately fire "You're crazy!" back at me, I decide I'm making progress.

"I know you don't want to get involved, but you already are. The challenge now is to get you uninvolved. If we do this my way, it will help both of us."

Still she says nothing, and my confidence grows.

"Doing this will really help me. It could help a lot of people. Think about all the others around the country who might eventually transmit. Volunteers or even paying customers later. How many of them will come through changed like me? Someone has to stop this from happening."

"And you think that someone is you?"

"I don't know, but if they don't catch me soon enough, my story will be all over the news."

"And what if these bigwigs don't want your story told? Your CEO and his friends in the media."

"Someone will tell it. The story is too big to ignore."

A good salesman knows to shut up at the end of his pitch. The next move is Nicole's.

"Well, I guess you've got it all figured out," she finally says, "and I don't know what the hell else to do. Where are you going to lock me up?"

I decide to use the master bedroom closet. A nearby armoire, large and solid, will block the door from opening. She informs me that her husband usually arrives home from work around six PM, which means she could be locked in the closet for more than eight hours, but we both know that nearly any amount of time is more welcome than a visit from NeuroStor.

She gives me directions to the interstate while we set the stage for her imprisonment. She's brought some tea, dry cereal, a paperback copy of Jeffrey Eugenides' *Middlesex*, and a laptop computer. "You'll wind through mountains all the way to Flagstaff. The town isn't very big, but I still don't know how she expects to find you."

"Me neither."

"What about your wife?"

"Batista might be bluffing. If he kills her, his leverage against me will vanish. I don't know. But I don't think it will help anyone if I just sit here and wait."

Barely ten minutes have passed since I read the instant message, but every second I remain here with Nicole seems like wasted time. We're in the closet, and I'm about to pull the door shut behind me.

"They'll probably find the room above the garage and know I was in there. Tell them you offered to help me—that will agree with what the Texaco guy saw—and that I turned on you in the guest room. I locked you in here and used your computer. You don't know anything else. If they don't come, tell your husband the same thing. Let him call the police. Repeat the story for them. They won't be able to track anything to me, because by then I'll be in Flagstaff. I'll park your car somewhere safe. Someone will find it and maybe you'll get it back without a scratch."

"Whatever."

"Don't forget to put this food and stuff away when—"

"I'll take care of it," she says. "Just get out of here."

I'm about to leave when I remember something else.

"Where's the gun?"

She doesn't say anything. Her silence is my answer.

"Have you ever fired a gun before?" I ask her.

"No."

"You had better be sure you can hit all of them, Nicole, whoever it turns out to be. There might be two, there might be more. I think you stand a better chance if you just play dumb."

"We'll see."

"I'm sorry about this," I tell her.

"You should be."

"I really appreciate— I mean, if you hadn't offered to help me, I—"

"Please," she says. "Just go. I didn't want this. Just go."

I don't know what else to say to her. Nothing, it seems. I push the door closed and then struggle with the armoire. Eyes shut, exhausted muscles straining, trying to slide the armoire far enough left to block the closet door from opening. But guilt steals through me, weakens me. I don't think I'm going to be able to push it far enough. This isn't right, locking a woman in her own closet, turning her into a sitting duck for Ivan or Ed or whoever might show up here after I'm gone.

If I'm gone.

I've been here too long since reading the instant message. They could be anywhere. Alarm pours adrenaline into my bloodstream, solidifying the muscles in my legs and abdomen, and the armoire moves. An inch. Two inches. Then four. A few more until there is no way Nicole can open the door.

I hope this isn't a mistake.

The street is empty, as is the main road, the one onto which I crawled from the canal last night. From here I turn left—north—because I don't want the Texaco guy or someone else to see me in the car and call the police. The next main cross street is about a mile away; I'll use it to head west until I reach I-17.

I don't even see the patrol car until I'm upon it. The officer reaches a stop sign and waits for me to pass. I watch the rearview mirror and wait for him to come after me. But he just sits there.

He's thinking about it, I bet. Probably saw me out of the corner of his eye. Somehow he knows this car isn't mine. My next turn is within sight. Why doesn't he move? Why just sit there?

And then the patrol car pulls forward. He doesn't go left or right, but straight across the street. After a moment I can no longer see him.

I reach the intersection and turn left. This street is full of cars. I head west under the bright sun for nearly seven miles, traveling into and out of civilization. The road is fresh blacktop, wide and smooth, and traffic lanes are marked with bright yellow and white paint. Everything is new. New homes, new banks, new grocery stores. Oversized parking lots packed full of shiny Japanese luxury cars, German luxury cars, American SUVs. The road winds through a range of desert hills and emerges at Interstate 17. Soon I'm heading north on a wide freeway, out of the city, toward a horizon of brown mountains. The monotonous sound of tires on pavement eases my tension, and I allow myself to relax just a little. With the speedometer pegged at seventy-five, I ought to reach Flagstaff in two hours.

I hope I'm doing the right thing.

I hope Misty is safe.

God, I hope.

five

▋▋▋

I t's hard to believe I've been married for fifteen years.

When I was a child, time, and my life, seemed like something indeterminate, an invisible, unreachable horizon. But initiation into the ritualistic working world brought a new understanding of time, and the monotony of eight-to-five employment erased mind-bending chunks of life that could never be reclaimed. Periods of boredom were intensified by the knowledge that human existence was cruelly finite. Five years of marriage passed quickly, then ten, and soon I was a man who could say his best years were behind him.

Misty knows I'm bored with the familiarity of expense evaluation, of calculating income tax refunds and payouts for my friends, of any number of mind-numbing, number-crunching accounting services. But what do you say to a husband who knows little else? Occasionally, I join a golf tournament at my country club, and I've won quite a few. But the victories are hollow because we're all just a bunch of amateurs. We play our little hearts out, sweat over our shaky putters and unsure tee shots, and still none of us are worthy of carrying Tiger Woods' dirty towel.

How does a person live with mediocrity? How do you reconcile the knowledge that you will never be the best at anything, will never be acknowledged for doing anything worthy of true recognition, will never escape the cloying stigma of your tedious middle-American, middle-class existence? Maybe you're better than ninety percent of golfers in the world, but what's the point of competing when it's obvious you will never challenge the best? What does a person do when denial no longer numbs the daily pain?

I suppose if that person is me, he agrees to transmit.

What exactly is going to happen when I don't show up in Houston today? My return transmission is scheduled for noon, which is less than three hours from now. I have to hope the instant message threatening Misty was a bluff, because my incentive to cooperate with Batista will be gone if he murders her now. Still, what the hell is she going to do when they tell her I didn't show up in Phoenix for my transmission? Try to call Tom first, I'm sure. And after a few agonizing hours, she'll probably contact the police. I don't know how long before they'll declare us missing, but eventually someone will investigate our disappearance.

In time, they'll realize that Tom and I vanished from the golf course. And unless anyone in the adjacent houses saw us running down fairways and across greens, there won't be any reason to believe our disappearance was the result of foul play. Tom and I will be reduced to an unsolved mystery unless I do something about it.

But let's be realistic. Can one person ever successfully stand up to a wealthy corporation? Especially a person who's driving a stolen car down an unfamiliar road in an unfamiliar state?

I am so alone.

The horizon changes gradually, sometimes near and other times farther away. Small towns are spaced every five or ten miles, and none offer more than one exit from the highway. The sky is blue and perfectly clear. The mountains draw closer, occasionally turning green with Ponderosa pine.

A gray Isuzu Trooper passes me in the left lane and seems to go by in almost slow motion. A couple of kids in the backseat have pressed their faces flat against the windows. A boy and a girl, both fair-haired, grinning at me. As the Trooper pulls away, the boy moves to the back window and waves. I close my eyes for less than a second, but when I open them the truck has somehow become a speck on the horizon.

I blink again and hear Tom's voice. He's talking to Crystal, asking if she'd like to come back to his place for a private dance. Music seems to come from everywhere, and colorful lights reflect off chrome-frame chairs and tables. A cloud of smoke hangs above us. I look over at Tom, who smiles broadly, and a great weight lifts from my mind. He is alive. Tom is alive. I thought for sure they had killed him.

The ground rumbles beneath my feet. Something is wrong with the music, it sounds like—

I've driven halfway off the road. My hands jerk the steering wheel violently to the left, and the car jumps back onto the highway.

Sweat trickles down my forehead and temples, into my eyes. I lock the steering wheel in a death grip.

Shit. If I'm going to do Batista's work for him, why fall asleep at the wheel? Why not find a gun and blow my head off instead? I mean, let's be as dramatic as possible.

My fingers switch on the stereo, and the tuner searches until it finds soft rock hits from who knows when. But that crap isn't going to keep me awake. The next station is screaming heavy metal, and this is a much better choice for morons who can't seem to keep their eyes open. I crank it up to one decibel short of intolerable and glue my eyes to the road. Soon afterwards I pass a road sign that tells me Flagstaff is only fifty-four miles away.

Forty-five minutes or so.

I see it first topping the distant peaks, but as I close in on Flagstaff, the snow stretches all the way down to the highway shoulder. Just a light dusting, but still something of a shock compared to the warm desert air in Phoenix. Directly ahead, mountains make the middle of the horizon tall and jagged. I'm twenty miles outside of town.

I wonder if anyone has visited Nicole yet. Is she all right? Did she tell them where I'm going? After all, if Ivan and Ed are parked beside the highway shoulder up ahead, they won't let me get away again.

The mountains ahead are higher than any I've passed so far, and their rugged, snowy peaks are startling. I must assume these are the San Francisco Mountains of which Crystal spoke. Flagstaff is still thirteen miles away, but already I'm passing A-frame houses and small log cabins built inside clearings carved out of the pine forest.

Interstate 17 ends ten minutes later. I can go west toward Los Angeles, east toward Albuquerque, or leave the highway completely. It looks as if the town continues north, so I exit on Milton Road and find myself in the middle of a traffic jam on a road five lanes wide.

People are everywhere.

Another road sign tells me Northern Arizona University is directly ahead. The San Francisco Mountains stand against the northern horizon as if guarding the town. Am I supposed to drive toward them? I was expecting a small town with three streets and a Piggly Wiggly, not a city with strip malls and universities and plenty of traffic. How in the hell am I supposed to find Crystal here?

I drive through town, past fast-food restaurants and gas stations and hotels, and soon I'm in the country again, traveling north on U.S. 180. Perhaps Flagstaff isn't as big as it seemed—the liveliness of the main road may have deceived me—but trying to find one person here will still be akin to looking for the proverbial needle in the proverbial haystack. A highway sign tells me the Grand Canyon is eighty miles away.

I turn the car around in someone's gravel driveway. The mountain looms before me—Humphrey's Peak, according to signs I've seen along the way—and there is something else up there called the Arizona Snowbowl. Ski resort is my guess.

I wonder if I'm supposed to look for her up there? After all, Crystal did say the "highest point in San Francisco." I can't believe she expects me to climb to the mountain summit, but what else could "highest point" mean?

I drive back into town and find a convenience store. The gas tank is nearing empty, but I still have no money or credit cards. Why didn't I think to ask Nicole for money? If I don't find Crystal soon, I'll be looking for her on foot.

The clerk inside is a college-age male with closely cropped hair and an earring. He's tall and lanky and glares at me as I approach him. According to the badge on his shirt, his name is Cory.

"Hi," I say. "Maybe you can help me. Those are the San Francisco Mountains out there, right?"

He looks at me as if I'm a narc. The distrust is obvious. "You mean the Peaks?"

"Yeah. I was—"

"Really it's just a volcano that blew its top."

"And the main mountain is called Humphrey's Peak?"

"Well, the highest peak is called that, yeah."

"How do I get up there? Is there a road?"

"We have maps here, you know." He points to a stand on the counter stuffed with maps for the Grand Canyon, for Arizona, for Flagstaff and Vicinity.

"If you could just tell me how to get up the mountain, if there is a road or—"

"The Snowbowl is up there. Ski resort. It's not open yet, so you'll only be able to drive to the gate. Sometimes people go there to watch the sun set. And the trailhead is there if you want to summit Humphrey's."

"Great. How do I get there?"

"You from out of town?"

"Out of state, actually. If you could just tell me how would I . . . how . . ."

And then all at once the store grows bright, as if someone just cranked up the electricity. My ears begin to roar. A metallic taste seeps into my mouth. The world begins to swirl away.

The guy behind the counter says something, but I can't hear him above the roar in my ears. I try to ask him for help, but someone must have stuffed cotton in my mouth. I can't say anything. My tongue seems to swell.

Now I'm on the ground. I don't think I fell, and yet the convenience store clerk is standing over me, looking at me with bulging eyes and a wide open mouth.

"Wha—"

"Don't worry, dude," he says. "I called an ambulance. They're on the way."

"When? When did you call?"

"Just a second ago, after I kept you from choking on your tongue. You epileptic?"

"Epileptic? Of course not. What did you do with my tongue?"

But I can taste it now, the salty flavor of his fingers in my mouth. Why can't I remember?

"Just relax, dude. You had a seizure."

I raise up, and he puts his hand on my shoulder.

"You should stay put. I've seen stuff like this before."

"No! I've got to get out of here."

"Why, man? You need to get to a hospital."

I struggle to get up, but dizziness sends me back to the ground. Determined, I try again, and this time manage to stay on my feet by stumbling around in circles.

"Please tell me how to get to that place on the mountain. Please."

"You're crazy," he says.

"Maybe, but I'm not a criminal or anything. Please just tell me how to get there, and then forget I was here. It's sort of an emergency. Please help me."

My mind is quickly clearing. It's imperative I get out of here now, even if this guy won't tell me where I need to go.

"Just head toward the Grand Canyon on 180 and watch the signs for the Arizona Snowbowl. Turn right and follow the road. It's a switchback that'll take you where you need to go."

"Thanks."

"You can't sue us," he says as I shuffle to the door. "If you leave, you can't come back and sue the store."

"Just tell the paramedics that I ran off," I tell him. "Then no one will even know who was here."

Distant sirens wail as I step outside again. I hurry to the car and drive toward the street, darting into traffic. The sharp, white mountain peaks beckon to me. I never see the ambulance.

Soon I'm out of town again, going the same direction as before. Toward the Snowbowl, and away from the convenience store . . . where something just went wrong with my body *yet again*. A seizure this time. What's next, a stroke? Will one of my arms rot and fall off while I sleep?

The terror rushes back, simultaneously hot and cold and electric. The transmission is only forty-eight hours in the past, and just look at the symptoms that have surfaced: faltering coordination, eighteen hours of unexplained sleep, and now a seizure. If all this so soon, then what about a few days from now? What about next month?

Will I die?

I so glibly embrace the exhilarative nature of this new life—running from armed gunmen, hoping to expose Batista's faulty product for heaven's sake—and then a seizure jerks me back into the real world where it becomes clear that I am nothing more than a frightened, unsure creature whose fate rests, in part, on the resourcefulness of an exotic dancer with whom I once spoke in a topless bar. Have I really escaped the boring constraints of my humdrum life? Or am I merely a doomed man trying desperately to make something of the last few moments of existence?

Confused, I almost miss my turn. The new road is a narrow stretch of asphalt barely wide enough for two cars to pass side by side. Trees close around me, perfect cover for Ivan and Ed to hide within while they wait to pounce.

The road weaves and curves, tracing a roundabout path up the mountain. I disengage the automatic overdrive, which can't seem to decide on its own what to do. So far, I've come upon no other cars, and none pass me. I look out the window occasionally and watch the peak slowly grow closer. How high up am I? Eight thousand feet? Ten? Mountainous terrain is unfamiliar to me. In Houston, freeway overpasses are considered high ground.

The road goes on and on. A jolt of adrenaline shoots through me as I remember the gas tank. The gauge rests on empty. Will I even—

And then the trees melt away on my left, revealing a spectacular, elevated look at hills in the distance. A gold Buick sedan is parked facing those hills. The road ends before a large gate, and farther ahead on the left I see what looks like a sign for the trailhead. Do I drive over there? Do I park next to the Buick? What if Ivan and Ed are inside waiting for me?

The passenger door opens and a man steps out whom I don't recognize. My first instinct is to turn the car around and go back down the mountain, but it's too late now. The driver's side door opens next. A mane of blond hair emerges. Relief gushes through me like warm water.

Wearing a white sweatshirt and faded jeans, Crystal's beauty in daylight is terrific. She jogs toward my car, and I am barely out the door before she takes me into her arms. Even now, in this time of duress, the swell of her breasts between us electrifies me.

"You made it," she says, releasing me. "What a long shot. I can't believe you actually found us up here."

"Guessing Flagstaff was easy enough, but it wasn't until I got here that the 'highest point' thing made sense."

"Hey, great minds think alike, right?"

Her friend walks up to us, hands jammed in his pockets, staring at his shoes. He's wearing a long-sleeve black T-shirt and gray pants, his hair a black cord thrown over his back. Crystal sees him and introduces us.

"This is Lee Garrett. He's an old friend from high school."

Thin and pale, he sports a scruff of fuzzy hair on his chin, and his hand feels ten degrees colder than mine when we shake. "Hi, Lee."

"Nice to meet you."

"Lee is going to help us get the goods on NeuroStor."

His eye contact with me lasts for about a nanosecond before his attention turns to the distant hills.

"Those people are wrong, man," he adds. "Money-hungry assholes."

"Well," I say, not really sure how to respond. "I certainly appreciate your help."

Lee nods, still looking at the hills. He's either painfully shy or doesn't want to be here. I can't tell which.

"I got another instant message after yours," I tell Crystal. "Batista said they knew where I was, and if I didn't wait there, he would kill my wife."

"Shit. And you left right then?"

"What could I do? He could be bluffing about my wife, but what if she's—"

"You did the right thing. If they decide to mess with your wife, it won't make any difference what you do. You can't let them find you, no matter what." She motions toward the Buick. "We should go," she says. "They'll figure out this ruse soon enough. Whose car is that?"

"It belongs to the woman in Scottsdale who helped me. I drove it here on fumes."

"What are you supposed to do with it now?"

"Park it somewhere safe and hope someone reports the license plate number to the police. Do you think it will be okay here?"

"It'll probably be fine, but you never know. I think the woman who lent you this car must have been willing to part with it. Pretty generous of her."

I place the keys under the Maxima's floor mat, lock the doors, and then join Crystal and Lee in the Buick. I have the backseat to myself.

"Generous isn't a big enough word."

Crystal starts the car, and we wind our way back down the mountain.

One of the forgotten joys of childhood is the blanket of security that lies waiting, ready to be called into action whenever danger looms. Mother's warm breast after a screaming nightmare. Father's iron grip when your new bicycle pitches toward the ground. The reassuring thickness of your locked front door when the neighborhood bully has been chasing you for two blocks.

Male adulthood offers few examples of such protection. When something goes bump in the night, it's up to you to check it out. Dangers are real. Mortality is severe. And when you want to cry out to your mother, reach for your father, you find the blanket disturbingly absent.

But here, now, if only for a fleeting, counterfeit moment, Crystal has stepped into the place long since vacated by my mom and dad. She has assumed the role of protector, and for the first time since the golf course, I relax.

Crystal asks for a recap, for a quick summary of the past thirty-six hours of my life, and I begin with the moment I left The Wildcat. My identification of Ivan in the parking lot, the initial encounter at the golf course, the moment when the chase began. Our standoff at the river's edge. My battle with the churning water. The choking incident with Nicole. I carefully weave around the scene where she ordered me out of her house at gunpoint and instead focus on her initial grace and willingness to help me.

"I thought you looked pretty clean for a guy who fell into a flooded river," Crystal says.

"You have no idea."

She guides the car to the bottom of the mountain and then back toward Flagstaff. The town opens before us. Houses, stores, signs directing us to this museum or that one. Back the way I came before.

"Is this the only road in town?"

"Pretty much," Crystal says. "Route 66 is the other. It cuts through town on a general east-west track."

A police car is parked in front of the convenience store where I stopped for directions. Through the glass windows I see two human forms. A cop and the clerk who watched me convulse, perhaps. I guess I should mention what happened to me there, but I don't feel like talking about it.

"Crystal, I really appreciate your help. Both of you guys. After I got away from those two men, I didn't know what to do next."

"We're glad to help," she answers.

"So what do you suggest I do now? The only thing I can think of is to call the police."

Crystal and Lee exchange glances.

"What?" I ask. "Is that the wrong thing to do?"

"There is a lot you don't know about this," Crystal says.

"Like what?"

"We suspect considerable government involvement. Politicians and federal agencies being paid to look the other way when NeuroStor goes public, for instance. Or worse."

Government conspiracies have always seemed like paranoid fantasy to me. How could a bunch of glad-handing politicians elected by special interest groups ever work closely enough to hold a conspiracy together? They already have this country paralyzed with their endless two-party bickering. Am I really supposed to believe they can somehow put aside their differences long enough to deceive the American public? And why? Why would they want to?

"Worse how?" I ask.

"Do you remember David Duke?"

"The KKK guy? From Mississippi or Louisiana or wherever?"

"Louisiana. You probably first heard his name when he ran for the U.S. Senate in 1990. He was an acknowledged racist, or separatist, or whatever it is he calls himself, and he was nearly elected."

"So?"

"*So?* He won over forty-three percent of the vote in an election for a United States Senate seat. And sixty percent of the white vote. *Sixty percent.* Almost two-thirds of the whites in Louisiana voted for a racist."

"Okay, but what does it have to do with NeuroStor? Is David Duke a big investor or something?"

"Of course not."

"Then what does he have to do with anything?"

"What he did was illustrate that our country isn't as tolerant as we'd like to believe. There are a lot of frightened citizens out there, people who think their culture is under constant assault from the media, from races other than their own, who feel as though they are backed against a wall and are being forced to strike. Voting for a white supremacist is just the tentative first step toward mobilizing forces for domestic terrorism."

"Nice speech, but you didn't answer my question."

"Your company is financed by extremists," Lee growls, contributing his first words to the conversation. "That's your answer. Freakos who want to use the transmission machine as some kind of weapon."

I can think of absolutely no response to this statement.

"Doesn't that bother you?" Crystal asks me.

"I can't really say. I don't think I understand."

"We don't fully understand ourselves, but the AFA almost certainly operates NeuroStor in some capacity. We also haven't fully grasped how they plan to use the machine offensively."

"The AFA?"

"American Federation of Aryans. Don't tell me you haven't heard of them."

"No, I haven't. But you're telling me that this AFA developed quantum teleportation as some sort of means to terrorize the country?"

"Terrorism is just the beginning of what they hope will turn into an all-out war," Lee says. "Those fuckers want either an entire new government or they want to assume control of a portion of the country and secede."

"That's nuts. Who came up with this theory?"

"It's not a theory. I know people who've been on the inside, who have left because they realized just how crazy and serious the AFA had become. A group of these defectors put their heads together and decided to do something about it, because the government won't. The FBI shoots their fucking wad at these standoffs like Waco and Ruby Ridge. Politicians are more concerned with legislating morality and raising money than working together to help the country. So maybe someone else has to pick up the slack. Put a stop to this shit before it gets out of hand."

"Before what gets out of hand?"

"I *told* you! It's a fucking war, man! A war in the cities, in your fucking middle-America cow towns! Blacks are tired of getting shit on. Hispanics are pissed, too, but they don't get much press yet. Just wait until they become a majority in Texas and California."

I fear the conversation is getting away from me. "Look, I know the race situation isn't as fair as it could be, but I don't see the war you're talking about. And I live in Houston, where Hispanics must be thirty or forty percent of the population."

"Oh, yeah? Do you work downtown?"

"Yes. So?"

"So it probably takes you an hour to get to work because you live as far away from the crime-infested city as you can. Am I right? And you get in your Lexus or Cadillac or whatever and drive on elevated freeways all the way into town. If some hood is going to rip you off, he'll have to climb onto the highway and try to catch you going eighty miles an hour. Tell me I'm wrong."

I can't. I drive a Lexus along Highway 59 into the city every morning. The road is ten lanes wide. Inside the Beltway, people call it "murder row" for reasons that don't require explanation.

"You don't see the war because you don't want to see it. You sit in your suburban fortress and—"

"Lee," Crystal says.

"—with your Midwestern pseudovalues that—"

"Lee!"

"What?"

"I think you made your point."

"If we're going to help this guy, I think he needs to—"

"I think he understands. Don't you, Cameron?"

"Sure," I say amicably. And because I can't think of anything else.

Silence follows this exchange, and I make a point of looking out the windows to avoid any more confrontation. We turn off the main road and head into an old neighborhood. The yards here are small, the houses either quaint or run-down. Another turn and then we pull into a driveway. The home is paneled with aging white siding and needs a new roof, the lawn a mixture of unmowed brown grass and weeds. An empty brick planter stands in front of the covered porch.

"This is Lee's house," Crystal says.

We get out and head up the walk. My eyes, automatically now, sweep the yard and adjacent houses for anything unusual. I turn a full circle and look everywhere. There are too many places to hide. We'll never escape if they've found us already.

"Worried?" Crystal asks me as Lee unlocks the front door.

"Can't be too careful."

The house could stand redecorating. The carpet is old, the paneling and fixtures ancient. Everything smells musty. Any minute now, my late grandma is going to step around the corner in a blue polyester pantsuit and ask me if I want some homemade cinnamon rolls.

"So what are we going to do now?" I ask.

"Lee has been trying to break into your company's computer system so we can look for sensitive information. Anything about their internal power structure, planned operations, that sort of thing."

"This is something we should do before calling the police?"

Lee rolls his eyes.

"What?" I ask.

He walks by me and disappears into another room.

Crystal takes me by the shoulder and together we follow him. "Lee can be kind of temperamental. Can't you, Lee?"

"Whatever," he yells.

We walk down a hallway and into a small bedroom. Lee is already sitting in the center of a U-shaped desk. Monitors of different sizes stand on all three surfaces, and the middle screen spans at least twenty inches or more. The rest of the room is a landfill of unused or discarded electronic equipment—monitors burned out (or perhaps deemed too small), circuit boards, computer cases, stereo components, an ancient Nintendo game system. An off-road bicycle wheel stands in one corner next to an aluminum baseball bat. Forty-five-rpm vinyl records litter the floor. And who could miss the dartboard with Bill Gates' face printed on it?

"Don't let the computer nerd decor fool you," Crystal says to me. "Lee's not as one-dimensional as he seems."

The computer screen blinks on, and a text prompt appears that I can't read from here. Lee turns around and begins typing.

"He's actually a physics instructor at NAU here in Flagstaff. And he's going to be an author."

"Really? What do you write about?"

When Lee doesn't answer, Crystal continues.

"He's doing a book on string theory, origin of the universe, stuff like that. I read the first draft a few months ago, and it was actually pretty good."

Lee grunts but doesn't turn around.

"So you must know a lot about quantum teleportation," I say to Lee, "since you teach physics and all."

"You could say that."

"I've been having some problems," I admit. "Little things, like balance and coordination. Oh, and I blacked out."

"You what?" Crystal asks. "When did this happen?"

For some reason I decide to leave out my visit to the convenience store. "When I crawled out of the river. I lay down on the concrete and didn't wake up again for eighteen hours."

"Jesus Christ, Cameron."

"I was wondering," I say to Lee, "if you might have any idea what could be wrong with me."

"I don't think I would."

"Why?"

"Because your company's machine doesn't employ quantum teleportation. At least not any way I understand it."

"What do you mean?"

"Physicists have been struggling for years to make even the tiniest steps forward using entanglement to transfer the properties of one particle to another. Charles Bennett first proposed quantum teleportation in 1993, and Zeilinger in Austria confirmed his work by teleporting single photons. There just isn't any way that your company has taken one of the most complex disciplines in theoretical physics and moved the technology forward a hundred years.

"NeuroStor," Lee goes on to say, "has tapped into something we do not have science to explain."

"Apparently it works, whatever it is. I'm here, aren't I?"

"Yes, but in what sense are you here? Quantum teleportation assures us an exact replica of the original. Is that what you are?"

Which is the question I was asking in the first place, about my blackout and coordination problems and my seizure at the convenience store. In what sense am I here, indeed?

"If not quantum teleportation, then what?"

"I wish I knew. The information transmission alone is mind-boggling. If you forget about recognizing atoms and measuring their velocities and just scan to a resolution of one atomic length in each direction, you're talking about 10^{32} bits. Transmitting this much information using today's technology would take around ten billion years, so obviously they must have overcome this problem using a new information transmission system with nearly unfathomable speed and bandwidth. The next two problems are examining an infinitely complex molecular structure and reassembling it on the other side. Besides EPR correlation, which invokes the quantum mechanics we ruled out, there is no known way to measure something so precisely without damaging or destroying it. And it's possible, in theory, to reorganize particles and atoms in whatever form you choose, but present-day physics, as far as I know, is a long way from being able to do so.

"And finally," he adds, "what would become of the original?"

These ideas are beyond my understanding and concern. "Can you even guess what their machine does, if not quantum teleportation?"

"I already told you we have no idea."

I want to throttle him. How can he be such a jackass when we're talking about my health? My *life*?

Crystal stands beside me, smiling compassionately, and for a moment I hate her as well. They pity me, for Christ's sake.

"So what am I supposed to do now?"

"We've got to get your story on the news," Crystal says. "But first we need some evidence, and that's what we're hoping to find in their computer systems."

Lee has turned back toward his monitor again, typing more commands onto the keyboard. Crystal still stands there, hands joined at her waist, eyes open and inviting. Waiting to answer more of my questions. Prepared for everything.

"I don't understand something," I say to her.

"What is it?"

"I don't mean to be insensitive, but you're just some random woman

I met in a strip club. Tom is the one who told me to find you, so when I sent you that e-mail, I didn't know what to expect. Maybe some Internet assistance, or maybe for you to help me decide whether I should go to the police or call a television station. Then, when you asked me to meet you in Flagstaff, I figured 'What the hell do I have to lose?' But this . . . this is more than that."

I gesture to Lee and the computers and the house in general.

"This is like you've been waiting for me."

Lee stops typing and moves to turn around, but Crystal doesn't let him.

"Keep after it, Lee," she says. "Cameron and I are going for a drive."

"Why?" I ask. "Where to?"

"This is going to take Lee a while, so we don't need to stand here and bother him."

"Did Batista get to you? Are you taking me to him?"

"Of course not."

She takes me by the shoulder, intent on leading me out of the room, but this time I jerk free of her grasp.

"I'm not going anywhere with you until you give me some answers."

"I'll answer anything I can in the car, Cameron. But there's a chance that someone might trace Lee's work back to this house. Do you want to be here if that happens?"

"But doesn't he need me to stay? My network log-in and password? Something?"

"They would have locked you out days ago," Lee says over his shoulder. "I'm trying for a back door, something I can use that won't immediately alert them to my presence. But they may sniff me anyway. Probably better if you take off for a while."

Crystal looks at me impatiently.

I stand there for a minute, trying to be obstinate. But in the end I agree to leave with her.

The air is cool now, nearly cold. Crystal takes us out of Lee's neighborhood, and soon we're heading through the main part of town again.

Questions swell in my head. I cannot understand how these people can possibly know so much about my company, know so much more about this situation than I do. They have answers to almost every question I pose, have developed theories and concepts that never even occurred to me. How is that possible? The odds against me meeting these two people must have been fantastically long.

Unless someone planned it that way.

"So what do you want to know?" Crystal asks me.

"What do I want to know? How do you know so much about NeuroStor? Why was Tom so sure I should contact you? How did you get my e-mail so damn quickly?"

"Well—"

"Hold on. Let me back up. When you were telling me about the AFA you kept saying 'we think this' and 'we haven't figured out that.' Who, exactly, is 'we'?"

"Lee explained this. When the government can't or won't fix something, regular people have to organize and do something themselves."

"I heard all that. But who *are* they? You two can't be the whole thing."

Instead of answering, she looks out her side window at the sky. "I heard it was going to snow again tomorrow, but it doesn't look like it now." When she looks back at me, her eyes have turned darker somehow. "Never does."

I wait silently for her to answer my question. When she doesn't, I press on.

"It's not like you picked me out of a crowd at The Wildcat after all. I could have just as easily gone to the stage when another girl had been dancing. And you didn't offer the table dance to me. *I* asked *you.*"

"Hell of a coincidence," she says. "Maybe it was fate."

I try to ignore the fear welling cold in my stomach, but it's already too late.

"You don't seem like the kind of person who would believe in fate, Crystal."

"Not really. I mean, I don't go to church or anything, but I've always thought there might be some kind of smart energy built into the fabric of the universe. Something that makes sure everything runs smoothly. For some reason I don't think many things are left to chance."

"So if this isn't chance, what is it?"

Crystal begins to say something and then stops herself.

And something in the way she's looking at me makes me think of Tom, how concerned he was that we were being followed, how sure that we should run.

"Cameron," Crystal says. "I haven't been entirely truthful with you."

"Not entirely truthful? What the hell is that supposed to mean?"

It appears she is taking me out of town again, toward the Peaks.

"What did you think, Cameron? That some blond exotic dancer just happened to be interested in your story? That she would just happen to know more about transmitting than you did and give you her e-mail address so the two of you could discuss it later?"

I don't say anything because, until just now, this is exactly what I thought.

"My hair is dyed and my tan is fake. I'm no more an exotic dancer than you are."

My mind roars, the fear returning yet again, and though danger is not immediate this time, even though my life does not depend on the speed of my feet or the strength of my arms, the uncertainty, the deception, somehow seems worse. As if the Herculean effort that brought me this far has been wasted by the possibility that I was manipulated into doing so.

"What do you mean," I ask again, "when you say 'not entirely truthful'?"

She almost says something and again stops, as if measuring her words. A moment passes, then another. The snow-covered peaks fill the windshield.

"This was sort of arranged, Cameron."

"Arranged?"

"You want to know? I'm telling you. We arranged to meet you, to bring you here, for us to help you and you to help us."

Now we're traveling in a different direction than I've gone before, east and then north on Highway 89. My hands shake. The pads of my fingers seem to have gone numb, although that may just be my imagination.

After a few miles she turns off the highway onto a narrow, uneven road that disappears quickly into the forest. We pass driveways, marked only by mailboxes and newspaper drops, that must lead to houses hidden in the trees. Some of these private roads are covered by fresher pavement than others, and a few are not paved at all. Affinity for seclusion apparently crosses all income groups.

"Wait a minute. Are you saying that Tom knew about this all along? That he brought me there to see you?"

Crystal finally slows down and turns onto one of the unpaved roads. The Buick has no easy time navigating the rain-carved ruts or the overgrown grassy hump between the tire tracks, but she manages to push us up a gentle grade until the road settles into a clearing. An outline of mountains stands in silhouette behind a horizon of pine treetops, and beneath it all sits a small, well-kept cabin on a plot of overgrown grass. The road forks, sending one branch into a semicircular driveway in front of the cabin and another into what must pass for the backyard. The skeleton of a half-built deck stands in front of a single door.

"You seemed so honest and sincere at The Wildcat," I say to Crystal. "I didn't think you'd turn out to be such a smug bitch."

Crystal drives around back and parks beneath the framework of what will eventually be a carport.

"That's a cruel thing to say."

"What am I supposed to think? You won't tell me anything!"

"I'm trying to figure out the best way to break this to you, Cameron. You're so damn naive. At first I thought it was sweet, but you're really going to paralyze us if you don't learn to think and act a little more broadly."

"Now who's being cruel?"

She leans close to me, her sky blue eyes shining and lovely. Here I am trying to be mad, and still I can't ignore her dazzling beauty. What kind of person am I?

"Let's think about it, Cameron. If you wanted to hook up with a transmission volunteer, how would you do it? You couldn't just sit around and hope for one to call you up on the telephone, could you?"

"Of course not."

"So first you'd have to figure out who the volunteers were. How do you do something like that? Well, since you haven't yet been able to hack into NeuroStor's computer system, you'd have to get a contact on the inside to help you. So maybe someone you know knows someone else who may have risked his life to get you a list. And with a stroke of luck it happens that one of the people on this list is transmitting to your part of the country. Your own *state*, for that matter. So now you investigate this person a little to make sure he isn't someone who might fuck up everything. And then you do a little more digging to find out if the volunteer is coming to visit anyone. What kind of person is he? Might he be of any use? What do you know, the friend is a thirty-five-year-old ladies' man. Turns out he can be bought. So now the transmission volunteer can be manipulated any number of ways. We can send the guy anywhere we want because his friend is going to help us do it. You get the picture? Not easy, but not exactly impossible either."

My mind whirls, a kaleidoscope of images. Tom's nervous, waiting face when I first saw him in Phoenix. Crystal and her velvety, voluptuous body at The Wildcat. Ivan and Ed chasing us through a hurricane-like rainstorm at the Sandy Canyon golf course, the gunshot, Tom going down, imploring me to find Crystal. . . .

"So what you're saying is that your stupid, covert plan got my best friend killed! I should kill *you*! For involving him—"

"Cameron—"

"—for involving *me* in your brainless crusade that no one on earth gives a shit about! So what if the people who run NeuroStor are psychopathic racists? How are you any better?"

"Cameron, I am so sorry about Tom. We had people at the golf course; we were going to help you, but that rain . . ."

"Wait a minute. You were there? You knew they shot Tom and you didn't help him?"

"We tried to help, but by the time we tracked you down, it was too late. He'd already lost too much blood. I—"

But I don't want to hear any more of this. I throw open the door and lunge out of the car. I want to yell. I want to scream. I'm so fucking mad and confused I could just run shrieking into the woods and never come back. Noise swells between my ears, fills my brain. Swirling noise blown in the wind. Red noise like north Texas dirt. Like rage. Fuck this. Fuck *this*.

"Cameron."

I try to answer, scream *Leave me alone!*, but what comes out is a tongue-twisted, garbled mess. My eyes sting and my nose runs. I'm weeping. Weeping so violently that I can barely stand on my two feet. Tom is dead. My best friend is dead, and it's my fault. *I* did this. Me.

"Cameron."

"I killed him. I can't believe I killed him."

"Tom knew what he was getting into, Cameron. He took money from us. Why don't you come inside and let me ex—"

But the noise drowns her voice, covering all ambient sounds like a layer of volcanic ash.

A voice. A sweet voice. The sexy, muffled voice of a young woman. Muted by the snowfall of red ash under which I am buried. Under which I am suffocating. I can't breathe. My diaphragm won't move, will not flex the same way it has done a billion times before. It will not flex it will not move I cannot *breeeaaathhhhe* . . .

The voice again, stronger.

Coughing now, violently, clearing my throat of this godforsaken red ash that presses me downward, downward into the—

"Cameron! Breathe, goddammit! Wake up!"

Weight upon my chest, pressing again and again.

"Cameron!"

Her mouth against mine. The burn of sugarless cinnamon gum. The soft flesh of her lips.

"Cameron!"

"Okay," I croak. "Okay. I'm okay."

My eyelids flip open. Crystal hovers above me. The planes of her face are flat and smooth. Her blue eyes are youthful. Beautiful. Staring into mine.

She pushes away and stands. I am lying on a sofa of some kind. Apparently I made it into the cabin somehow.

"Jesus, I was afraid you'd *never* wake up. What the hell happened?"

"I don't know."

"You just got out of the car and started convulsing. Earlier you mentioned blacking out, but you didn't say anything about seizures."

I sit up and then look away from her.

"When?"

"When I first got to Flagstaff. I stopped at a convenience store to ask for directions, and I . . . well, you know the rest."

"Did anyone see you?"

"The guy working there. A young kid, maybe twenty or so. He said I convulsed pretty badly."

"Did he call an ambulance?"

"Yes, but I left before it got there. He gave me directions to the mountain and told me I was crazy for not seeking medical attention."

"Cameron, what if he calls the police? When they find the car, this town will be crawling with cops, FBI, everyone. I thought we could lie low in this cabin for a few days, but now it looks like we'll have to bump our schedule forward a little."

"I'm messed up, aren't I? Something is really wrong with me."

She frowns. "Don't jump to conclusions. We'll get you to a doctor, and whatever it is, I'm sure he can find a way to treat you."

But somehow I don't think so. If the transmission has altered my body somehow, it could be at the atomic level, at the *quantum* level, even. A doctor can prescribe medicine to ward off infection, or to alter your body chemistry, but what can he do if your body had been changed in a more fundamental way?

What the fuck did Batista do to me?

"How do you feel now?" Crystal asks.

"Okay, I guess."

"If your arms hurt, it's probably because I had to drag you into the house. You pretty much collapsed out there in the carport."

I look away from her, at anything but the pity in her eyes. I don't want it. I don't want to need it. Acknowledging her compassion is the same as admitting something is drastically wrong with me, something that sends me into convulsive fits. I cannot face this. I have managed to push my fear out to the periphery, into mere background noise, and I want it to remain there.

Crystal senses my distress and slinks away. She disappears around a corner and enters what sounds like the kitchen. Drawers open and close. Water runs.

I'm sitting in what must be the great room, and another sofa and two overstuffed chairs join the sofa on which I awoke. A television stands beside the fireplace. Out of nowhere I remember Tom, that he's dead, and tears blur my vision.

I kept hoping he had survived somehow, had made it to a hospital and was wondering when I was going to show up there. But he is not waiting for me. He'll never be waiting for me again, will never beat me in golf again, will never laugh at me as I down a pitcher of beer in his favorite strip bar. He's gone.

After a moment, Crystal rejoins me, bearing mugs of what appears to be coffee or hot chocolate. She sits in a chair beside the sofa.

"How much did you pay him?"

"What?"

"You said that Tom took money from you. How much did you give him?"

"Does it matter?"

"I want to know how much my friendship is worth. How much money it costs to sell me out."

"Cameron—"

"Will you please just tell me?"

"One hundred thousand dollars. Tom asked for a year's salary."

"He doesn't make a hundred thousand dollars a year."

"We checked. He filed ninety-seven and change last year."

I don't know why I'm surprised. It doesn't make much difference now, does it?

"Don't be so hard on him, Cameron. When we first approached Tom, he told us to shove it. We kept upping the money and he kept ignoring us. He only agreed to help after we convinced him that you would be a whole lot worse off on your own than if we were involved. And we couldn't really get involved without his help."

Tears flood my eyes again. I can see him there, on the ground, imploring me to run.

"That man, Ivan, he knew Tom was onto him. When he caught me by the river, he demanded to know what I knew. He thought we'd set him up. I guess we had. I just didn't know it."

"You'd only have been more at risk if we had told you. If you knew before the transmission, you probably would have spilled the beans to Batista, and in that case he would have killed you. If we had told you afterward, those men would have known for sure. You wouldn't have acted normally. They might have grabbed you right away instead of just watching."

"So the tests they performed on me after I arrived, those aren't enough to tell if I'm messed up? Someone has to observe me?"

"It's no secret why Batista wanted you to stay a couple of days before you went back to Houston. Transmission-related neurological problems typically take a few days to manifest themselves."

"Take a few days to manifest themselves?" Terror sends a short burst of adrenaline into my bloodstream, and its electric taste forces me to take a sip of my hot chocolate. "It's only been forty-eight hours since my transmission. Are these problems going to get *worse?*"

"I don't know," Crystal says.

"Have the other volunteers had problems like me?"

"I don't really know, Cameron."

Silence floats between us, and I try to get my mind around all of this. So much doesn't make sense.

"You know the volunteers are at risk."

Crystal nods.

"But you don't tell the volunteers or the media or the FBI or anyone."

"We know you are at risk, but we don't have any proof. That's a big difference. If I had flown to Houston and told you not to transmit, how would you have reacted? Would you have believed me?"

"It certainly would have made me think twice about going through with it."

"Would you have approached Batista about me? Asked him if what I said was true?"

"I guess I might have."

"See," she says. "And when he realized you were onto him, he would have killed you both."

"Killed us? *Then?"*

"This is serious business, Cameron. Batista isn't taking any chances."

Crystal reaches forward and puts her hand on mine.

"I am so sorry about Tom. You may think he sold you out, but he honestly believed you were better off with us than dealing with NeuroStor by yourself."

I look away, because otherwise she'll see my eyes shining.

"And sure, I have my own motives. I won't deny it. But I'm also honestly trying to help you. If you look at the situation objectively, I think you'll see that."

"It's hard to be objective about anything when your best friend is dead. And I don't know whether to blame Tom or myself."

"How about no one, Cameron? We all made decisions that were the best choice at the time. You transmitted. We offered Tom money to help us track you. Tom took the offer to help you and us and make some money in the process. There is no way to know how things would have turned out for you and Tom if I had never entered the picture. But they wouldn't necessarily be better."

A good point. Assuming nothing about the transmission itself played out differently, which Crystal had nothing to do with anyway, I would still have been followed by Ivan and Ed. Without Tom's prior knowledge, we both probably would have been caught on the golf course. And even if *that* had played out in similar fashion, who would I have turned to after I got away? No one but myself. So it's like Crystal said: She has her own agenda, but she's still trying to help me.

Hell, of course I want to believe her. Of course I want this striking woman to be looking out for me, fighting for me, acting as if I am the most important person in the world to her. I'm a man, aren't I?

"Are you involved with Lee? Romantically, I mean?"

Crystal's shoulders relax and she reclines in her chair. "Lee would sleep with me if I let him. He's nice enough, and I've thought about it, but I think it would just screw up everything."

"Do you have a boyfriend?"

"Why, Cameron? Are you going to get fresh with me?"

"I was just asking."

"You're blushing."

She has embarrassed me into silence.

"I'm surprised Tom was able to drag you into The Wildcat. You don't seem the type."

"I don't seem like the type of guy who is attracted to dancing nude women?"

"No. More like you'd think it was demeaning to them."

"I used to think so. But no one forces women to dance nude. How can a voluntary action be demeaning?"

"Does your wife mind?"

"Misty? No. She posed for *Playboy* once. One of those coed pictorials."

"Did she make the cut?"

"Yeah. I was the envy of all my college buddies."

"That's sweet, being married so long. So, you don't have any children?"

"We had a son. He lived three weeks. We tried again but were never successful."

Normally, when someone broaches the subject of Luke with me, I answer with the cool, detached demeanor that comes from being thirteen years removed from my son's brief life. But for some reason, the pain right now seems closer than ever, as if his tiny form was taken from me just yesterday.

"I'm sorry," she says.

"It was a long time ago. You don't have to be sorry."

Crystal leans toward me. "But it still hurts you."

"Not usually. I guess the stress . . . everything that's happened to me since I got to Arizona . . ."

"It's okay," she says.

"It's not. I mean, he died thirteen years ago. He was barely an infant. I can't remember what he looked like without a picture."

"He was your son."

"He was also a vegetable whose cerebrum was the size of a pencil eraser. I loved him because he was my son, but really he was nothing more than a human shell."

A description to halt any conversation. Misty would slap me.

"I can't imagine how painful it must have been," Crystal says. "But thirteen years is a long time, Cameron. My dad passed away four years ago, a man I idolized for twenty-two years, and I've let it go. Time passes and the pain fades."

Crystal is speaking pure logic, of course. Anyone who has ever lost a loved one to death knows this to be true. What she doesn't understand is that Luke's death signaled my own, because that's what I've been for more years than I care to remember. Dead.

But now I want to live.

"A person can't mourn that long, Cameron. Your mind protects itself from that sort of degeneration. I think it's something else."

"You think what is something else?"

"Your pain. It's caused by something other than your son."

"What do you mean, 'my pain'?"

"Come on, Cameron. Don't bullshit me."

I look away from her. How can I get out of this gracefully? Is there someplace I can go, like to the bathroom or over a cliff?

"Cameron, look at me."

I don't. The trees outside are beautiful through the windows. Ponderosa pines reaching for the sky, as if their branches request salvation.

"Come on. I saw it in your eyes when we first met. You slump when you walk, you don't make eye contact, you hardly smile. I bet it took every bit of your courage to feign bravado with me at The Wildcat."

"What the hell do you know?" I say, still staring out the window.

"If we're going to talk, Cameron, I want to talk to *you*, not some fucking facade you've created to deal with the real world."

"Who said I wanted to talk? I don't remember initiating this conversation."

Crystal doesn't say anything for a few moments. I feel her eyes burning into my side, but still I don't turn around.

"It scares the hell out of you, doesn't it?" she asks. "To admit your weakness. To reveal your fear."

"That's really brilliant," I say. "Did you read that in *Cosmopolitan*?"

"Poke fun at me if it makes you feel better. But we wouldn't be having this conversation right now if you'd already had it with your wife."

Like a surgeon's scalpel she makes her incisions, carefully but quickly, until the skin is laid open, the damaged organ exposed. I turn around, finally, but cannot hold eye contact with her.

"I've known Misty for eighteen years. We used to talk like brother and sister. Nothing was sacred, no secrets, no lies. After Luke . . . every year it gets worse. We still have polite conversations, but we don't . . . we don't talk."

"What don't you talk about?"

"Our problems."

"Like?"

"Like the family we never had."

"Is it Misty or you?"

"Misty."

"And you wanted to have children."

I'm struggling to fight away tears again. "More than anything in the world."

The questions stop firing for a moment, and I use the reprieve to collect myself. Crystal might as well be pulling the very teeth from my jaws.

"I bet it hurts Misty as much as you. It's her body."

"She was crushed, apologized for failing me, for being defective. Offered to divorce me. I assured her a thousand times that I didn't hold it against her, and eventually she went on with her life. But I didn't. I pretended to, but I didn't."

"She must've known by the way you changed afterward."

"We were both offered antidepressants after Luke's death. Misty didn't bother, but I took them and they helped at first—made the symptoms go away, at least. But they couldn't touch the source."

"If you wanted kids so badly, why didn't you take Misty's offer of a divorce? Or why not a surrogate mother with your sperm?"

"A surrogate would make her feel like a third wheel. And what would you think if your husband left you because you weren't fertile? I couldn't hurt Misty like that."

"Don't you think it hurts worse being married fifteen years to someone who holds a grudge against you?"

"I never told her that."

"But she knows, Cameron. I promise you she knows. You can pretend all you like, even be good at it, but this grudge . . . it makes you treat her differently than before. Women are sensitive to this. She's known for a while, I'm sure."

"If that's true, why doesn't she say anything? Why stay with me for so long?"

"The same reason you've stayed. Because it's easier to hurt a little every day than all at once."

Hearing such a thing spoken aloud is finally too much. Two days of invasive fear have dislodged the pain I have tried to ignore, that I have kept buried for so long. My mind spins, overheats, squeezes out tears that blur my vision, and I stand, ready to leave, ready to head for the bathroom or some other place where I can lock a door behind me. But Crystal grabs my arm.

"Come on, Cameron. Don't leave now."

The sobs shake my body, so deep I can barely catch my breath. At first I try to control them, aware that real men are not supposed to break down and cry in front of others, but even this ancient filter is stripped away by the power of my pain. I am exposed, a bare nerve standing in the great room of this secluded mountain cabin, and jerk involuntarily when Crystal puts her arms around me.

"I love my wife," I say between breaths. "I just don't know if we belong together anymore."

Later, I'm lying on the sofa again. Crystal sits behind me, alternately rubbing my shoulders and temples. An eye of calm has settled into the storm of my emotions, but I know it is only a matter of time before the winds and rain return.

"I don't know why I've ignored it for so long. It seems obvious when I tell you now."

"Probably because it's hard to imagine your life without her. You can't remember anything else."

"And because I still love her. I don't know many people who've voluntarily ended a loving marriage."

"Have you considered adoption?"

"I thought about it before, but it . . . I don't know. Adoption is great for a lot of people, but I just want a child of my own. That is part of me. I suppose that's really selfish."

"Yes, it is kind of selfish."

"But this isn't just about having children. The gulf between Misty and me is much more than that now. We seemed to . . . I don't know . . . take different paths after Luke died. On the surface nothing seemed to change, but beneath that we grew into different people. We lost our desire to be intimate. And I think, in a good marriage anyway, the opposite is supposed to happen. Over time you should slowly grow more into the same person, you know? Your likes and dislikes. Your attitudes. Political views. Even your personalities seem to merge into one over time."

"I know what you're saying," Crystal agrees. "My grandparents even look like each other."

"Exactly. To me, that's part of what marriage is. And I'm not sure if Misty and I have that. I think maybe we had a window after Luke died to either grow closer or farther apart, and I don't think we picked the right one. I'm afraid that even though I love her more than anything . . . I'm afraid love isn't necessarily enough anymore."

Crystal doesn't answer that, and I don't know what to do with the things I just said. Why am I addressing these issues only now? Does it have anything to do with the beautiful woman sitting beside me? Am I convincing myself that my marriage isn't working so that I can—

"What are you thinking?" Crystal asks me.

The lie comes easily. "I'm wondering if it would be worse to split now, after all these years, than to stay together? I'm thirty-five. I'm getting old."

"You're not that old," Crystal answers. "And you don't have to date someone your age anyway."

"I'm not going to hit the bars looking for nineteen-year-olds. Besides, they wouldn't look at me anyway."

"I promise you there are plenty of young women who are mature and who are attracted to guys in their thirties and forties. We don't all want to date twenty-five-year-old pricks who don't have any clue what to do with that club hanging between their legs."

Crystal's hands find my head again, this time exploring my hair with her fingers.

"You don't look thirty-five, Cameron. You still have all your hair, and it helps that you work out. Women notice that sort of thing."

Just like that my blood simmers, surging to my dormant organ. I relish the feeling and hate myself for it. What else can a man feel when a gorgeous, intelligent woman runs her fingers through his hair and tells him how handsome he is? Married or not, what else can he feel?

Life is organic. Humans are chemical creatures like all others. Our conscious, reasoning minds may separate us, in part, from our wilder, less-evolved animal relatives, but don't be fooled. We haven't come as far as we think. When Crystal strokes my hair with her fingers and speaks those words to me, I don't choose my reaction. Sensory input is received. Chemicals are stirred, dispensed. My response is predicated upon them.

Now I have a choice—unlike the horse or the dog or the duck, I have a choice—but really, how much of the decision is left to me? *Morals!* others may implore. *They make the choice for you!* And who am I to question such common sense? You can't just sleep around, right? But maybe, instead of choice, what we really have is a continuum. The continuum is this: How successfully can I fend off a sexual opportunity presented before me?

To illustrate, let's examine two unrealistic examples:

Say I've been married for three years, have a son who is two years old, and I'm in the hospital delivery room with my wife, who screams my name as she births the first of our twin daughters. A woman walks into the room. I took her to the senior prom eight years ago. She's gained forty pounds and wears polyester pants that stretch across her expanding ass. She turned me down for sex that night, after the prom dance, and has come to offer herself to me now. Do I turn her down? Of course. This is a no-brainer.

Let's try again. This time I'm nineteen years old, second semester of college. I haven't been on a date in six months, and yet my roommate, Jake, buys condoms more often than toilet paper. In fact, he's at the lake right now, in the boat he borrowed from his dad, making his own waves with some sorority babe he met last week. I'm on the sofa watching *Star Trek*. Then a naked *Playboy* model enters the room and sits next to me on the sofa. Her perfume is exotic. Thick maroon lipstick. Heavy eye makeup. Perfect body. Gorgeous skin. Everything is waxed, everything except that narrow landing strip. She says she'd like nothing more than to do me all night long, however I like, except she talks dirty when she says this. Uses the word *fuck* five or six times. Anything I want, she says. Do I say no? Is there even a question?

These scenarios will never happen, of course, but we can use such examples as the bookends of our scale, our freezing and boiling. Everything else falls in between. Maybe it seems like a choice, but really, when sex is presented to a man, he either does or doesn't depending on where he currently stands in that continuum. Is he married? Engaged? Just dating? Single? Is he happy with his female partner? Is she anywhere nearby? Will she ever find out? How powerful is his desire for this potential sexual partner? And yes, how strong are his morals? All these factors, and a hundred more I haven't thought of, go into the chemical computer and out pops an answer.

Men and women don't always understand each other because our minds, our bodies—our chemical balances—are different. Women go through cycles that confuse and anger men. Their desires differ from ours, or occur with unpredictable frequency. They abandon intelligent, sensitive men for those with large biceps or bankrolls or for those who exude power and confidence. Should they be judged for these things? On this earth, after all, who can say what is right and wrong?

No one can.

No one.

And Crystal behind me, her head now resting on my shoulder. I could reach for her. I could take her face in my hands and draw her to me, her lips toward mine, and she would climb around me, on top of me. I would lift her shirt off and expose those beautiful breasts, her precious skin, and her soft heat would be resting upon something hard of mine. We would begin to move, slowly at first, and I would reach for her pants, bring down the zipper, her panties, tiny, almost unseen, and her smell, so soft, so moist, and I could . . . I could . . .

"I think I'll call Misty," I blurt. Like a spring, I'm off the sofa, looking for a telephone. I spot one on a bar in the kitchen.

"No, Cameron!" Crystal cries. She appears before me and reaches for the telephone.

"I have to! I have to hear her voice and let her know I'm okay."

"You can't! They'll trace the call!"

"But—"

"No buts." She takes the phone from me, replaces it on the bar. "Don't give yourself up after all this running. You can try calling her when we go back to Lee's house. His computer can make untraceable phone calls."

My eyes shift away from her, to my feet, to the living room. I walk back to the sofa and collapse into it. "You're right," I say. "I'm sorry."

"Don't be sorry. You care about your wife. You'll talk to her soon."

"But what if she's not there? What if Batista has done something to her because of me?"

"That would be stupid, Cameron. Your phone is tapped, sure, and there is no doubt they're watching the house in case you show up. But she's the only leverage they have against you right now. There's no question she's still alive."

I can't think of anything else to say, so I look away from her again, this time at the television set. I'm thinking about her hands in my hair again. The smell of her. Goddammit, what kind of insensitive prick am I? Worried about Misty's safety and five seconds later lusting after Crystal again? The only thing I can hear is my own breathing. Where am I in the continuum right now? Much closer to boiling than freezing, I'm sure. Misty is a thousand miles away, Crystal is my *Playboy* model, and only inches separate us.

How many men in the world could sit where I am and not try to seduce her?

This is a question for which there is no clear answer.

"What time is it?"

Crystal looks at her watch. "Almost five o'clock."

"*Five?* You've got to be kidding."

"You were out for a while, Cameron."

"A while?"

"You were unconscious on the sofa for almost two hours before you started choking."

"My God, I thought I was only out for a minute. Seconds, even."

"I was worried sick. I nearly took you to the hospital."

Seizures. Minutes and hours gone from my life. What have I done?

"So I guess she knows now."

"She?"

"Misty. She was expecting me in Houston at two forty-five today. It's close to six there. What did she do when I didn't show up?"

"I imagine she demanded to know something from Batista, and he probably told her there was an unforeseen delay."

"Then what?" I ask. "She would want to talk to me. Make sure I was all right."

"They would have had to make something up," Crystal points out. "Who knows what it was. But it had to be believable enough for her to wait patiently. They couldn't have her call the police."

"Batista might have kept her there. As long as she's alive, I guess it doesn't matter where she is."

"Look, Cameron. We've already gone over this. You can't help Misty if you compromise yourself. The only way she'll be safe is if you continue to be safe as well."

"I just want to talk to her. Is that so wrong? Just because we may not be right as a couple doesn't mean I don't love her."

"You can try her from Lee's house, all right?"

Again this makes sense, even if I don't want it to.

"So what do we do now? How long are we going to stay here in this cabin?"

"Not much longer. We should get back and check on Lee. But since it's nearly five o'clock, we might as well wait until then. I'm curious to see if there is anything on the early news about your stop at the convenience store."

"I don't know why there would be."

"Probably there isn't, but you'd be surprised what passes for a story around here. If a television reporter picked up something on a police scanner, he'd be there in no time."

The remote sits on a shelf below the television. I switch it on just as a talk-show host is introducing Jack and John, a couple of skinheads who strut onto the stage in an eruption of censored profanity. The studio audience immediately berates them.

"Are those the kind of people I'm up against?"

"Yes and no," Crystal says. "Men like this comprise the bulk of the neo-Nazi movement. Many of them are members of the AFA I told you about. But they're also the least likely to do anything serious, the least likely to organize something pervasive and powerful enough to threaten the country. And a lot of skinheads eventually give up the lifestyle, anyway. Aggressively hating everyone requires more energy than they think."

"So who is the real enemy?"

"Well, some might say Jeff Ender, the leader of the AFA, or William Pierce, the head of another neo-Nazi organization called the National Alliance. But I'm not so convinced. Those two are politicians, not action-oriented leaders who can organize and direct any sort of offensive against the U.S. government. I think the real enemies are people we don't know. Or worse—maybe we know them but we don't yet realize what they are."

"Offensive against the government? Are you really sure about that?"

"We're not sure about anything. But we hear a lot of disturbing rumors from people who have been on the inside, Cameron. You can't just ignore something like that."

"But don't you think the government can take care of itself? I mean, they've done a pretty good job so far. I think I would leave this sort of thing to the FBI."

"You would, huh? I guess you say that because the FBI has such an excellent track record handling extremists in the past. They really saw the Oklahoma City bombing coming, didn't they? September eleventh?"

"What about all the good stuff they do that doesn't make the news?"

"My point is that there are weaknesses in the system."

"But this network that you claim exists, how does it propose to do any better? Without the resources of the FBI, how can you possibly hope to combat anyone who could seriously threaten the government?"

"Who said we didn't have the resources of the FBI?"

"I don't understand."

"The government is made up of people, Cameron. Human beings with opinions and prejudices and faults and weaknesses. A lot of our representatives are like you, completely ignorant of the wars going on in this country every day, but many others are quite aware. Most of these fall on either one side or the other. Those whose opinions match ours might be willing to help if they could be assured there was a need for their help."

The talk show ended a few moments ago, and now that the commercials are ending, it looks as if the local news is about to begin.

"You're saying you have contacts in the FBI?"

"I'm saying that if there was a dramatic need for assistance, it's possible that we could obtain such assistance from organizations you wouldn't necessarily expect. Public *and* private. After all, who do you think stands to lose the most because of NeuroStor?"

"Airlines, I guess."

"And?"

"Other transportation companies. Bus and train lines."

"How about Big Oil? Automakers?"

"Yeah, I guess. But . . ."

"But what?"

"What the hell *is* your group, Crystal? You haven't really told me anything."

"I don't know what else there is to tell."

"Oh, come on. How many people are in it? Do you have a leader? Where does your money come from?"

"We get money from the members. They donate for the cause."

"*What* cause?"

"I told you: to answer the extremists who want to terrorize our country and infect it with their separatist agenda."

"What are you, Batman? People don't just go around taking the law into their own hands."

Crystal smiles. "Oh, yeah? Who was it that e-mailed me instead of calling the police after he got away from a couple of NeuroStor hit men?"

That shuts me up.

"Come on, now. Tom or not, you contacted me because you thought I would know how to retaliate against NeuroStor. That I could help you get on the news or something that would make them answer for what they did to you."

"I—"

"Tell me I'm wrong," she says.

The evening news theme saves me, trumpeting theatrically, and our attention turns again toward the television. The news anchors appear, their faces contorted with an apparent mixture of gravity and excitement, and suddenly I get the feeling that something is desperately wrong.

The camera frames both anchors initially—a stout, fair-haired fortyish man (Steve Johnson) and a twentysomething brunette (Kelly Smith)—as they introduce themselves. Then a second camera angle zooms in on Steve, who immediately opens with the evening's top story.

"A Good Samaritan's deed turned deadly in Scottsdale this afternoon, and her attacker is still at large."

Now the picture cuts to Kelly Smith, who offers the next bite of information.

"That's right, Steve. Thirty-one-year-old Nicole Shepherd was found by her husband, local attorney Matt Shepherd, apparently murdered in her home this evening. Early reports suggest that Mrs. Shepherd accepted a drifter into her home sometime around eight AM, and while details are sketchy, it appears this mysterious visitor is currently the prime suspect in what can only be described as a vicious murder. Let's go to Abbie Bishop, our reporter on the scene in Scottsdale."

My heart beats frenetically as the anchors are replaced by an attractive brunette reporter standing in front of a store of some kind. For an instant I wonder why she isn't reporting from the crime scene, and then I realize she's at the entrance of the Texaco where I first met Nicole.

"Thank you, Kelly. While police are currently going over Mrs. Shepherd's house looking for clues and forensic evidence, Channel Three has learned of the victim's first encounter with the suspect here at this Texaco station at Pima and Greenway. Mr. Clyde Chambers was the main witness of this encounter. Mr. Chambers, please describe to our viewers what you saw this morning."

And here is the buffoon from the Texaco station, the fellow who blundered into my encounter with Nicole and hammered me with his fat fists.

"I had just sold this nice lady a doughnut and coffee, and not ten seconds later I hear screaming outside. I go out there and here is this guy who I can tell has been, you know, had his paws on her. So I start yelling at him to get the heck off our property, to leave our customers alone. He gets mad, of course, and tries to attack me, so I hit him back a few times. I guess the lady felt sorry for him because the next thing I know she's letting the guy get into her car."

"Right away?" Abbie asks. "Did you hear any of their conversation? Surely they must have said something. Perhaps they knew each other."

"I don't know about that. This guy didn't look like your average . . . I mean, he didn't look like he lived around here or anything. The customers here, they kind of fit a pattern, you know? I recognize most of 'em, anyway. This guy looked like he'd been hiking across the desert."

"But did you hear what they said?"

"No, I went back into the store and watched them from the counter. I think she gave him some money and then must have offered him food or something, because the next thing I know he's getting into the car with her."

"What did you do then?"

"I went back outside and asked if everything was okay. She didn't say anything. Just kind of ignored me. I knew something bad would come of it, though. I just knew it."

Cut to the reporter, Abbie, again. "Kelly, from what we've been able to piece together from all sources so far, it appears Mrs. Shepherd drove the drifter back to her house, fed him, and allowed him to take a bath. Maybe she angered her visitor at some point, or perhaps his plan all along was to attack. At some point Mrs. Shepherd appears to have locked herself in a closet, because that's where she was found. The door, police say, was forced open. She was shot at least twice, gangland-style, in the head and chest."

I can no longer breathe.

Cut back to the anchors again, who are now looking at a large, studio TV monitor where the reporter is still pictured. Now Steve speaks. "Abbie, have the police found any trace of the man? Any way to identify him?"

Cut again to Abbie. "Steve, the police have declined to answer questions about possible evidence. They would say, however, that the suspect apparently fled the scene in the Shepherds' car, which was last seen by a police officer heading north on Pima. The car is a late-model silver Nissan Maxima. License number E-R-L-four-zero-nine. The suspect should be considered armed and extremely dangerous. Contact the police immediately if you see this car. We've also been told that a sketch will be ready for our six o'clock broadcast."

The anchorman appears on the screen again, makes a final statement, and goes on to some other story. Crystal sits down beside me.

"That woman was just in the wrong place at the wrong time, Cameron. You even thought up an alibi for her. What else could you have done?"

"I could have turned her down. Stayed away from her house. Not used her computer."

"And then you wouldn't be here. You'd still be running instead of fighting back. The only problem is that we don't know what she told them. They probably tortured her, and we have to assume she gave in and told them about Flagstaff."

"You don't understand. Two people are dead. Dead! I don't know how much longer I can . . . I mean, how can I be a party to—"

"You've gone too far to back away now. Lee and I have put ourselves in danger to help you. Others are waiting to do the same. You have to see this through."

I hear the words, but they make little sense to me. A fog bank has rolled into my head, obscuring thought, beclouding reason.

"Why would they kill her?" I wonder aloud.

"Because she knew about you. That's why you can't talk to your wife again until this is over. You don't want to—"

"That's where you're wrong," I say. "I *have* to call her now. Just to hear her voice. To make sure she's alive."

"Cameron, you don't even know if she's—"

"I'll use Lee's computer so they can't trace the call. If she's still home, I want to hear her voice. This is very important to me."

"Cam—"

"Let's go," I say. "We're driving back to Lee's house. Right now."

"Someone is going to find that woman's car. When they do, the whole town will be after you. Now that we know the cops are looking for you, it's better to stay here."

"But how would they find me? No one here knows what I look like."

"What about the guy who saw your convulsion? He even saw the car, didn't he?"

"Oh, shit. He did. He saw the car." This throws me, because if that kid sees the news, he'll call the police for sure. But this knowledge still doesn't lessen my need to talk to Misty.

"We're going," I say again. I grab Crystal's keys from the kitchen counter. "I just want to hear her voice. I have to know if my wife is alive."

six

≣

For some reason, I'm a little nauseous as we get back into the car. So of course the ride back to Lee's house seems to take forever. Crystal drives slowly to minimize the chance of being stopped by a police officer, and every traffic light is red. I stare at the horizon and concentrate on not vomiting, point the air-conditioning vent into my face and inhale deep breaths of icy air. For a while I think I've got the nausea under control, at least long enough to get back on solid ground, but then we get stuck behind the fits and starts of an eighties-era Chevrolet driven by an old woman who either has forgotten where she is going or never really knew in the first place. Time crawls to a stop.

"What comes next?" I ask Crystal, trying to direct my attention away from my stomach. "You must have devised a plan well before you met me."

"It depends. If you spill your guts to your wife, then I don't know what we're going to do. Our only advantage right now is surprise. If you tip our hand—"

"I'm not going to do that. If she answers I'll just hang up."

"Like that won't be obvious."

"Okay, what if I act like I'm a telemarketer calling the wrong number? They won't be able to trace the call anyway."

"Maybe you should stick with your first idea. She might figure out it's your voice."

"Anyway, what do you have planned? What are you going to do with this surprise advantage?"

"Expose them to the public. On national television."

"How do you propose to do that?"

"The exact details are still being worked out. It depends on what sort of support we get."

"Support?"

"How many men and supplies we can arrange."

"Supplies for what?"

"We're going to record admissions from NeuroStor and broadcast this on national television."

"I don't understand. How are you going to get anything on *national* television?"

"I told you, I don't know the exact details right now. But we have to do this. We have to get your story, your proof, on TV. It's the only way to mobilize the millions of apathetic people out there who have no idea what's going on."

"Apathetic people? Just because everyone doesn't run around fighting conspiracies, that doesn't mean we're all apathetic."

"I know. I just wish more people would take time to learn about the world around them. There are people—millions of them, all over the world—who would gladly take away your freedom if they had the chance. The last thing we need is that same threat from our own citizens."

"So you're going to somehow get on national TV and tell them what to think?"

"No! But I want to provide the information people need to make a good decision. That's one of the ways a repressive government or organization works, by limiting the outside information available to its constituents. When people find out who NeuroStor is and what they want to do, they'll be furious. That's all I want. For people to know."

I remember Nicole, the gun wavering in her hand as she pointed it at me. She was so frightened, so sure that she had unknowingly brought death into her home. And I left her there. But I honestly didn't think they would . . . I wasn't even sure they would *go* there, let alone *kill* her.

"Who are these people, Crystal? These 'extremists'? Why are they so damn brutal?"

"I told you. They're racial separatists who—"

"I know, I know. American Federation of Aryans. But I want to know who they *are*. What the hell are they trying to do with the transmission machine that makes them kill?"

She brings the car to a stop, and I realize we are in front of Lee's house. The sun is low in the sky now, the street painted dark with shadows.

I open the car door, and immediately something is wrong. Nausea rushes back into my throat as I step onto the curb. My head begins to spin, and I can't figure out which foot to put where.

Crystal says, "Like I mentioned earlier, we're not exactly sure what—"

The ground swirls toward me. Crystal extends her arm to break my fall, but I push her away and sink to my knees.

"Cameron!"

What's left of Nicole's Chinese food urps out of my mouth, along with a slick of sour bile. My stomach clenches again, but this time the heave is dry. Clenches and clenches and clenches some more. I'm turning inside out.

"Cameron, honey," Crystal says, kneeling beside me. "I'm sorry, but let's get inside. We don't want anyone to see—"

"Fuck them!" I say. "Who the hell is going to recognize—"

Again my stomach clenches. Again. And again.

"Oh, God," I moan. Pain like I've never felt before spreads throughout my gut. I wipe the spit off my lips and bring back something red.

"You're bleeding. Let's get you into the house."

My head stops spinning long enough for me to stand. Crystal takes my hand and leads me into the house, where Lee meets us. His mouth opens wide.

"What happened to him?"

"I don't know. He got out of the car and couldn't stand. Started throwing up blood."

They lead me to a sofa. I don't lie down. I'll throw up again if I lie down.

Crystal goes into the kitchen to clean her hands. Already the blood and bile are drying on my own hands and face. I must look stunning.

"I'm sorry for yelling at you," I say. "I was out of my head."

Crystal comes back into the living room and sits down beside me. She's brought a wet paper towel with her. I try to grab it, but instead she wipes my lips and cheeks herself.

None of us speak for a few moments. For the first time I realize what an incredible liability I am to these people. Certainly I have every reason to be angry and frustrated for the way they manipulated me, for the way they used Tom to get to me, but do I have the leverage to yell at Crystal? Can I afford to lash out when she is the only chance I have to get out of this situation intact? I don't think so. I don't know why they're even bothering to help me anymore. They've already gotten what they wanted from me. They already know NeuroStor is trying to cover up a botched transmission.

"She's dead," I finally say.

"Who's dead?" asks Lee, who sits in a chair beside us, watching Crystal's every movement.

"The woman in Scottsdale who helped me."

"No way."

"We just heard it on the news," Crystal adds. "Cameron wants to call his wife with that emulation program you have. He wants to make sure she's all right."

Lee looks at me like I'm the worst thing that has ever happened to him.

"What's been going on here?" Crystal asks him. "Any luck?"

"Not really," he says. "Got through, finally, but they've isolated their other systems from the Web server as best as I can tell. I'll have to try something else."

Crystal nods. "I figured that."

"We need to get into one of their local offices," he says. "I think the computers there have access to more than just the transaction programs."

"What makes you say that?" Crystal asks.

"You remember that friend I told you about in Phoenix, the one who works for the Tempest company? I finally got in touch with him. I fig-ured it would be worth a try to use some of their detection instruments, but he told me that NeuroStor fully shields all of their workstations. Like every office is the damn Pentagon or something."

Crystal frowns at this, but Lee has lost me.

"What is 'Tempest'?"

"Monitors and other computer instruments emit radiation that can be detected and interpreted if you have the right kind of equipment. For instance, someone could stand outside this house and see what is on my computer screen. Sort of like using an antenna to receive television signals. It's not cheap to shield this radiation, though, so it's mostly done by governments and contractors who do sensitive work for them."

"And NeuroStor," I add.

"Like I said, the Phoenix office must have access to sensitive information. If we can just figure out a way to—"

"We're not going to have time for that," Crystal says.

Lee again looks at me as if passing judgment. "Why not?"

"Cameron had contact with someone before he found us on the mountain. He had a seizure in front of a convenience store clerk."

"So?"

"So the clerk saw his car. And if he also saw the news tonight, it's not going to be long before a shitload of cops and whoever else are looking for him. We don't need that kind of heat."

"How am I supposed to get anything out of their computers if you don't give me more time?"

"We'll have to go to Dallas without it."

"And then what?"

"And then we'll figure something out!" Crystal yells at him. Her cheeks have gone red and her eyes are narrow. "Now get in there and run this program for Cameron. After that, we'll call Clay and tell him to proceed with Stage Two. Then we're getting the hell out of here."

Lee vanishes like an apparition. Crystal turns to me and the red is magically gone, her eyes wide and smiling.

"Feeling any better?" she asks.

"A little. What was that all about?"

"Lee is a smart guy, but he needs direction. You have to raise your voice every once in a while to keep him focused."

"What's Stage Two? Something to do with our home office in Plano? That's near Dallas."

"Exactly."

"We're going there?"

"Sure we are. If we're going to incriminate them on camera, they're not going to come here. Come on, let's go back and call your wife."

I follow her back to the computer room. Crystal finds a bare spot beneath a window, and Lee pulls up a rickety office chair.

"Sit down, dude," he says. "Let's call your wife."

I take a seat in front of the computer screen. The interface is basic. Two input fields (ORIGINATION NUMBER and DESTINATION NUMBER) and two buttons (DIAL and CLEAR FIELDS). The origination number has already been populated.

"This program talks to AT&T's long-distance network. It will confuse the router and make it think we're calling from some other phone number. So if someone tries to perform a simple trace, they'll get bogus information. But you can't stay on too long, because sophisticated equipment can get around this misdirection eventually."

"Okay."

"I used the Internet to find the phone number of a carpet cleaning service about ten miles from your house. Hopefully when you hang up, whoever is listening won't get suspicious."

He's thought of everything. Now all I have to do is dial the number. Connected speakers and a mike have turned Lee's modem into a speakerphone.

"Punch the numbers and hit enter to dial?"

"You got it."

And then maybe I can hear Misty's voice.

If she's home.

If she's alive.

I reach forward and slowly press the numbers. My area code is 281. It only changed a few years ago, but it'll probably change again soon. All the modems and faxes and cellular phones have crowded our telephone lines. It's hard to believe that just a few years ago—

"Cameron?" Crystal says. "I don't want to rush you, but we don't have a lot of time here."

I depress the ENTER key.

From the speakers, a click. A dial tone. Rapid touch tones.

One ring.

Two.

Three, then another click. I already know what's coming next. My own voice, the joke I made before I left for the—

"You've reached 5-5-5-1-1-1-9. We can't come to the phone . . ."

But this is not the joke. This is not the same announcement that was on the machine when I left.

I'm about to say something to Crystal about this when the message is interrupted. Someone picks up the phone. Answers.

"Hello?"

My next breath doesn't come. It's a man's voice on the other end of the line. A *man's* voice. Why the hell is a *man* answering *my* telephone?

"Hello?" he asks again.

Only . . . only it sounds like the voice I just heard on—

On the answering machine.

It sounds like *my* voice.

"Hello?" the man asks a third time. "Who is this? Charlie, is that you?"

Charlie is one of my golf buddies. He's a terrible player. I have to spot him thirty strokes just so we can bet money.

Commotion behind me. I look around and find Lee dragging his index finger across his neck. He wants me to end the call.

But I can't. I have no idea what to do.

Lee lunges across my body and hits the ESCAPE key. The speaker crackles. The dial tone hums.

"You shouldn't have stayed on so long!" he yells.

I don't know what to say.

"Are you trying to get your wife killed?"

"But didn't you, I mean didn't you—"

"Hear your voice?" Crystal says, finishing my thought.

"How could they do that? Are there programs for that kind of voice emulation? And why? Why would they bother? Why the hell are they in my house? What have they done with my wife?"

Crystal puts up her hands. "Hold on just a minute. Before you lose it, let's go over what just happened."

"You heard what just happened! Someone or some*thing* is at my house impersonating me!"

"No, it isn't."

"Then who the hell was on the phone?"

"Who do you think it was?"

"Look, don't play any fucking games with me! This might be your crusade, but it's *my* fucking life!"

"Then why don't you pull your head out of the sand and look around? 'Who the hell was on the phone?' you ask. Think about it, Cameron! If it quacks like a duck and it acts like a duck, then maybe, just maybe, it's a fucking duck!"

I sit there staring at her, still beautiful but no longer an angel, her chest heaving, her brow beading with sweat. For the first time I realize that I'm not the only one under pressure here. And maybe I'm not the only one about to crack.

"You know that guy I told you about," Lee says to me, "the one who works with the Tempest equipment?"

"Yeah?"

"This guy's brother worked for NeuroStor for a little while. Client-server maintenance, that sort of thing."

"Yeah?"

"They didn't let this guy near the transmission computers," Lee continues. "But he got drunk one night with one of the other guys, the *real* IT guys, who let slip something about what they call the Central Bank. A mountain bunker in Wyoming he claimed was the largest memory storage facility in the world. And he talked about the latest memory technology you guys had come up with, shit with crystals that can store zettabytes of information in something the size of a three-and-a-half hard drive. Did you ever hear anything about that?"

"We have a distribution center in Denver," I tell him. "That's the closest office I know of."

"Well, this Central Bank, he said it's where they plan to store everyone. Every person who transmits."

"Store us?" I ask. "What the hell does that mean?"

"Quantum teleportation assures the original, scanned information is disrupted, right? Essentially destroyed. You kill your body and then send it somewhere else to be reassembled.

"But really, disrupting the original information is a good thing. Otherwise, what you'd have is a human fax machine. If you put a person in, send a copy of him off to some other place, and then take the original person back out again, you're left with two people instead of one."

Where they store us. Where they store US.

"Quantum mechanics says you can't do the fax machine bit," he continues, "that you can't scan something closely enough to duplicate it. You disturb the information before you can extract everything you need to make the copy."

"So what the hell did they do to me?"

"I don't know. They did something, because you're sitting right here in front of us. But just because you look like you, that doesn't mean you *are* you. Not exactly."

Lee's earlier words, never really gone, now burn themselves into my consciousness. *In what sense are you here?* In what sense am I here, indeed?

The dread, the fear—it comes full on now, beginning in my neck as a physical sensation, almost as if someone has rubbed menthol cream on my skin. Hot and cold at the same time. The hairs there stand up like soldiers. A moment or two passes before my bowels begin to churn. My hands are shaking. My mouth tastes electric, as if I just stuck my tongue on the leads of a nine-volt battery. I think I'm going to faint.

"Cameron!"

I hear the voice, but my ears are roaring now. It sounds like someone calling my name from across a crowded football stadium. A stadium enshrouded by silvery fog.

Hands on my face, slapping me. Once. Twice. I smell her before I see her. Crystal. Her sweet smell.

"Cameron!" she says again.

"What?"

"Don't faint on us!"

"I'm not."

She slaps me again.

"I'm *not*!"

I push myself upwards in the chair. Maybe if I'm sitting up straight she will believe me.

"I know this is hard to hear," she says, kneeling in front of me. "But now is the time to be your strongest."

"No! Don't try to force this bullshit on me!"

"But you heard him on the phone."

"Do you think I'm an idiot? That I'm just going to throw up my hands and believe that a facsimile of me is living in my house?"

"We don't know that *he's* a copy," Lee says.

"Of course you don't. It's bullshit."

"No, I mean *you* would be the copy."

When no response forms on my lips, I just glare at him.

"My best guess is they held your original while observing you, the simulacrum—"

"The what?"

"The facsimile. Whatever. They held him until they decided you weren't a good enough copy. Then they figured out some way to get the original back home, some kind of story both he and his wife would believe. That's why they're after you now. Two Camerons could present a few problems for them, if you know what I mean."

"I am not a copy!"

"Then who was on the phone?" Crystal asks.

"I wish I knew."

We all stare at each other, at full stalemate. What they've said makes sense, and I don't necessarily fault the logic they used to draw this conclusion. But something about it just doesn't feel right. Wouldn't I know if I wasn't really me?

"Let's assume for a moment that what we say is true," Crystal offers. "Why do you think NeuroStor invented the machine? Surely they never planned to really go public with the thing. Not as a public transportation service anyway. If it really preserves the original, after all, I don't think there is any way they could keep that a secret. Not if they rolled out the machine on a national scale."

"You guys have already told me they want to use it as a weapon. As a terror device against the U.S. government."

"Yeah," she agrees, "but how? Size constraints on the transmission portal make sending a large number of troops or significant military supplies unfeasible."

"That's also why they might have trouble marketing the machine as a shipping carrier," Lee adds.

Crystal nods. "But even that doesn't make sense. If they can fit a person in there, they can fit a lot of envelopes or boxes or whatever the hell someone wants delivered the same day."

"But who would spend a thousand dollars to send a package today when they can spend fifteen dollars and get it there the next morning?"

"Someone would."

It seems silly for us to debate such things when we really have no idea what the leaders of NeuroStor are plotting. Who are we to think we can somehow come up with the smoking-gun issue that will blow their covert plan wide open?

Crystal smiles, as if she's read my mind.

"You know what we think the machine really is, Cameron?"

"I can tell by the look on your face that you're about to tell me."

"A cloning device. Only instead of placing both terminals beside each other like you would in a laboratory, you might have them separated by hundreds or thousands of miles. The information transmission poses problems, of course. Maybe they're using advanced compression algorithms, I don't know. Obviously they've figured something out, because here you are."

"But that's where you're wrong," I tell her. Something Lee said before finally makes sense to me now. "It can't be a cloning device because you can't create something out of nothing. That's some kind of physics law. If I'm really a copy, if the original Cameron Fisher is still in Houston, what did they use to construct me? Molecules don't just form from thin air."

"No, but the molecules *in* air could be reconstructed," Lee says. "When you break matter down into its constituent pieces, it's all basically the same stuff. What makes iron and gold and carbon different is, to simplify, just the organization of quarks and leptons. So if you had the ability to manipulate matter at such a level, you wouldn't necessarily need any special material."

"But you said that sort of molecular assembly wasn't possible."

"I know, but—"

"Besides, if you guys are right, then you could scan someone and reproduce them over and over."

"You could build yourself a special forces unit," Lee adds. "All you need is one sympathizer, some Green Beret or Army Ranger or whatever, and you could churn out a whole battalion of him. If you lose some, just make more."

"That's nuts."

Lee shrugs.

"NeuroStor put my original back because they think the transmission didn't work, that's what you're telling me?"

"As soon as you ran from them, the other guy had to go back. They couldn't let you blow their story."

"And if they catch me, I'm dead."

"They can't let you go back."

"But something about this doesn't make sense. There were four other volunteers. Surely some or all of those were transmitted successfully. What does NeuroStor intend to do with the originals if their copies turn out fine?"

"They would have to kill them, don't you think?" she says matter-of-factly. "What else could they do?"

"*Kill* them?" I say to her. "Innocent volunteers?"

"They probably have themselves convinced it isn't murder," Lee suggests. "Since the copy is still alive on the other side."

Crystal stands quickly, as if remembering something. "This is how we'll bring them down, Cameron. The whole terrorism concept would be pretty hard to prove, but not what they're doing now. If we can make people understand that they are killing volunteers after the transmission— their very own employees—we can bring them down. But like I said, they aren't going to come to us. This is why we're going to Dallas. To—"

The computer beeps, and a window pops up with some sort of warning sign. Lee leaps in front of me before I even begin to read it.

"Someone's coming," he says.

"Where?" Crystal asks. She runs out of the room without waiting for an answer.

"The front!" He reaches beneath his desk, into a maroon metal box, and pulls out a pistol of some kind.

"What's going on?" I ask.

"I've got infrared motion detectors installed around the perimeter of the house. Two of them just tripped."

"You don't think it might be someone you know?"

"I'm not expecting anyone," he says. "We'll know soon. Stay here and watch this screen."

A new window on the screen displays what is obviously an outline drawing of a house floor plan.

"If any of the sensors in the backyard trip, tell us so we don't get surprised from behind."

"Okay."

He steps out of the room, and I sit there, staring at the screen. A bird sings a repetitive song from a nearby tree, and a frustrated dog farther away barks wildly.

Something solid shakes the house. Wood splinters and glass shatters. I whip around, watching the door, and then four sharp reports—muffled, but each succeedingly louder—split the air. Heavy whispering. Unintelligible. I'd feel better if I could get behind the desk or try to escape out a bathroom window, but my assignment is to watch the screen. In the corner I notice the baseball bat again, standing there innocently, waiting for a neighborhood game that is never going to come.

"Get your hands up!" I hear Crystal yell. "Drop the gun and show me your hands!"

"Fuck you," a man's voice says. "Wait until—"

His voice is cut off by a single gunshot, this one decidedly louder than the previous silenced rounds.

"You fucking bitch!" the man yells. I know this voice. It's the man who left me to suffocate in the muddy riverbank. Ivan.

Another loud gunshot. Then more struggling. Crystal screams—in anger or pain, I'm not sure—and her distress galvanizes me. I rush forward, grab the baseball bat, and run for the living room.

Another muffled gunshot.

"Lee!" Crystal yells.

As I turn the corner with the bat raised, I find Crystal on the ground struggling with Ivan. She's on top of him, pressing his face against the floor with one hand and trying to reach for his gun with the other. The carpet beneath them is red and soaking and makes squishing sounds as they thrash against it.

Ivan is obviously shot; Crystal could not have wrestled him into this position if he wasn't injured. I stand there for a moment assessing the situation, and that's when Ivan uses a burst of energy to wrench his hand from beneath his body and smack Crystal in the face.

Reason abandons me.

I step forward and swing hard for Ivan's head, but the bat misses, slamming instead into the blood-soaked carpet, spraying droplets everywhere, against his face and my pants and into Crystal's hair. I pull back the bat and swing forward again, this time connecting solidly with Ivan's skull. The impact of aluminum slamming into bone sends electric vibrations into my arm, and the sound is sickening, but Ivan ceases to fight at once. Ceases to fight and in fact begins to bleed from a hairy, matted wound near the crown of his head. I stand there looking at him, picturing the way he struck Crystal, remembering how he left me for dead near the flash flood, remembering that Tom is dead. I swing quickly again with the bat. Hit him again in the head. This motherfucker deserves no sympathy, at least not from me.

"Cameron," Crystal says as she rolls away from Ivan. "That's enough."

"Motherfucker," I say aloud.

"Cameron!" she says again. "Lee is shot. And we need to get the hell out of here in case the cops come."

Her voice is lucid, the words make sense, but still I cannot move from where I stand. I cannot believe this man, this goon who chased me and tormented me and left me for dead is now lying across the floor in a heap, bleeding and perhaps dying from a head wound inflicted by me. It seems almost too easy. After all, he was shot already. All I did was prematurely end his struggle with Crystal.

"Cameron! Don't just stand there. Get some towels from the kitchen so we can wrap Lee's arm. I think it's just a flesh wound."

"Right," I answer and then head for the kitchen. That's when I realize there is another body in the room, one that lies across the entrance to the kitchen. It's Ivan's partner—Ed, if I remember correctly—and I'll have to step over him to get the towels Crystal requested.

The only dead people I've ever seen before have been lying peacefully in caskets, painted with makeup to bring life back into their faces. This man's blood is soaking into the carpet on his left and pooling on the vinyl floor on his right. I know he must be dead, but as I step over him, I expect his hand to shoot out and grab my ankle.

"Cameron, hurry!"

My hands root through drawers until one of them reveals a stash of formerly white hand towels stained brown by years of kitchen use. I grab a handful and bring them to Crystal, who sits on the floor with Lee's torso in her lap. His long-sleeve shirt is ripped and matted red with blood. She folds one of the towels lengthwise until it's about four inches wide and then wraps it tightly around his arm. His muscles twitch beneath the bandage. The smell of blood is heavy and metallic.

"Can you hold this towel while I tie another one around it?"

I do as Crystal asks me, and soon she has fashioned a workable bandage for Lee's wounded arm.

"Crystal, that hurts," Lee slurs. He appears to be in shock.

"It's okay, honey," she says to him. And then to me, "We need to get him in the car. Probably in the back where he can lie down."

"Are we taking him to a hospital?"

"The wound isn't bad enough to warrant that kind of risk. We have to get the hell out of here before the cops come. And there may be more NeuroStor men where these two came from."

"Don't need a hospital," Lee adds. "Need computer, though."

"You know," I tell Crystal, "I haven't seen anyone else follow me besides these two guys. It might take them a while to send someone else."

"Cameron, these two may not even be the ones who followed you around the golf course. Here, help me carry him out to the car. You get under his shoulders, and I'll get his legs."

Together we carefully move Lee out the front door and toward the car. The neighborhood is miraculously quiet, as if no one heard the two unsilenced gunshots. Crystal is forced to lay his feet on the concrete driveway to open the back door, and then I pull him onto the seat. When Lee is comfortably positioned—ranting again about his laptop computer—we close the car doors and hurry back into the house.

"What do you mean these may not be the guys? Believe me when I say I recognize them. Especially that guy you were fighting with."

"Of course they're the same *people*. They just may not be the same *version* of those people. These two are probably really well trained, so it makes sense that NeuroStor would clone as many of them as possible to get consistent performance out of their covert security ops."

This is something that didn't occur to me. Possibly because I'm still not sure I believe what they've told me about the transmission machine, even though there seems to be no other explanation for the voice that answered my telephone.

"Are you serious?"

Crystal nods and hands me her keys. "I'm going to get Lee's laptop bag from his room. You go start the car."

I head outside and get into the Buick's driver's seat. The engine catches on the first try. Crystal appears a few moments later with a black laptop case and another, smaller duffel bag. She places the items in the passenger side floorboard and then walks around to my door.

"Ready?" I ask her.

"I think I'll drive, if you don't mind."

"Does it matter?"

"It will if you have another seizure while you're behind the wheel."

This silences me.

"I'm sorry, Cameron. But you have to consider the possibility that—"

"Don't be sorry," I tell her and get out of the car. "You're right."

A few moments later I've taken my place as the passenger, Crystal is behind the wheel, and Lee is mumbling in the backseat. She engages the transmission and pulls out into the street.

"We going to Plano?" Lee asks from the backseat.

"That's where we're going, Lee. Lone Star State or bust."

seven

∎∎∎

We pass the first few minutes without breaking the tense silence. All the way, in fact, to Winona, where we enter the rough, beaten lanes of I-40. Tractor-trailers stretch to the horizon—great, rectangular beasts bound for Albuquerque or Oklahoma or points farther east, heading in the direction from which I came. Pulled forward by an internal combustion engine. How quaint. And how safe.

We collectively relax as the sun falls into the mountains behind us. Questions fill my mind now, questions about the transmission procedure, about the safety of my wife, about how Ivan could find me again so quickly. I don't know if Crystal has the answer to any of these questions. When you think about it, I really have no idea at all what she knows.

"So you honestly think there could be more of those men who came to Lee's house? More Ivans and more Eds?"

"It fits perfectly with our Green Beret theory: seek out loyal subjects and build yourself an army."

Can it really be true? Is the transmission machine really a *cloning* device? The idea is impossibly difficult to swallow, and yet how else can you explain my voice on the other end of the telephone?

I reach forward and turn on the air conditioner. For some reason the car interior is already too stuffy.

I don't know where to go from here, what to think or what to say. The idea of simply refusing to believe it appeals strongly to me. If I don't believe, perhaps the scorching fear will go away. Perhaps there is still a chance that all this is a mistake, that if I can just get back home everything will be okay.

"Do you feel betrayed?" Lee asks in a voice that sounds somewhat off-kilter.

"Betrayed?"

"That your company used you to test their machine? That your original is back at home, millions of dollars richer and no worse for wear, while you're left on the run with no place to go?"

"Lee!" Crystal says. "Why don't you lie down and get some rest?"

"You're just a casualty, Cameron. A casualty of the war being waged between true Aryan Americans and the multiculturalists. Between white storm troopers and politically correct robots. That's what the crazy investors behind NeuroStor would say if they were here."

"Well, I don't understand that sort of bullshit rhetoric. Really, I'm not sure I even believe these neo-Nazi types are helping fund the machine. Why would they hire Batista? He's not white! And how does the transmission machine really benefit them? How would they even arrange the expertise to develop it?"

"You'd be surprised how easy it is to line up funding when the potential payoff is so high," Crystal says. "More than anything else in the world—except sex, I guess—people want to make money. The poor want to be rich. The rich want to be richer. The difference is that rich people have enough power to get it done. To do just about anything they want."

"But what you're talking about is a multimillion—no, multi*billion*—dollar conspiracy. I just can't believe anyone could secretly organize something so complicated."

"Our lives are controlled by giant corporations," Lee nearly yells. "Manufacturers sell you goods and media conglomerates sell you lies. Arrogant monsters control your life and you don't even know it. You're told what to like, what to wear, who to idolize, what to think. You're helpless to stop it, because the endless procession of pretty people on television and in the movies is too impressive for the average, plodding American to ignore. We celebrate the best actors instead of the best fathers! We celebrate the best quarterbacks instead of the best engineers! Celebrities are the secret weapon of the media conglomerates, Cameron. They use these friendly faces to lead the herd."

This is where I should voice opposition, the place where I point out the weaknesses in his theory. Only this particular theory sounds dangerously similar to my own desperate life. Isn't it me, after all, who can't enjoy golf anymore because I don't play like Tiger Woods?

"Why do you think so few people in this country help choose their leaders?" Lee rants. "Because at some point the American public realized their votes no longer mattered. If they *ever* mattered. Politicians speak in evasive half-truths designed to be both media-friendly and ambiguous enough to be altered at any moment. Congressmen who veer to the left or right stand no chance of achieving significance without eventually shifting their platforms to the middle. The goal today is to be politically correct. Alienate no one. And hope the media picks you to become the next president of the United States."

It's ridiculous to have a debate like this right now. I'm tired and nauseous and not at all in the mood. But Lee doesn't seem to realize this.

"By the way," he says, "you never answered my question."

"Which one?"

"Do you feel betrayed? That you had no idea you were a clone?"

"You're an asshole."

I sit quietly for a while after that. It must feel good to be Lee and Crystal right now. All unique and everything. They don't have to worry about the "other," the one living in my house, sleeping in my bed, making love to my wife. That must be really neat for them.

"Highway patrolman," Crystal says.

Her hands squeeze the steering wheel, and the muscles in my neck tighten under an epidermis of gooseflesh. I look out the window, my eyes searching across the median for the patrol car. At seventy-five miles an hour, and with the cop driving toward us at a similar speed, we ought to pass each other quickly. The equivalent of approaching a still object at 150 miles an hour.

"I don't see him," I say.

"He's coming up behind us," Lee answers. "He'll pass us in thirty seconds."

I turn around to look for the patrol car. Although tractor-trailers rumble toward Flagstaff in steady numbers, the eastbound traffic is thinning. We're the only car in the vicinity. Nothing else to distract the officer's attention. When he changes lanes to pass us, our car will be mere feet from his. Maybe he'll have a police sketch on the seat next to him. Perhaps he'll recognize me.

"Look away, Cameron," Crystal says. "Don't move suddenly or try to duck. Just look away."

My initial, knee-jerk thought to that is, What difference does it make? What difference does any of this make? Why bother to go on when I have no home and no wife waiting for me?

And why are Crystal and Lee even bothering to take me to Dallas, anyway? All I am is a liability to them now. They'll be implicated as accessories to murder if the police catch them with me. Who knows if I'll have another seizure or bout with nausea? I don't understand why they think they have to drag me across hundreds of miles of desert.

After a few seconds, the nose of the patrol car overtakes the trunk of ours, and then he is driving by. It seems to take forever. As his front windows come even with ours, I imagine his eyes boring into the back of my skull. He can tell somehow. He recognizes me from the side—it's the shape of my head, no doubt—and now he's on the two-way, calling for backup. Before you know it, I'll be handcuffed in the backseat of his car, on my way to Flagstaff again.

He goes by and by and by. Forever he goes by. But then, after forever, the patrolman moves back into the right lane, and drives away toward the darkening horizon.

Silence again.

I keep thinking about that other Cameron Fisher, the one who is really me. He doesn't know about any of this. How will he and Misty reconcile their different perspectives on what happened?

"What do you think they told my wife?" I ask Crystal. "When that other Cameron showed up? Wouldn't she have asked questions, wondered why I couldn't remember anything about Arizona?"

"I'm sure they had something figured out," she says. "About how the scan must have altered his memory somehow. You signed a waiver, of course, so it's not like she has any legal recourse. And beyond not remembering the transmission, everything about you would be fine anyway. Maybe she's just happy you're back safely."

I try to remember my visit to NeuroStor that day, to guess what the other Cameron must remember. I stepped into the portal, took off my clothes, and then waited. My next memory is waking up in Arizona. I don't remember the scanning process, and I certainly don't know what happened to the other "me" after the transmission. What would they have done with him while they waited to evaluate me?

I guess if I really wanted to know, I would have to ask him. But when I try to picture myself talking to, well, myself, I realize just how unbelievable this whole story really is.

Darkness overtakes the last rays of orange daylight, and the car grows quiet again. For a while I sit with my eyes closed, hoping to will myself to sleep, but of course that doesn't work. Strobelike images flicker behind my closed eyes. Running from Ivan through a thundering rainstorm. Batista's greasy smile when I agreed to volunteer. Misty's confused tears as I climbed into the transmission portal and out of her life.

That's what I am now, isn't it? With the other Cameron there, the original one, what am I? Where do I fit in?

Nowhere.

I've been so worried about the state of our relationship, about whether we are better off staying together or trying to find happiness with someone else, and now it appears my feelings are irrelevant. I'm not her husband anyway. Not anymore.

I can't even picture that man in my house. With my wife. Do they still argue about transmitting? Does Cameron feel vindicated in his decision to go through with it? Is his life changed for transmitting?

"Where are we?" I ask.

"We just went through Gallup," Crystal says. "I guess we're two hours from Albuquerque."

"Oh."

"What were you thinking about, Cameron?"

"Nothing, really."

"Were you thinking about your wife?"

For some reason I don't want her to know that I was.

"You can't try to see her until we do something about NeuroStor, you know. They'll be waiting at your house in Houston."

"So what *are* we going to do about NeuroStor?" I ask. "How do you plan to confront them or get the story on television?"

"Well, we could go to the media with what we have now, but I think the story would be much more explosive if we got someone from NeuroStor on videotape. This Batista, for instance. We need to confront him with our proof and see what happens."

"What proof?"

"Well, *you*, of course. You and the original Cameron."

Ah. This is why they need me, why these relative strangers are so willing to put up with my naïveté and frustration and bouts of nausea. Because I'm their best piece of evidence.

"How are we going to get Batista on tape?"

"We'll have to get inside their Dallas office."

"And what happens if they capture us in the process?" I ask her. "They would kill us. Then we'd never get to tell what we know."

"I won't argue that. It's a game show now, Cameron. We can take our sixty-four thousand dollars or try for the million. What do you say?"

"I don't know. We've got a long time to talk about it, I guess."

"About twelve hours to Dallas. How are you feeling?"

"Pretty good right now."

"From what you've told me, it seems like all of your episodes have come during times of high anxiety or stress. If that's the case, maybe you'll be okay when all this is over."

"Sure I will. I've lost my wife and my job. About the only thing left of any interest to me is golf, and I don't know if I can even do that anymore."

"Why can't you play golf?"

"That's the first thing I noticed after the transmission. Tom and I played the next morning and something was wrong with my coordination. I couldn't hit the ball."

"Maybe you could relearn. Practice a lot and be able to play again."

"I don't think practicing is going to change the problem with my balance or my hand-eye coordination. The transmission effects are intermittent. One moment my dexterity is there and the next my hands and arms and legs don't do what I tell them. I'm certainly not going to keep playing golf if I can't compete."

"Are you a pro or something?"

"No. But . . . I don't know. It's complicated."

"Complicated how?"

"I'm almost good enough to play on tour. Not the PGA, but maybe one of the semipro tours. Except that really I can't play on any of them because being almost good enough and actually good enough are light-years apart in golf. It doesn't matter that I can beat almost anyone I play. What matters is that I can't beat tour players."

"Have you ever played against professional golfers?"

"Not directly, but Tom and I once tried out for a tournament in Austin together. I shot eighty-one and he shot eighty in the qualifier. Ben Crenshaw won the tournament with an average score of sixty-eight."

"That's the only time you tried?"

"Tom went to qualifying school four times, and four times he tanked. He was thinking about trying out for the U.S. Open before this all happened, but I haven't bothered."

"Why?"

"Because golf is not just striking the ball well; it's striking the ball well when people are watching and big money is on the line. Apparently my nerves aren't that strong."

"That's all golf is about? Playing well when big money is on the line? Don't you make pretty good money yourself?"

"Maybe, but I'm not happy doing it. I could walk away from accounting today without a second thought. But golf, it pisses me off that I can't compete with the best. No matter how good you are, there is always someone better."

"But how many people can really be the best, Cameron?"

"I don't know," I admit. "There are a lot of things to be the best at."

"But what you really want is to be the best golfer, right?"

"Of course."

"And who is the best golfer?"

"Tiger Woods."

"See what I mean?" Lee says from the backseat, apparently not asleep after all. "The gods you worship? Celebrities, all of them. Created and used by the media to lead you around like a donkey."

"That's bullshit," I growl. "You can't arbitrarily make someone the best at something."

"But you can turn anyone into a celebrity," Lee counters. "Look at Anna Kournikova. A decent tennis player, someone who shouldn't get all that much press, except that some sports management company got the idea to turn her into a sex symbol, and now that part of her image is much more important than what got her noticed in the first place—a pretty good backhand."

"What the hell are you talking about? I'm sitting here fighting for my goddamn life, wondering if the lingering effects of my transmission are going to permanently damage my body somehow, and you're back there trying to convince me that *celebrities* are what's wrong with our country? Why the hell are we even talking about this at all? I just want to get to Dallas and do whatever it is we need to do to make Batista or whoever the hell runs NeuroStor fucking *fix* me so I don't lose my goddamned *mind,* so I can have my fucking *life* back and play fucking *golf* again without having to chase the ball all over the goddamned *course,* so I can make someone pay for killing my best *friend,* and you're sitting back there with a bug up your ass trying to piss me off because I like to watch golf on television, because I think Tiger Woods has built a game every-one should aspire to? Who the hell do you think—"

But the rest doesn't come out because suddenly I'm ill. In my head, up there where the works are usually rock-solid, I notice a change, a loos-ening in my sense of balance and orientation. The car begins to spin slowly around me. Nausea stirs my stomach, and the car seems fifteen degrees warmer than it did a moment ago.

"Cameron," Crystal asks. "Are you all right?"

I sit up straight and swallow a few times. Wipe my forehead, bring back a slick of sweat. Someone has pumped poison gas into my stomach, and now it's spreading upwards, into my throat. I need to burp. Release this awful poison.

"Cameron?"

I don't want to open my mouth to answer. Lee sits behind me in silence. My stomach is rolling now. Hot down there. My heart beats double-time as I struggle against the urge to throw up. When you get sick in a car full of people, everything and everyone is forced to stop just for you. This has only happened to me once, when I was eighteen and drank way too much beer at an Astros game. It was miserable. Imagine sitting in the backseat of a '78 Nova between two drunk buddies who keep punching each other every time they see a Volkswagen Beetle. No air-conditioning. Dry, musty seats. Sitting there, still as a mouse, hoping the nausea will go away. But of course it didn't. I waited so long that when I finally opened my mouth to yell "Pull over!" vomit sprayed all over the front seat. What a fucking riot everyone thought it was. Everyone except the guy who owned the car, who brought us to a screeching halt in the freeway breakdown lane.

I'm about to ask Crystal to make an emergency stop when a short burp bleeds off my belly like a pressure valve. My heart slows down. I can breathe again.

"Cameron?" Crystal asks me again. "What's wrong?"

"I think I'm okay. I think it's going to pass."

But what I'm more afraid of is that it's only going to get worse. This is the second time I've experienced nausea since the transmission, the last time being in front of Lee's house where I threw up blood. And usually I'm the kind of guy who loves roller coasters, any ride that rotates, anything that is supposed to make the stomach turn somersaults.

"You think *what's* going to pass?"

Now here comes the nausea again, clawing its way into my throat much more quickly than before. This is what I hate the worst, this expansion, this feeling of fullness, as if someone in my stomach is pushing a Ping-Pong ball up my throat. My heart races again, sweat rolls into my eyes, and if we don't stop soon, if I don't get out right now—

"Pull over, Crystal," I say. "Stop the car."

The pause before her foot hits the brake sucks away precious seconds. "What's the matter, Cameron?"

"Just pull . . . og . . . I'm gonna be siii—"

I lean into the floorboard. My stomach clenches like a giant fist. A glut of brown liquid urps out of my mouth. Crystal has already jerked the car into the breakdown lane. I'm thrown forward as the car slows down, and I vomit again.

"Okay, honey, we're stopped now. Do you need me to—"

Grope for the door handle. Into the cool night air. Much better. I heave again, dry this time, then stumble around as my head spins wildly. The car idles beside me, puffing exhaust in quick bursts. Interstate traffic hums in the distance. I move toward the car and reach for its solidity. Everything spinning. Turn sideways and rest my cheek on the cool steel. A door opens. Hands upon me.

Crystal.

"It's okay, Cameron. It's okay. Do you feel better now?"

"My stomach feels better. But my head, the spinning, oh God . . ."

"Do you think you can ride in the car?"

"Not right now. I'll throw up again if I do. I can't even stand without leaning against the car."

"So you're dizzy? Disoriented?"

"I can barely stand here and talk to you. Nothing is still."

"You've got some kind of inner-ear problem. Are you prone to motion sickness?"

Fear tightens my scrotum, rushes up my spine like ice. "No. I've never been motion sick. Not once."

"If we give you a few minutes, do you think you could ride then?"

"I don't know. I'll have to wait and see."

"Okay. Just stand there and relax. Let your balance come back."

Her hands leave me, and I turn my head to cool the other cheek. She leans into the car and says something to Lee. I hear him curse something back. A tractor-trailer roars by on the interstate and shakes the car.

Thank God they need me. If I wasn't their precious smoking gun, Lee would probably be willing to leave me right here on the highway. I better hope they don't have second thoughts.

Crystal is still leaning into the car. Arguing, from the sound. I see her narrow waist and curvy hips, her beautiful bottom, and I'm almost too sick to care. Almost.

She walks around to the back of the car and then reappears on the shoulder with me. "I'm not sure what to do, Cameron. We can't just sit here on the side of the road. You might be sick all night."

"I don't want to hold anyone back, but I may throw up again if I get back in that car."

"I found a couple of plastic bags in the trunk. You could use those if you're willing to go."

"Okay."

It's hard to pry my face from the car, the only solid entity in my swirling existence. Crystal pulls out the soiled floor mat and tosses it into the weeds beside the road.

"Are you ready?" she asks.

"I guess."

I slide back into the seat, immediately aware of the car's new fragrance: Bile of Cameron. I'm sure they're both happy about that.

"Feeling better?" Lee asks me.

"No."

"Do you think you'll throw up again?"

"Probably be dry heaves if I do. I'm surprised there's anything left in my stomach considering I threw up a couple of hours ago."

"Any blood this time?" Crystal asks.

"None that I noticed, thank God."

"We'll stop and buy you some Dramamine in Albuquerque," she says. "But that's over an hour from now."

"I don't know if Dramamine will solve this particular problem."

"Then maybe you should try to get some sleep."

And so we're going again. Once Crystal reaches cruising speed, I close my eyes, but immediately sense myself going into an uncontrollable spin. My stomach grumbles. I open my eyes. They seem to be looking in all directions at once, even when I hold them steady.

Though our headlights only push the darkness back a short way, I find it comforting to stare straight ahead, as if watching the horizon. My fingers find the two closest air vents, and I point the gusts of cold air directly into my face.

Fifteen minutes later, though, I'm sweating like a football player in summer practice. The poison is back in my stomach. I grab a plastic sack and spill more bile into it.

"I'm sorry, Cameron," Crystal says. "I know you're suffering. I didn't expect this."

I close off the sack and relax against the seat. An hour or so to Albuquerque, and then another ten to Dallas?

Jesus, I'm never going to make it. Right now it feels like my stomach is trying to cannibalize itself. And when we get there, what then? Sure, maybe I'm proof that will help Crystal expose NeuroStor's sadistic volunteer program, that will provide the catalyst she needs to wreak havoc on the titans of industry she thinks rule the world. But what about me? Where do I stand? With my seizures and my uncontrollable nausea and my eighteen hours of sleep, what sort of future can I possibly hope . . . what can I . . .

Something is different. Something about the car. I've been asleep. I know this because my mouth tastes like shit and the skin on my face is smeared with oil. Because dried tears have formed a crust in the corners of my eyes. I can't open them to see—I'm so incredibly tired, but . . .

The road is smoother. That's the difference.

I bet we're in Texas. As a citizen here, you don't realize it until you leave, but our roads are among the best in the nation. I read somewhere that Lyndon Johnson had something to do with it.

Home.

Where my wife lives. Where that man—that other me—is sitting with her, or perhaps cuddling with her, smelling her chestnut hair.

At the very least, however bad I feel and whatever terrible things may happen later, at least Misty believes I'm okay. At least she feels comfortable and safe. For now.

But could that change? If we attempt some kind of hidden camera campaign against NeuroStor and don't accomplish what we want, is it possible that Batista would retaliate somehow? Would he go after Misty, use her as leverage against me or even kill her in anger?

Is that something I really want to do? Take the chance of hurting Misty to further my own agenda? It's easy to be angry, to go after

NeuroStor to get my life back, but should I do so if it means placing my wife in danger?

Just thinking about this is making me sleepy again. My eyes flutter, almost opening, but I give up.

I mean, shit. Why bother?

eight

≡≡≡

Distantly, I hear music. Rock music. Can't recognize the group, but the sound of guitars is familiar. Beneath the tires I can tell the road has turned rough again, only this time because of spaced, uniform bumps beneath the tires. My eyelids struggle open, and I see amber light. Streetlights.

Are we there?

Trees off the road, then a hotel, then a wide ravine under a bridge. We might be passing over a river, and now I see a waterfall of some kind. But I'm confused, because it seems out of place, as if it's not part of this river at all.

The music ends. A disc jockey prattles about a weekend showdown between Rider and Old High. Those names sound familiar but I can't place them. Sleep seems to fade in and out. Someone on the radio exclaims: "Olney, Windthorst, Wichita Falls! . . . ninety-two-point-nine . . . KNIN."

Now the connections are made. The artificial waterfall, the local high schools. This is where I grew up, where Misty took me to be buried in the recurring nightmare that precluded my trip to Arizona.

I'm falling again, away from the Wichita Falls radio station and into an orbit of sleep, but before I go, something occurs to me, something I had forgotten but that must be related to the memory of the recurring dream. It's Misty's proposal that my soul could be lost during the transmission. I dismissed her, of course—I no more believe in God than I do the Force—but for some reason now I feel like entertaining the idea. Could that be why there was no eulogy in my funeral dream? Because the body being buried was nothing more than an empty shell? A shell that is beginning to show cracks, buckling under the increasing pressure of an inaccurate transmission?

The car is much brighter. I've woken up again. We're crossing another bridge of some kind.

"That was a long nap," Crystal says.

"Where are we?"

"Between Dallas and Fort Worth. Look over there."

I look out the window and see, of all things, Texas Stadium. Which means we're in Irving, only a few miles from Plano now.

"How do you feel?" she asks me.

"Not too well. My head is still spinning. My stomach feels terrible."

"Can you make it another thirty minutes?"

"I think so."

But I don't. We're going over an elevated freeway interchange when the nausea comes again. I throw up into the same bag as last time. Brown spittle. Nothing more. By now the muscles in my stomach are beginning to cramp, and my throat is raw.

Fear still rumbles within me like a constant, nearly inaudible bass line, but now another track is being laid into the mix—anger. Because I shouldn't be here, sweating, shuddering, throwing up in this car. Certainly I agreed to transmit—I accepted the risk—but I did so with incomplete information. I'm here because I was lied to. By that brash, young little fuck whose ideas, whose profits were more important than the lives of my wife and myself. Batista. Motherfucking Batista.

Neither Crystal nor Lee say anything to comfort me. I just sit there and broil in my own contaminated juices as we drive into Plano on U.S. 75, a freeway nothing less than ten lanes wide. Our set of northbound lanes, which head away from downtown Dallas, moves quickly, but the southbound side crawls at a snail's pace. Newly built restaurants and car dealerships border the road. Fast-food signs tower above us—

McDonald's, Burger King, Denny's—and normally I would be salivating at the thought of scrambled eggs, sausage, and hash browns. Not today. The way I feel right now, maybe never again.

We exit the freeway and turn onto a surface street. The Hampton Inn appears after only a minute or two, and Crystal jumps out as soon as we reach the carport, leaving Lee and me behind. We wait for her in silence.

Crystal returns to the car a few moments later and guides us to a parking spot. Into the room we go, where the air is crisp and cool, where two beds stand sterile and flat.

"We've rented the two adjacent rooms as well," Crystal says. "Others will join us soon, and this is where we'll stay tonight."

"Who are these other people? What are they going to do, exactly?"

"I don't suppose you're hungry," she says. "But would you like something to drink? A soda to soothe your stomach, maybe?"

"What kind of answer is that?"

Crystal takes me by the arm and leads me toward the door.

"A Coke would do wonders for your nausea," she says. The morning air is warm and muggy. The door slams shut behind us.

"Would you please—"

A cramp of pain interrupts me, a hot flare in my stomach, and I double over. When Crystal puts her arm on my back, I shrink away.

"Cameron."

I don't want her to touch me. Not this way. Not with pity.

"Cam—"

"Leave me alone," I say and stand up straight again. "I'm okay."

"You're not well."

"But there's nothing you can do about that, is there?"

Crystal offers no consolation, for which I am supremely grateful. The last thing I want right now is for her to lie to me.

"I guess I'll take that Coke now," I tell her.

We get into the car, and Crystal drives us away from the motel. Several fast-food restaurants stand within sight, in the direction of the freeway, but she heads in the other direction.

"These 'other people,' " she says, "are acquaintances who are going to help us get into the NeuroStor complex in Plano."

"When?"

She makes a right turn and now we're on a narrower street. We've driven by no less than a dozen places that serve soft drinks. Where exactly are we going instead?

"The day after tomorrow," Crystal says.

"What? How?"

"We'll try to sneak inside, but at some point, force will be necessary. We have guns and explosives. We have a mobile satellite uplink facility, which we'll use to interrupt network television if Lee can hack into one of their satellites. He's been trying NBC for a while, but I don't know if it's going to work."

"What the hell are you talking about? You have all this set up?"

"Cameron, we've been ready for a long time. When you came along, we just mobilized what had been acquired and planned well before."

"You're telling me Lee can hijack a network television satellite and interrupt programming?"

"I told you I'm not sure it will work."

"But if it does, what about afterwards? You'll be hauled into jail for unlawful entry, airtime theft, firearms violations, and who knows what else. And Batista will just claim his admissions were made under duress. Your crimes will be only a public relations hassle to him."

"Not if we broadcast with definitive proof," she says with a devious smile.

We round one more corner and end up on a street populated by medium-size warehouses of the corrugated steel variety. Rick's Home Security Specialists, B. Tate Heating & Air, AAA Body Shop. We turn into one labeled D&D Mechanical. The main warehouse is painted a boring tan color, and a smaller, brick office stands before it. A red Dodge truck is parked in the parking lot out front.

"By proof, you mean me. Or should I say 'us'?"

"Imagine it, Cameron. The two of you on national television confronting the people who created this abomination. How could they explain it?"

"But why risk so much? When we break into their building, they'll try to kill us. Isn't it more practical to tell our story on *20/20* or *Dateline*?"

"First of all, *you're* not going in. That would be ridiculous, because you're right, some of us are likely to get hurt or even killed. Second, we can't do it the way you mentioned—go on the news by ourselves—because an interview like that would do little to damage their credibility. I don't think we can really get people's attention until we get NeuroStor on camera. Don't you want them to answer for what they've done to you?"

"Sure I do."

"Then this is it. Let's go inside. I want you to meet someone."

She pulls a magnetic key card from her purse and uses it to unlock the door. We walk into a typical blue-collar office. Cheap desk, cheap telephone, cheap coffeemaker standing on a cheap table. Open doors stand on the right and left sides of this room, and another one on the back wall leads to the warehouse.

Footsteps creak across the floor in one of the adjoining rooms. A figure steps around the corner and looks at us.

I've never seen this man before. He's shorter than me, sports a receding crop of dark hair, and looks as if he could bench-press five hundred pounds. The sleeves of his black polo shirt are stretched tight around arms that might have been chiseled from pure granite. He walks toward us with no expression at all.

"Crystal," the man says. His Texas accent is heavier and slower than my own.

"Hi, Clay."

"You brought the copy. Good work."

She smiles.

Now Clay looks at me, surveying my body as if it was a particularly choice cut of meat. I don't know what to think or say, so I just stand there.

"How do you feel?" he asks.

"Fine. How do *you* feel?"

"Any symptoms of transmission sickness?"

"Still a little nauseated."

"Dizzy?"

"Not too much."

"Disoriented?"

"I was earlier, but right now—"

"It'll come back," he says. "Even stronger. We've got a doctor who can take a look at you later today, but I'm afraid there's little to be done. He's got painkillers if you need them."

I'm about to ask him what he knows about transmission sickness—that's a term I haven't heard before, not even from Crystal—when movement on the left catches my eye. Another figure walks out of the side office.

My God.

This is someone I *have* seen before. About a million times. And always in the mirror.

nine

▌▌▌

Initial thoughts are incoherent. An overwhelming feeling of artifice, of falseness, comes over me, as if my eyes can't be trusted. As if what I'm seeing is a well-designed movie special effect, or maybe extremely high resolution camcorder footage broadcast onto the wall. It must be an optical illusion of some kind. It *must* be.

These thoughts are evaluated and rejected by my mind in fractions of a second. I know what I'm seeing. I know who this person is. I know him like no one in the world, but I don't know what to say to him. Or how to address him. By his name? By *my* name?

His thoughts must be similar to my own. He doesn't seem surprised, but I know he is a person who can easily mask emotions.

"Hello," I say. I want to offer my hand, but he has not ventured much farther than the office doorway. Several feet still separate us.

"Hello," he returns.

Neither of us knows what to say next.

"You two are gonna have to work close together," Clay says. "I suggest you get on speaking terms. In the meantime, let's go out into the warehouse and look at what we've got so far."

Clay starts toward the rear door, and Crystal immediately follows him. Cameron and I both stay put.

"Have they told you what happened to me?"

"Pretty much," he says. "You must have had a terrible time. It certainly shows."

"How do you mean?"

"You're very pale. Your eyes are red. You look tired."

"I was sick in the car. We came a long way."

Where do we go from here? What do we say? The only thing that comes to mind is to catch up, to brief each other on everything that has happened since the transmission, since we separated.

"How is Misty? Is she okay?"

"Misty's fine. And for the moment has no idea what's going on."

This is a relief.

"And you know about Tom?"

"I'm still kind of in shock. I can't picture him dead. This is all so unreal."

"So what do you know about everything?" I ask him. "What do you know about me?"

"I know Tom picked you up from the transmission station in Phoenix. You guys went to a strip club that night, where you met Crystal, and then you played golf the next morning. That's where NeuroStor first tried to apprehend you."

"What else?"

"I don't know a whole lot more except these guys want to use us to help bring down NeuroStor. What have they told you?"

"Nothing more than that. And they really haven't told me anything about you at all. I don't understand how NeuroStor returned you. I talked to Misty while I was in Arizona. What the hell could they have told you guys to reconcile that?"

"You'd be surprised how believable the story was," Cameron tells me. "I woke up in a transmission portal two days ago, but to me, of course, no time had passed. I didn't even know I was still in Houston. But when I went to put my clothes on, they weren't the same as what I had been wearing before. The door opened after I dressed, and that's when I saw the same NeuroStor employees who were there before. I was disoriented. Upset. When I asked what the hell had happened, Batista and some other guy whisked me into a room and closed the door."

"What did he say?"

"That there must have been some kind of problem with the transmission. As far as they knew, I came through fine in Phoenix, but at some point had stumbled back into the terminal asking to be sent back to Houston. According to Batista, I couldn't remember anything after I arrived. He rattled off a bunch of unclear technical talk that was supposed to be an explanation. Then he apologized profusely and offered more money for my promise not to go public."

"What a motherfucker. What a moneygrubbing prick."

"There was no point in fighting with him. I signed the release. He didn't have to give me anything. And to be honest, I was just happy to be alive."

Of course, Cameron didn't know, as we all do now, that he never left at all. He didn't know everything I was going through, or that I even existed.

"What was it like?" he asks. "The transmission, I mean."

"Just like we expected. Like I fell asleep and woke up in Arizona."

"What does it feel like now?"

"Hard to describe," I say. "You know how it feels when you take a nap in the afternoon, how—"

"When you wake up, you feel like you're not yourself. Like you're just . . . off."

"Right. Sort of like that with nausea and dizziness thrown in. And I had seizures."

"They told me that. I really don't know what to say. Somehow I think I should apologize, but it was . . . I guess it was *your* decision, too. Of course, if I had known something like this was going to happen, I would never have—"

"You don't have to apologize," I say. "I know how you feel."

"But in a way, I did this to you. You're the victim. It's like I . . ."

"Like you what?"

"I don't know what it's like. It just makes me feel badly, because what—"

"What am I going to do now? Now that I don't have a wife or a job or a place to live?"

"I'm sorry. I didn't mean—"

"Don't worry about it. Please. Don't feel sorry for me."

For a little while we are silent. We search for a new subject, and now something else occurs to me.

"Since Misty doesn't know what's going on," I ask him, "how did you get here? Crystal told me the house was being watched."

"We came to Dallas to accept the settlement from NeuroStor and to stay at her mother's for a few days. I went to play golf this morning, and the guy they paired me with turned out to be one of Clay's hired soldiers."

"Hired soldiers?"

"For the assault on the NeuroStor building. You know about that, right?"

"Crystal told me they were going inside to get someone from NeuroStor on tape."

"Kind of reckless if you ask me. I thought a less aggressive approach, like going on a news program to tell our story, would be more prudent. It would accomplish the same thing, anyway."

I nod my head. Not much of a shock that we think alike.

"So this guy at the golf course, what did he tell you? How did he convince you to come with him?"

"He just told me the story. Most of what I just told you is what I found out on the course. I was even par until he started talking about this, and then I made three double-bogeys in a row. Finished with a ninety."

Cameron smiles at this.

"What?"

"I thought you'd be disappointed," he says. "I mean, we haven't shot ninety in probably ten years."

This man obviously doesn't know what it's like to be presented face-to-face with his own death.

"Look," he adds, "I know that sounds stupid. But you've got to understand, this shocked the hell out of me. I didn't want to believe it at first. I *couldn't* believe it. But when they told me you were sick, how Tom had died trying to get you away from those goons, I had to at least come here and see if it was real. And if it was real, I was willing to do whatever I could to help you."

Clay pokes his head through the warehouse door and looks at us sharply.

"What are you two waiting for? A wrapped invitation?"

A wrapped invitation. What a yahoo.

"Get in here and take a look at what we've got," he tells us.

Cameron and I follow Clay into the warehouse. The collection of equipment is nothing like what I expected.

"Is this everything?"

"What'd you expect?" Clay says. "We don't have an army."

Indeed. There are two wooden worktables, one on each side of the door, and I count a total of six large weapons—machine guns of some kind. Beside each of these sits a holstered handgun, extra ammo clips, a harness, and a brown utility belt. A white van stands beyond the worktables.

"Each of us will be outfitted with two weapons—an MP-5 machine gun and a .45 Sig Sauer. The MP-5 will be your primary weapon. The Sig will be concealed. We also obtained several pounds of C4 plastic explosive."

Six people. He expects us to go into the NeuroStor main building with six people? I look at Crystal, surely she must also recognize this as futility, but I don't catch her eyes.

"The last item you'll carry is a hidden video system. A camera is fitted into each helmet and will be wired to a broadcast-quality digital video recorder. An FM transmitter will send the video signal to a receiver in the van. We'll all be live, and our man in the van will select the best angle for broadcast. He'll beam the signal to the NBC satellite. The affiliates could preempt us, of course, and many of them surely will. But we'll likely have at least a few minutes of nationwide coverage, and of course all stations will tape the entire broadcast."

"How are we supposed to get inside the building?"

"First of all, you two aren't part of the assault. You don't have any combat training, and if you get killed before the broadcast, then there isn't much of a point, is there?"

"I suppose not."

"Anyway, to answer your question: We have someone inside. There will be a fire. We'll be disguised as firefighters and go in through an emergency exit. You two will be with us at first, but then you'll hide in a designated room while the rest of us take the building. After everything is secure, we'll bring you to the action and begin taping."

"So basically we're staging a fire drill?" I ask him.

"It sounds crude, but the employees will be running scared, and I don't think their security will expect a full-on attack in broad daylight."

"Who are we going to capture on tape?" I ask. "Won't everyone be running out of the building?"

"Our target is the boardroom," he says. "We want to talk to the men who really run this fucking thing. All these men have their own offices, of course, but our information says Batista is meeting with them on the morning in question. We'll use their 'sophisticated' security system to turn that room into a jail cell."

Crystal walks closer to Clay and leans against his shoulder.

"You really came through for us, Clay. We couldn't have organized this without you."

"What are the explosives for?" I ask.

"After our broadcast," Clay says, "we might need to destroy the building."

"Why?"

"If something goes wrong—if the broadcast isn't successful, or if part of our team is disabled and we aren't able to arrange the video at all— we'll cripple them in another way: by destroying computers and hard-copy files. C4 is a devastating explosive. Strategically placed, we have more than enough to level their building."

He grabs the duffel bag and shoves it toward us. Cameron and I both shrink away.

"It ain't gonna bite you," he says. "Watch this."

He tosses the bag into the air above us and grins as Cameron and I fall backwards trying to get away. The duffel bag drops onto the concrete floor with a harmless thud.

"This stuff is stable. You can even set it on fire and it won't explode. But an electric charge, that's a different story. All I have to say is you better be far away when it detonates."

He points to another, smaller duffel bag.

"Those are blasting caps and simple wind-down timers. Maximum time: five minutes. That's not any time at all, especially if we detonate on the top floor. The NeuroStor building is nine stories high.

"If something very bad happens, something that prevents you from leaving the building, there are hand devices that you press and release for instant detonation. We'll practice that later."

I shudder at the thought of hand-detonating a lump of plastic explosive. Whoever did so would be nothing more than carbon goo scattered among the ruins. And how likely is it that "something very bad" will happen? Would Clay answer honestly if I asked?

But I guess it doesn't matter. This is never going to work.

The car is quiet on the way back to the motel room. Clay doesn't come with us—he lives in Irving and promises to meet us later today for a midafternoon lunch—so it's just Crystal, Cameron, and myself.

I want to talk to the guy, but what is there to say? I can't ask him what his interests are or what he does for a living or who his favorite sports team is. And what's strange is that, instead of wondering what differences there might be between us, all I can think about are the many embarrassing things about myself that I've never told anyone. Autoerotic idiosyncrasies. The huge crush I had for the cheerleading captain back in high school. My failed first effort at sex after the senior prom. How I've always secretly hated pizza but refused to tell anyone because they might think I was weird. Everyone likes pizza, don't they? And if Crystal wasn't around, I would ask him if he's thinking the same things. Our responses to the world, after all, are nothing more than the accumulation of all experienced stimuli. Cameron and I share everything. Everything, that is, save one notable exception: the past three days. Three days that have been the most important of my life.

Perhaps we do have something to talk about.

Stoplights, oak trees, and ugly, brown buildings roll by as we drive, and I begin to tell Cameron my story. Everything from the very first sensation after I awoke in Phoenix until I arrived in Plano this morning. I know he's heard a lot of it already, but I suppose he can identify more closely with the experiences as I tell them. I play loose with the facts when I explain how Crystal and I met, and skip altogether our encounter at the cabin. He should know these things, of course, but I'm uncomfortable speaking about them in front of her.

When we get back to the motel, Crystal surprises me by taking Lee out to get some food. "Clay probably won't come by for several hours," she says, "and I'm hungry *now*. Besides, I'm sure you guys want to catch up."

When they're gone, I don't know to how to begin about Crystal, but Cameron steps in to fill the silence.

"You asked about Misty before," he says, "and I kind of fudged because I didn't want to worry you right away. But she went nuts when she realized I didn't remember anything about the transmission. She wants to sue in spite of the waiver."

"You probably can't take the money and then sue."

"I know."

"Was she angry at you?" I ask him. "For going through with something that turned out so poorly?"

"There wasn't a lot of 'I told you so.' I think she was so relieved to get me back safely that she didn't think as much about the argument before. I think she had resigned herself to losing me . . . us . . . whatever."

"Cameron," I say to him. "Let's get something out in the open right now. I'm, well, I don't know how to say this, really. I'm more than just sick, man. Something is drastically wrong with me, but I don't really know what it is. I don't think anyone does, except maybe Batista and his fucking friends at NeuroStor, and it probably doesn't matter anyway. There isn't any way to reverse what they did to me."

"How do you know that?"

"I just do. Whatever this technology is, this scanning and reassembling that Crystal's physics friend told me was impossible, there isn't going to be any way to repair that. It's like shattering a vase into a million tiny pieces and then trying to put it back together. Even if you could get really, really close, there would always be problems. Maybe at first the vase would look fine, but at some point cracks would develop along lines that didn't quite match up, and eventually the whole thing would fall apart. I think something like that is going to happen to me."

"You don't know that."

"But I *do*! I can feel it, you know? Something isn't right."

Again silence swells between us. The discomfort is tangible.

"Look, what I'm trying to tell you is that I don't. . .oh, shit. This is going to sound ridiculous."

"What is it?"

"I don't expect you to share Misty with me. That's what I'm trying to say. Probably such a thing never occurred to you, but for me, well, assuming we survive this business with NeuroStor, I don't know what I'm supposed to do. But I'm here to tell you that I'm not going to pester you guys. I don't expect to even talk to her."

"Cameron—"

"I'm not joking. I don't want Misty to have to deal with this. And I don't really want to either."

"The money—"

"If you can spare some money, that's fine. I don't know how long I'll be around to spend it, anyway."

"I was going to say that we haven't received the money yet, anyway."

"Well, when you do, I don't expect—"

"You don't have any idea what's going to happen with this transmission sickness," Cameron says. "It could stay the same as it is now. It could go away. You're not necessarily going to get worse."

"If it goes away, then I'll find another life. I've sort of realized during the past few days that I was looking for another one anyway."

"What do you mean by that?"

"You know what I mean."

"You're talking about Misty? You don't want to be with her anyway, so you're letting me have her?"

I get up and walk to the window. The parking lot outside shimmers under the Texas sun.

"What I'm feeling," I say, "is what you've been feeling for a long time. I didn't come up with this during the past few days."

He looks at me through squinting eyes. I move away from the window and pull the drapes closed.

"I know," he says. "But something is different with Misty and me since I got back. We realized just how far we had fallen, how we weren't talking, how we didn't really know anything about each other anymore. And we *do* want to know. Both of us."

"Really."

"You came to a different conclusion?"

"I guess I did. I felt like we had grown into different people. I've been wondering why neither one of us had ever mentioned getting a divorce."

"You sure the girl didn't have something to do with that idea?"

"Crystal?"

"Of course. Sounds like you gave up on Misty because something else appeared on the horizon."

"We didn't do anything, if that's what you're thinking."

"You didn't have to. You know like I do that even the thought of something developing is enough to make a man question his marriage."

"She doesn't have anything to do with it."

"Well, that's good, I guess. Because I think she and Clay might be . . . I think they may be more than just friends."

This hits me a little hard, unexpected, but for some reason I don't want the other me to know that. So I press on with the conversation.

"Hey," I tell him. "It's great if you guys are talking more, if you think you're back on track again. That's wonderful news. But I don't know—I wish you could have been with me the past few days."

"What does that have to do with Misty and me?"

"It doesn't. That's not what I meant. But I know how you've felt, how *we've* felt for so long. How we've been sitting in a cubicle twiddling our thumbs while years pass by. How we've never done anything of any consequence in our lives."

"Until the transmission, that is."

"But you didn't transmit."

"Yes," he says, "I did. I did everything to transmit that I could. Just because the technology is different from what we thought, just because you came out on the other end instead of me, that doesn't mean I didn't do it."

"Yeah, but I don't know how to explain the transformation I've undergone since I stepped out of that portal. It's like I've thrown off shackles. Escaped the prison of my previous life."

"So have I."

"Okay," I say. "Let me ask you this: What if you never get the money Batista promised?"

"What do you mean?"

"Well, who knows what's going to happen after this assault Clay has planned? You might never see that money. What are you going to do for a living?"

He thinks about this before answering. "I guess I'll find another job somewhere."

"In accounting?"

"What else?"

"But you can't do that. Batista was right when he said we'd never make it at another corporation. You have to find something else, use this opportunity to start a whole new life."

"And what are we supposed to do about the house while I fart around looking for a new career to solve my midlife crisis?"

"Sell it if you have to. Get a job as a golf instructor. Move to Arizona or California. Misty can be a writer anywhere."

"Don't you think that's a little rash?"

"Not any more foolish than agreeing to transmit! That's what I'm trying to tell you. Carry this thing out, man. Go all the way with it. If you get the money, that's great. But do something even if you don't get it. *Do* something, Cameron."

This is surreal. Talking to myself like this. Only I need to remember that it's *not* really me, not if you define self as the lifetime sum of experienced stimuli. Because even though we've separated for only three days, that time apart has been the most important of our lives. And now I want him to know what I know. Feel what I feel. Because if anyone can help open his eyes, it's me.

Cameron smiles.

"What is it?" I ask him.

"I was just thinking that if you and I didn't go through with this assault that Clay has planned, I would probably get the money. I mean, he doesn't really have a lot of proof without us, right?"

"Yeah, but—"

"Hold on," he says. "Let me finish. I was thinking that, but I didn't say it because I realized that if you're right, if I need to carry this thing out—if I need to do something, as you say—then I guess this is the first step toward that. Sure, maybe we won't get the money, but we'll be doing something worthwhile. Something that makes a difference. And isn't that what we set out to do in the first place?"

Cameron rises to go to the bathroom, and I step outside to get some air. The motel parking lot is mostly empty. The sun explodes with heat.

The moment I saw Crystal and Clay together, something told me they might be lovers. I didn't really think much of it at the time—didn't want to, of course—but now Cameron's suspicions have confirmed my own. Jealousy makes me wonder if Clay won't somehow get killed during his planned assault on NeuroStor. Or maybe be hit head-on by a tractor-trailer on his way to the motel. Or something.

Crystal didn't really say when she was going to be back, and I have no idea what Cameron and I are supposed to do in the meantime. Talk more, I suppose. But at some point we're going to run out of things to discuss. What I am right now is hungry. But I'm not really sure if I should eat, because I haven't exactly been keeping my food down lately.

When I return to the room, however, Cameron has already ordered us a pizza. "I'm starving," he confesses. "And I don't have any idea when everyone is going to be back."

I start to ask something, but Cameron has already thought of it.

"Sorry about the pizza," he says. "But since we don't have a car, there wasn't much choice."

We chat about Tom while we wait for the food to arrive. Cameron is decidedly unforgiving of our best friend at first, but relaxes his position as he hears in detail the unselfish way Tom helped me elude Ivan and Ed. I describe how well he played golf that day, even under what must have been unbelievable pressure, and I suggest that he finally had a real chance to qualify for the U.S. Open. When the pizza arrives, we are both relieved.

Plain cheese is all either of us can stand—who the hell wants to eat meat and vegetables swimming in a lake of mozzarella?—and the smell of it makes me realize just how hungry I am. We both inhale several pieces and wash them down with the root beer Cameron ordered. A sense of calm settles over me as my stomach welcomes the sensation of being full, and for a moment I think I might be able to relax a little.

But soon it becomes apparent that eating was indeed a bad idea. I stand, suddenly sick to my stomach again, and a rush of blood swirls into my head. My feet cross. They stumble on the carpet. I swoon toward the bed, my spine bending backward against a mattress corner, and then I roll onto the floor.

A voice shouts above me. My voice.

The rush fills my ears, a sound like the roar of waves rolling onto a beach. My eyelids flutter open, and I see Cameron hovering above me. He's yelling something, but I can't hear his voice above the roar.

And now red noise obscures my vision. Waves crashing inside my brain. I'm falling. Away.

Away.

Awake.

Voices.

This is what I hear:

". . . be nausea, vomiting, and diarrhea, that may . . . days and then seem . . ."

Now the voices drift out of my reach, pulled away from me like the tide. A moment or two later I hear them again. They come and go.

". . . days to a week, the symptoms will . . . he . . . diarrhea and vomit blood as the lining of his . . ."

Blood? Who's bleeding? Not me.

"But we need him. We haven't even told him the real . . ."

The real what?

". . . begin to shed . . . his bone marrow and . . . blood . . . if his white cell count . . . sores . . ."

Primal fear envelops my heart and spreads into my stomach. Distantly, I feel my bowels release, though I'm almost sure this is really happening to someone else. Who shits in bed? Not me.

". . . lower the number of platelets, cell fragments that help blood to clot . . . hemorrhage into his skin . . . the intestines and stomach . . . probably dying . . . dying . . ."

Who's bleeding? Not me.

Who's dying? Not me.

Not me.

Cataclysmic thunder. Screams of the dead. White heat. Sacred fire.

Later now. Whispers. A moan. Quick breaths and the creak of a mattress.

"Kiss me down there," she says. "Love me."

A soft cry. A grunt.

"Oh, yes."

I will myself away from this, back to the maternal comfort of sleep.

Later still. More voices. This time they are hollow-sounding, electric. Someone is laughing, announcing what a beautiful morning it is today, predicting thunderstorms in the Midwest, humidity in the southeastern part of the country, and here's what's happening in your neck of the woods . . . and a good morning to you from NBC 5 Today, looks like another hot one this afternoon, it's like summer again with a high in the mid . . .

I open my eyes and wait for them to focus. A toilet flushes on my left. A door opens, the faucet squeaks on and then off. Crystal turns around. Looks at me. She's wearing a terry-cloth robe. Wet hair hangs on her shoulder. The flat planes of her face are smooth and clean, the tanned skin of her high forehead more beautiful than ever. She's not wearing a single smudge of makeup. She's beautiful.

"Cameron," she says, moving quickly to the bed. "Honey, are you all right?"

"I think so. What time is it?"

"A little after seven thirty. Does your head hurt? Are you dizzy at all?"

"No. But I'm a little stiff. How long have I been lying here?"

"Since yesterday around noon. Eighteen hours or so."

"Eighteen hours! Again?"

"You don't remember anything?"

I do remember something, maybe it was a dream, but I don't know.

"I was having lunch with Cameron. That's the last thing I remember."

"He wanted to take you to the hospital, but we couldn't risk it. A friend came by, a doctor. He said all we could do was wait."

"Where are the others?"

"Lee and Cameron are in the next room. Clay is running errands."

"Did you stay with me all night?"

"Yeah. I was awake most of the time watching you. You didn't move all day, but after nine or ten o'clock last night you started to toss and turn. You screamed a couple of times—scared me to death—and once you yelled something about fire. It was kind of creepy. I never heard anyone talk in their sleep before, at least not so clearly."

I sense something, a memory just outside my reach, something about fire or an explosion. Something that seemed wrong, like betrayal. Whatever it is, it's turning the skin on my arms to gooseflesh.

"Can I get you some water?"

"No, but I do have to pee." Actually, my bladder feels full enough to burst. But when I pull my hands backwards and attempt to push myself off the bed, I don't feel anything. My arms move, and I see the hands going in the right direction, but there is no sense of control between them and my brain.

I roll over and shake my right arm violently. The hand moves before my eyes, but I can't feel it.

"Cameron, what's the matter?"

"I can't feel my hand. The whole arm is numb to the elbow."

"You probably slept on it wrong."

"Yeah, but the other hand feels the same way."

I roll over and try my other hand. Nothing.

"Goddammit."

"They're asleep," Crystal says. "Get some blood into them. Stand up and let your arms hang at your sides."

I wiggle toward the edge of the bed. My feet nearly trip over each other, but somehow keep me from falling over. Balance, I've learned recently, is easily taken for granted. Never before have I been so concerned—and thankful, when it's working properly—for that innocuous fluid somewhere inside my inner ear.

"Better?" Crystal asks.

Already I feel blood draining into my hands and fingers, awakening cells that had felt dead.

"Yeah."

"Feel like taking a shower? The water is hot, and we bought you some new clothes yesterday." She points to a large Dillard's bag beneath the vanity.

"I guess so."

She steps back into the bathroom and grabs her used towels. As she walks out again, a pair of panties falls to the floor. They are tiny, lacy, a thin sheaf of material that would snap any man to attention. When she bends to pick them up, the lapels of her robe fall open, and through them her breasts are plainly visible. Full and tanned and beautiful. I cannot help but stare.

And of course Crystal catches me.

Our eyes lock for a brief, electric instant, though it seems to last much longer, and then she walks to the bag of clothes. Smiling, she pulls out an orange tank top and khaki shorts.

I step past her and into the bathroom. Close the door behind me. A few moments later, I'm standing beneath a curtain of steamy water. Thinking. Feeling sorry for myself.

Crystal couldn't possibly want anything to do with me. But what if I'm wrong? Did I just miss my chance? I could have . . . *we* could have . . . I think I'm in love with her. So beautiful, intelligent. What if I'm not that sick? What if a doctor can help me? Could Crystal and I, later on, of course, after the assault, could we have something together?

Ah, shit. I heard what they said. About platelets and white blood cells and the digestive problems. I heard all that. But this only confirmed what I've known for some time now. That I am dying. On the golf course, the day after I arrived in Phoenix, I knew something was fundamentally wrong with me, and I tried to deny it, tried to tell myself that I would be okay, that I would heal just like always. I tried to tell myself that nothing was so serious that I might actually die.

But that was a lie.

I *am* going to die.

Do you know the urban legend about a man named Jerry, whose attitude toward life is uncommonly positive? Well, let me tell it to you. Jerry always smiles, always has something good to say, always tries to do right by everyone. It is his belief that every encounter in life presents us with a choice, a point where we can decide to look upon the positive or negative side of that encounter. And one day, when he is shot by a burglar, Jerry is rushed to the hospital with a devastating prognosis: He is not expected to live. Bullet fragments are scattered throughout his body. And when the operating doctor, going through the motions, asks if he is allergic to anything, Jerry says, "Bullets." Everyone in the ER has a good laugh at that, and then Jerry says, "I have a choice now: to live or die. I choose to live. Please operate on me as if I am alive, not dead."

And because this legend was written to promote a good attitude, Jerry, of course, lives. But happy stories like this are bullshit, chicken soup for the fucking weak-minded, for the losers who think positive thinking can overcome physiology. I am not going to live. There isn't enough good cheer, there aren't enough smiles in the world to prevent that now. I can't even begin to comprehend the end of a life, can't understand what will happen to the consciousness that is me. My understanding of the universe does not reach that far.

But my inevitable demise doesn't have to be fruitless. Just because I can't change the ending of this story doesn't mean I can't shape it. All I need is the courage to channel my fear, the resolve to hone my anger at Batista into something sharp enough with which to stab.

And perhaps a little help.

Crystal is not in the room when I finish my shower.

I find a bathing suit among the clothes she bought for me—a red-and-blue number with POLO stitched in large white letters on the side. I don't know if I'll be able to swim, but a few rays of sunshine would feel good right now.

The pool is long and rectangular. A fortyish couple sit at one corner—a beached walrus of a man with his ninety-pound wife—and a long-legged brunette in a green bikini basks at the opposite corner. I find a chaise lounge between them and lie down on my back. Sunshine washes over me.

For a while my mind flips through the events that brought me to this situation. My trek down the flooded washout, the vigilante convenience store clerk who pounded me with his soft fists, those few moments in the transmission portal before everything went dark.

Strange how that last memory, and all others that precede it, aren't really mine. I can remember things that never happened to me, not to this body anyway. You could say I am a reincarnation of myself. In fact, you could say I was born only four days ago. But from what? From what was I born?

I don't understand quantum teleportation as well as Lee does, but I did gather that one set of particles transfers its properties to another set of particles, essentially destroying the original and re-creating it somewhere else. True teleportation is achieved with this method, not replication, although its success so far has been limited to photons and other ridiculously small atomic elements. NeuroStor's process is something altogether different. There are two Cameron Fishers in the world because they do not, in fact, teleport anything. It's replication, pure and simple. Scanned data is sent from one place to another, where it re-creates a copy of the original. But how? What sort of scanning process do they use?

"Hey, Cameron."

Involuntarily I jump, brought out of my trance by the sound of Crystal's voice, and sweat burns my eyes as I open them.

"That girl over there is checking you out."

I look over at the brunette in the green bikini, but of course she's not looking in my direction.

"Right," I deadpan.

"I'm serious. She keeps glancing over here. I watched her on my way from the room."

Crystal's white bikini is tiny and beautiful. The bottom rides high on her hip and makes her legs look a mile long.

"Why are you telling me this?"

"Because the other day you were trying to convince me that you were too old to meet someone. And I'm calling bullshit."

"I appreciate what you're trying to do," I tell her. "But you've got to know I'm not really that concerned right now about my ability to pick up women."

She looks away from me.

"Look, Crystal. You know I . . . I really . . ."

"You really what?"

The words are right there, I know what they are, but I can't make them come out of my mouth.

"It's hotter out here than I thought," she says, and moves to stand up. "Maybe I'd be more comfortable back in the room."

I reach out and grab her wrist. "Don't leave."

"Then make me want to stay."

"Sit down."

Crystal relaxes and combs her fingers through her hair. Now is the time I'm supposed to say it to her. Whatever it is I think I should say, now is the time to do it.

But I can't.

Jesus Christ, it's like I'm in fucking junior high again. I can't count how many girlfriends I missed out on back then simply because I was too frightened to act upon what we were both thinking. Because if you aren't man enough to tell a woman how you feel about her, why would she want to have anything to do with you?

My excuse now, of course, is that I've been married for fifteen years. I can't remember what the hell I'm supposed to do or what I'm supposed to say. But I don't think Crystal gives a shit about that.

She looks away from me again, so I just blurt it out.

"I like you, Crystal. A lot."

When she looks back at me, the sparkle in Crystal's eye is bright enough to light up the city of Houston for a year.

"I like you, too, Cameron. A lot."

"I can't say I understand why."

"Why analyze it? Is it too much to just accept when a girl's attracted to you?"

"It's just that, well, considering my physical condition . . ."

"Cameron, that doesn't matter to me. Oh, I suppose it should. Neither of us knows what's going to happen to you, after all. But that doesn't change the way I feel about you. In fact . . ."

She trails off.

"'In fact' what?"

"Well, you were an accountant before, right? Not that there's anything wrong with that, but it certainly didn't prepare you for what's happened during the last few days. And you haven't backed away from any of it. You've been really brave."

"Thank you," I answer, even though I don't think "brave" is the way to describe how I've been feeling or acting.

Crystal leans forward and puts her hand on mine.

"That kind of thing really attracts a woman."

Now what am I supposed to say to that? If Tom was around, he would probably toss out something like, *Moron! She's throwing herself at you! Take her back to the room and fuck the shit out of her!*

But do people really do that? Do people really make the leap from civilized conversation to *Let's go back to the room and fuck*? I've slept with five women in my life, and none of them accepted me into their beds before several dates and plenty of get-to-know-you. There have been other opportunities, of course—alcohol-induced make-out sessions at college parties; the inevitable, pathetic come-ons that occur at accounting industry conventions—but I've never actually stepped across that line. What do you say? How do you make the transition?

"Crystal," I say finally, "everything about you is the kind of thing that attracts a man."

Now she just stares at me. Her eyes are so blue, the color of a bright summer sky, and so full of intelligence. Calculated intelligence. She leans toward me and I toward her. I see my reflection in those beautiful eyes, I see myself as how she must see me, and—

I jerk away from her. Again.

"What's the matter?"

"What's the matter? What the hell is happening to me, Crystal? I heard you guys while I was asleep. About platelets and white blood cells and hemorrhaging. Am I going to die?"

She straightens and crosses her arms over her breasts.

"I don't know, Cameron."

"But what do you think? What did your doctor think?"

"If you heard him, then you know."

Even though I've guessed as much, my hands shake as I ask the next question.

"How long does he give me?"

"A couple of weeks. Maybe a month."

Weeks. A month. How can I begin to believe such a thing? People don't really die, do they? I mean, it's just a big act, right? The earth is only so big, a fixed ecosystem, so when humans reach a certain age, we're shipped off to another galaxy, another dimension. Tell me it's true. Tell me we're sent to a place where we grow young, where we become children again.

Oh, please tell me something.

"I'm sorry, Cameron. I really am. But that's just one doctor's guess. He doesn't know. No one knows anything for sure."

I lie down on the chaise lounge and look up at Crystal through squinting eyes. From here she is nothing more than a silhouette before the blazing, white sun.

"It doesn't matter what's wrong with me," I tell her. "Because this whole thing is going to fail anyway. Clay's plan is so simple it borders on childish, and the resources earmarked for the 'assault' tomorrow seem meager at best."

Crystal doesn't have an immediate answer, so I press on.

"This doesn't seem like a well-funded outfit to me. It seems like something thrown together by a couple of kids who are in way over their heads."

"You think kids could come up with a half-dozen MP-5's and enough C4 to level a building?"

"I'm just saying that I expected more. I think something about what you've told me doesn't add up. I think you've been misleading me."

Crystal looks away.

"Well? Am I right?"

"Maybe," she says. "But if I'm going to tell you, I don't want to do it here. Let's go back to the room and talk."

Crystal pulls a T-shirt and shorts over her bikini and then closes the drapes, cloaking the hotel room in shadows. I rummage through the Dillard's bag until I find a white linen shirt of my own. We each sit on one of the queen-size beds and face each other.

"You're right, we've sort of misled you," Crystal says. "I guess it was really me. *I* misled you."

My heart accelerates to just over one thousand beats per minute.

"About what?"

"About who we are. When I told you we were a nationwide organization, that we had contacts in Congress and the FBI; when I told you all that stuff about airlines and Big Oil being involved—that was all bullshit."

"What? You lied to me? Why? Why would you do that?"

"We needed your help. *I* needed your help. And I didn't think you would cooperate if you knew the real situation."

"The real situation? What the hell does that mean?"

Crystal looks away. First at the dormant television, then at the closed motel room door.

"The man who created this whole mess—NeuroStor, the volunteer program, the idea to use an electronic storage company as a front to build the transmission machine—his name is Stanley King. He's one of the officers who was waiting when you came out of the transmission portal in Phoenix."

I remember this fellow. A big man in his sixties. The imposing one who questioned me as I struggled to suppress my excitement upon making the trip in one piece.

"And he has nothing to do with Aryans or white supremacy or anything like that," Crystal continues. "Lee's best friend was the victim of a hate crime a few years ago. It affected him a lot and he wanted to, you know, fight back. All he really ended up doing was learning way too much for his own good about the white supremacist movement." A guilty look settles over her face. "It was the rest of us . . . we decided to use what he knew as our cover story."

Crystal's eyes break contact with mine as she says this last piece, angling toward the floor, as if anything down there would surely be less threatening than looking at me.

"Wow," I say to her. "I guess at this point the average person would begin to wonder if anything you've *ever* told me was true."

"I expected you to say that, and the only answer I have for you is that the intention behind what we're doing is true, just not the details."

"But how am I supposed to trust someone so selective with the facts?"

"I'm sorry, Cameron. You would never have given us any credit if you knew the intimate nature of our battle."

" 'The intimate nature of your battle'? What are you talking about?"

"Well, I didn't want to . . . I mean, you don't have to know every—"

"Jesus Christ, Crystal! Can't you be honest with me now? After everything that's happened, as hard as I've tried to—"

"Okay, okay. I was Stanley's administrative assistant. His secretary. Here in Plano. I'm not from Arizona."

"And?"

"And we sort of got into a relationship, and—"

"And you were fucking him? Is that what you're trying to tell me? The man is forty years older than you, Crystal! Jesus Christ!"

"What the hell does his age have to do with anything?"

She's right. His age has everything to do with nothing. I suppose I should at least attempt to contain my jealousy for the time being. It's not like Crystal is a virgin. Just because I'm smitten with her, just because this anger has somehow intensified my electric desire for her, that doesn't mean I'm the only man who has ever felt this way. Certainly she must have slept with several men, perhaps a score of them, I mean, *look* at her. She must have to beat men away with a stick when she goes out on weekends, and I have the nerve to be jealous of her because some rich old man impressed her with his baritone voice, his command of power, his—

"It didn't last long, Cameron. I realized pretty quickly that I was being shallow. And you're right, the age thing was always going to be a problem."

"So what happened? You dumped him, and he fired you?"

"No," Crystal says with a distant look in her eyes. For a moment she doesn't answer, but just when I'm about to say something, she continues. "Stanley was a bigger man than that. When I told him I didn't think it was going to work, he gave me the option to leave or stay. I decided to leave."

"Did you know what was really going on? About the transmission machine and what he planned to do with it?"

"Eventually I did."

"Is that what made you leave?"

"Yes and no. Stanley admitted to me early on that the whole NeuroStor thing was just a means to an end—the storage technology was important, but certainly not the crown jewel. He couldn't really keep the transmission machine from me because of the administrative work I did for him. He told me all along that he planned to market the machine as a transportation device, something he claimed would eventually change the way all Americans traveled. But later . . ."

I wait for Crystal, but here she has decided to stall.

"Later what?"

"Later, I met the guy who ran the R and D offices in Wyoming. No one at NeuroStor knew about this facility because it wasn't on the books.

The R and D guy was much younger. You could say he was Stanley's right-hand man, because without Rodrigo there never would—"

My mouth opens, noticeably, and Crystal waits for me to say something. Instead I fill the room with silence.

"—have been a machine," she decides to finish.

Batista.

Thunderous silence, still.

BATISTA!

"Cameron?"

I get up from the bed and walk over to the window. The parking lot is sunny. A ten-year-old boy glides across the asphalt in Rollerblades.

"Crystal, pardon me for saying this, but is there *anyone* in this soap opera—this real-life fantasy—that you *haven't* slept with?"

Her eyes shrink, dark and wounded.

"What do you mean by that?"

"What I mean, Crystal, is that you and Lee have sucked me into this . . . this lover's spat, and yes, maybe it's more than that because of what's at stake, because of this machine that someone created, that someone somehow built in spite of the physics laws it seems to ignore. Yes, maybe there are bigger consequences at stake, but in the end you got yourself caught in a love triangle, with King and that slimy, greasy motherfucker, and the only way you saw fit to extricate yourself from said situation was to find *another* boyfriend, another man perfectly willing to stick his dick in you, a muscle-bound soldier of fortune with just enough knowledge of guerrilla warfare to help you break into the offices from which you've been banished, enabling you to put a stop to *something*, God only knows what the *real* purpose of the machine is—"

"Cameron—"

"—to make you look like a hero—"

"Cameron!"

"What?"

"Clay is my brother."

"What?"

"Why would . . . why did you think we were—"

"I heard you while I was asleep."

"What did you hear?"

"I thought I heard you . . . well, I thought you were having sex. With him."

"Jesus, Cameron. Of course you didn't hear that."

I just stare at her.

"You also said you heard an explosion. You were obviously dreaming."

I walk back to the bed and sit down again, still with nothing to say.

"I'm sorry if you think I'm a slut. I don't see how dating both of those guys makes me different from any other girl out there. But—"

"But *Batista*? Come on, Crystal! He's—"

"You don't know anything about him, Cameron, so shut the hell up about that, all right?"

"Believe me, I know plenty about—"

"You don't have to help us, Cameron. I will understand perfectly if you don't want anything to do with me, considering how I've misled you. But the rest of us . . . we still have to go through with this. We can't just sit back and let them test this machine on innocent people—people like you, for instance—and then sell it to a foreign government that will just end up using it against us at some point."

"What? They want to sell it to a foreign government?"

"Israel has sent over representatives. Saudi Arabia and Pakistan. I even heard that a former KGB agent turned Russian mob boss got wind of the machine and threatened Stanley, who of course isn't afraid of anyone. But it did convince him to move the timetable forward, and that's why we have to act now. I think he wants to sell soon, even before all the problems are completely worked out."

"I don't understand where the money is coming from. You sure he doesn't have a buyer already, someone pumping money to him? Because a project like this would take an extraordinary amount of investment capital."

"Stanley made a fortune off the Internet. I think he was in on the Yahoo IPO a few years back and owned a bunch of Oracle stock. And because he needed liquidity to form NeuroStor, he cashed in just about everything well before the NASDAQ nosedive."

"Still, if that netted him, say, a half-billion dollars, would it be enough for this?"

"Regardless of where he gets his money," Crystal says, "we can't let him sell the machine. If it gets into the wrong hands a lot of innocent people will die, Cameron."

"Crystal, I have to admit that doesn't matter a whole lot to me. I don't care a whole lot about battles in faraway countries. Even though I'm supposed to now because of the constant battle against foreign terrorism, I don't. I don't care. And right now I can't really find the desire to care about any of the rest of this considering how you used me."

"Look, Cameron. I'd be angry, too. I hate it when people lie to me. But I needed your help. Badly. And I was afraid you wouldn't want anything to do with me when you learned the real truth."

"But this isn't about you. It's about King and Batista. I don't understand why you thought it would be better to lie to me than to admit you slept with them. Because from what you told me, that's the limit of your involvement in their plans."

"I was embarrassed, Cameron," Crystal says. Her eyes gleam as she tries not to cry. "Look at how you reacted when you found out. Imagine if I had tried to tell you that before we got to know each other. I'd have lost you right away."

Knowing full well that her tears could be artificial, that she could be manipulating me again, my anger softens anyway. What a predictable fool I am.

"You don't know that."

"I do! I do know that! You have such a good heart, such strong moral convictions, and I'm just a pretty face who got into this shit because a couple of guys wanted to fuck me."

Of course, here I sit, condemning her lies, when all I want is to fuck her, too.

"Crystal, don't cry."

"This is just so overwhelming. I'm not as stupidly confident as Clay. I don't think we can pull this off. Especially when the most important evidence we have—you—doesn't trust us anymore."

"I don't know if we can pull it off either, but you know I have to try."

Crystal looks up at me.

"You do?"

"Look, it pisses me off that you lied to me. But in the end I'm still better off than if you hadn't helped me. By now, without your help,

Misty and I might both be dead. And even if I don't make it out of this intact—who knows what's going to come of this 'transmission sickness'—I can't just stand by and let Misty suffer at the hands of Batista. Because if I don't do something to help, he could kill her."

Crystal absorbs this information, knowing as she probably did that I would be forced to come to this conclusion whether I wanted to or not.

"But I'm not going to do it the way Clay explained. I don't want to be pulled into the mix after you guys have already done the hard part."

"What do you propose, then?"

For a moment I hesitate, unsure what to say, even though somehow my mind has already made a decision—that this is my battle, not theirs. Certainly we both agree that NeuroStor must be stopped, but no longer do I care why Crystal thinks so or what she and her friends have planned. I stepped into that transmission portal four days ago to make a difference in this world, to do something with my life, and now, finally, I have found a platform upon which to do so.

"I'm going in alone."

"Alone? Cameron, that's suicide!"

"If we catch them by surprise, I don't think it matters how many go in."

"I'm telling you it won't work," Crystal says.

"And I'm telling you I won't do it any other way."

"But this is my battle, too, Cameron. I was getting ready for it a long time before you stepped into the picture."

"Yeah, but now I *am* in the picture. And I'm the only one here who is likely to die no matter what we do."

"I understand that, but—"

"I don't think so, Crystal. I just said that I'm likely to *die*. One minute I'm going to be a living, sentient organism, and the next I'm going to be gone. Dead. The whole world will just go on, just like it always has, but I won't be part of it anymore. Because of this fucking machine! I don't know if you understand that at all."

Crystal looks into my eyes—whether with pity or compassion, I can't tell—but doesn't say anything.

"I don't think anyone understands that," I continue. "Until you're staring death in the face, I don't know if you can comprehend it at all."

Silence invades the hotel room as we sit there at an impasse.

"What exactly do you want to do?" she finally asks me.

"We all know why we're here," Clay says through a mouthful of food. In addition to Clay, Crystal, Cameron, Lee, and me, we have added four new members: Scott Warren, David Stone, Randy Temple, and Brandon Richards. The nine of us are scattered about the small motel room, munching on Whataburgers and fries. Well, except for me. I'm just having fries. About three of them so far.

"We're here to expose NeuroStor for what they are: racial separatists. White supremacists. Terrorists who want to divide the United States and make part of it a white-only state."

According to Crystal, our new members have been fed the white supremacy story that I was originally led to believe, and for the same reason—to hide the truth of Crystal's disagreement with her former employer. As far as my plan to go in alone, I've decided that only Cameron, Crystal, and I need to be involved. So I sit here, privately amused at their elaborate story, knowing as I do that it's now all for nothing. Because they aren't using me anymore, I'm using them.

"Buncha fuckin' cowards," Randy says. "Fuckin' Nazis."

"They aren't just neo-Nazis," Crystal points out. "It's a lot of separatist groups who have finally learned to pool their resources. National Socialists, religious fanatics, neo-Nazis. Other, smaller organizations that the average American has never heard of. Groups that have existed separately for years, with different motivations and platforms but with the same general ideas about the United States: that our government has become too strong and corrupt, that minorities are taking over the country and must be stopped, that the moral fabric of America has become poisoned and must be set right again."

"Right," Clay says. "None of us would be here if we didn't want to see these people bear responsibility for their actions. Not just what they've done to Cameron, but also the bombs and murders and hate crimes they've supported for years. Am I right?"

General nodding of heads from our assembled team, a couple of affirmative grunts.

"Good. So let's dispense for now with our own propaganda and start preparing for the strike itself. Crystal and I have decided the best time to storm the building is tomorrow morning at around ten o'clock. This should be right in the middle of the board meeting that is scheduled from eight to noon. Does anyone have a problem with a midmorning broadcast?"

I hate it when people ask questions to which they already know the answer. Guys such as Clay (and Batista, fuck him) like to hear themselves talk, but even more they love it when people agree with them. It affirms their perceived intelligence, their power. We've all worked under a manager at one time or another (Batista) who got a kick out of saying, *Don't you think the best course of action is blah-blah-blah?* because he knew you'd have to agree.

"Good," he says. "Crystal and I have put together a schedule of events, a time line that includes assignments for everyone here. For those of you who don't know, Brandon and David went through Ranger school in the Army, Scott is a former SWAT team member, and Randy once flew helicopters in the Navy. Our attack team will include me, Crystal, Brandon, and Scott. Later the two Camerons will join us."

Or so he thinks.

"We'll broadcast from their boardroom on the ninth floor. This evening we'll have blueprints of the building, and that'll allow us to devise the exact route from first floor to ninth. Lee and David will be assigned to the TV van. Then we'll have to find a way to the roof, where Randy and his helicopter will lift us to safety.

"There's a good chance we won't all get out of there. I want everyone here to understand that. Every precaution will be taken—and with the cameras rolling, surely they'll be hesitant to fire on us—but your personal safety cannot be guaranteed."

No one says anything. Everyone here knows the risks. We're much too far along to pull back now.

"After lunch we'll all drive over to the warehouse, and those of you who need it will be trained to use the weapons. We'll go over some basic tactical maneuvers, and then Scott will demonstrate more advanced entry techniques. We'll practice those. By then we should have the building blueprints, and we'll devise the most advantageous route to the boardroom. We'll look at alternate locations if there is no board meeting. Then, after dark, we'll load everything into the van and drive back here. This is where we'll sleep tonight and start in the morning. After the broadcast, the helicopter will fly from Plano to a farm road just west of Nobility, a small town northeast of the city. Four cars will be waiting for us. The driver of each car will have disguises ready for us."

"I wanna be Bill Clinton," Randy says. "Chicks still dig that guy."

"Congratulations, Temple," Clay shoots back. "First to smart off gets to be the transvestite."

Laughter from our military friends. I guess they live for this shit, but somehow I don't share the humor.

"Each car will head toward a different destination. In Car One, me and Crystal will drive to Little Rock. Car Two, Cameron One and Randy will drive to Tulsa. In Car Three, Cameron Two and David will head for Oklahoma City. Brandon, Scott, and Lee will take Car Four and drive to Amarillo. Each car will be fueled and furnished with a detailed map. Any questions so far?"

And of course, everyone's silent.

Evening. At the warehouse. Fluorescent lamps cast sickly light upon the eight of us, standing in a circle, watching Clay as he explains the weapons.

"The MP-5 and Sig are so simple a first-grader could operate them."

"Or some asshole with a first-grade education," Scott adds.

Clay explains how the safeties and triggers work, we go through a few exercises, and then move on.

"The C4 is easy to detonate. Each of you will be issued several bars, which are wrapped in plastic like cheese. The bars will be prepared so that all you'll have to do is set the timer and run." He pulls out a bar and shows us how the timer works. The device looks like a video game controller with an LED readout on the side and a button on top. "You can also detonate one or more bars instantly by wrapping them together, flipping the safety switch to 'off,' and pressing and releasing the top button. This method is primarily a defense mechanism—no one would dare attack you while you held the button down, because anything that disturbed your grip would result in detonation."

Later, Clay turns center stage over to Brandon, who introduces basic maneuvers, and then to Scott, who explains entry techniques. We're going in dressed as firefighters, wearing heavy vests underneath. He blabbers on about tactical distractions and how proper planning is critical for raid success. He speaks in the trite, robotic tone of a drill instructor. I absorb the information I need and ignore the rest.

Then, for nearly an hour, sweating like pigs in the hot warehouse, we run through what seems like an endless parade of drills. How to run with the weapon, how to dive with the weapon, how to use the weapon in close-quarter battle. Failure drills and backup weapon transitions. What to do if a team member goes down.

The building blueprints arrive just before his hour-long lesson ends. I'm about to ask for a fifteen-minute recess when Clay offers us a break. Everyone heads for the office, looking for water and air-conditioning, and I find a quick minute alone with Cameron.

"What do you think about all this?" I ask him. "Think they can pull it off?"

"I have my doubts. I understand why he doesn't want us to go in with the first assault—if one of us gets killed, obviously, their proof could be lost—but I don't know if separating the group is any better."

"What if I told you I had other ideas?"

"What do you mean?" he asks me.

"Crystal and I bought some equipment of our own earlier today. A computer and a digital camcorder. I think I'd like to try this a different way."

"Different how?"

"I want to go in by myself."

"What? We don't know how to mount an assault like this."

"I think we can do plenty of damage to NeuroStor without stepping foot on their property. You and I are really all the proof anyone would need to believe what's going on."

"But you said you wanted to go in on your own."

"I do. Once we've documented our situation—my existence as your clone—then any extra proof I can get will only help build our case. And I've got a personal score to settle, if you know what I mean."

Now the door opens again, and Crystal steps out. She sees us and walks on over.

"Don't be too obvious," she says. "Clay doesn't miss much."

Cameron looks at Crystal, then back at me. "I hope you know what you're doing," he says.

Cameron, I think. *You know I don't.*

"There are two enclosed stairwells designated as fire escapes, encased by walls designed to hold off fire for three hours, and two other stairwells that carry no such designation. The fire-safe stairwells end in exit doors that open at ground level. We'll be entering the building at one of these exits."

Clay clears his throat and continues.

"The primary exit for most buildings like this is out the nearest door, preferably something high volume. Our fire will be set to help direct employees to the front doors. Many people will even use the elevators. The less traffic we encounter on the way up the stairwell, the quicker we'll make it to the top. In any case, since all the door locks in the building are operated electronically, our contact inside will make sure the board members don't go anywhere at first. But there is no way to predict how long it will take someone to break down the door or go through a window. We shouldn't count on much extra time. The success of this operation will depend largely on surprise. We must move quickly."

"How will you get the boardroom door open if your contact has locked it electronically?" I ask.

"There are closed-circuit video cameras all over the building," Clay answers. "Including one that points right at the boardroom doors. When we arrive, he'll unlock them for us."

"Oh."

Clay continues. "Our suits have been outfitted with a special pocket to conceal our automatic weapons, but keep your hand on the MP-5 at all times. The nearest fire station is a little over three miles away.

Someone will realize soon enough that our response time was a little too quick. The faster we move, though, the more likely we'll be near the top floor before encountering resistance."

"Camerons, you will remain in the fire exits." He points to a small room on the first-level floor plan. "We'll hide you in this utility closet until we've secured the boardroom. You'll wait exactly five minutes for someone to retrieve you. If no one comes by then, get the hell out of the building and run away from it as fast as you can."

For the next forty or so minutes we go over the designated route, as well as two backup plans if the first fails. The soldiers choose their attack formation. And then we discuss the actual broadcast itself.

"A miniature hidden camera is mounted into each helmet. It will be wired to a digital video recorder and an FM transmitter. We'll send our signals to the van and Lee will transmit the best shots to the satellite. Once the boardroom is secure, we'll switch to a professional-style camera. This will assure the best possible picture for the money shot."

Now Clay makes a dramatic body turn and faces Cameron and myself.

"Then the spotlight will turn on you two men. We need strong emotions, stuff that will play well for a television audience. I know you guys must have mixed feelings about all this, but we need the public to know how outraged you both are. And you"—he looks directly at me now—"it will be your job to describe the horror of being a scrambled version of your former self. I don't mean to sound insensitive, but you'll have to really play it up for television. On the small screen, we need big. Lots of emotion. And know what you're going to say."

I picture myself standing in front of Batista, my machine gun trained on his head. Or maybe his cock—the one he stuck into Crystal. I imagine him quivering before me, begging for his slimy, useless life, exhorting me not to kill him, explaining to me in his patronizing, conceited way that there is no call for violence, no reason why there can't be a solution agreeable to—

"In fact," Clay says to Crystal, "we should have scripted his dialogue."

"It wouldn't sound real if we did that," she replies.

"We could have given him an outline or something."

"It's too late now. And we really should get everything over to the motel soon. This team needs to be well rested."

It's shocking how they talk about my ruined life with such detached indifference. I'd like to strap Clay into a transmission portal and see what he thinks when his twin comes out on the other side. He probably wouldn't care. After all, it wouldn't be *him*. Just a clone.

Of course, I can't tell I'm a clone. I feel as real as any other person would. But do others see me that way? Is my life any less important than the original Cameron's?

To surviving friends and loved ones, what is death, exactly? An empty place in your heart once filled by the deceased, perhaps. But what happens when there is no void?

Without that void, what is death?

Clay decides to heed Crystal's advice. We pack the weapons and fire suits into the van and then head back to the motel. By now it's nearly nine o'clock, and a few dim stars have poked through the light-polluted firmament that passes for the Dallas–Fort Worth nighttime sky. I look out the window and try to remember what it was like to live in a world where none of this had happened.

It's a world I don't miss.

I agreed to transmit, in part, to change my life for the better, to invigorate my life. Has Cameron achieved such a thing? I'm not sure. Maybe he's found a small taste of excitement during the past few days, but if he knew what it was like to nearly die, perhaps he would know what it is to really want to live.

I read once that, as late as 1920, the average life expectancy in the United States was fifty-five. Which means that until medical science learned how to tamper with nature, the average person in the United States barely lived long enough to raise his children to maturity. At the time such a thing seemed significant to me. Why should we live any longer? For what natural purpose?

But now I realize that, even without the basic function of species propagation, a person can find fulfillment, a noble purpose to make life worth living. I just hope I have the strength to see mine all the way through.

It's a party here in the motel room, as boxes of pizza are devoured, as six-packs of beer are sucked down in front of the blaring television set. After today's preparation and exercises, Clay has afforded our team with a little time to unwind before we turn in for the evening. Governor Arnold Schwarzenegger is destroying entire legions of terrorist bad guys in the evening's pay-per-view presentation, and our military commandos cheer him on with disconcerting fervor. These men worship him because they want to be him, and in some ways they are. Physical strength, determination, and the ability to fight are central to their occupations, to their lives, and their bodies reflect this. Their demeanors reflect it. Do I really expect to accomplish on my own what four soldiers have been brought here to do?

I've stayed away from the pizza, obviously, and after one beer I elected not to put anything else into my stomach. The nausea is under control now—barely—but I don't want it to return at an inopportune time. So instead I sit on the bed, pretending to watch the movie when really what I'm doing is watching Crystal. She's quiet, too, distracted it seems, and I wonder what she's thinking.

After the movie, the team retreats to their respective hotel rooms. Brandon, Scott, and David will bunk in one room, while Clay, Lee, and Randy will sleep in the other. Crystal, Cameron, and I will remain here. Crystal gets her own bed, of course, while Cameron and I share the other one.

Crystal uses the bathroom first. From behind the closed door we hear the typical sounds of nightly hygiene.

"She's beautiful," Cameron says to me.

"Yes, she is."

He seems ready to say something else when the bathroom door opens and Crystal emerges in a navy blue T-shirt and plaid boxer shorts.

"Which one of you is next?"

"I'll go," I tell her. "And now that we're alone, why don't you go ahead and fill Cameron in on the real situation? What you told me this afternoon. He's going to find out soon enough."

In the bathroom, I brush my teeth first. It seems silly to perform this kind of maintenance considering the short life span that likely remains for me, but mainly what I'm trying to do is clean my stale breath. Next I wash my face. And then, as absurd and pointless as it may seem, I go ahead and wipe down my crotch with a damp washcloth. There is no doubt that I am not the first man to do such a thing in the presence of a woman like Crystal, considering how many of us entertain dreams of sudden, impulsive sexual encounters that defy reason. Of course I could never summon the nerve to make the dream a reality, but I freshen myself anyway.

Cameron goes next, briefly leaving Crystal and me alone in the room. Her skin is tanned velvet, her blond hair a waterfall reflecting evening sunshine.

"I hope you know what you're doing tomorrow," she says to me.

"So do I."

"It's not too late to change your mind. If you decide between now and in the morning that you'd rather do it our way, just wake me up."

"Okay."

God, she is so gorgeous. Right now I think I would go crazy if I wasn't able to look at her, if I wasn't able to sit here and absorb her beauty. I want to touch her. Hold her. I want to kiss every square inch of her body, taste her precious skin, smell her golden hair.

I must be insane. Tomorrow I am going to thrust myself into a situation that could likely result in my own death, and yet I cannot control my lust for this woman, this woman who has lied to me since the day I met her.

Cameron opens the door then and emerges from the bathroom. He looks at us briefly and then crawls into bed on the side facing the wall. I lie down near the nightstand.

"Want me to turn off the lamp?" I ask Crystal.

"Sure," she says, and pulls the covers up to her neck. "We're going to need plenty of sleep."

But of course I don't sleep at all.

The room is still now, dark and quiet except for the low rumbling of the air conditioner. Something about this situation reminds me of summer nights in South Padre during high school and college. Hotel rooms with sand-matted carpet that stunk of beer and pizza and where sleep was as foreign as the ruble. I lost my virginity in such a room, to my girlfriend of three years, a nineteen-year-old goddess with skin so tanned that when her navy blue bikini disappeared, I thought for a short, drunken moment that she was wearing another, white bathing suit underneath. And when my eyes fell from her white breasts to that closely shaved triangle of hair, sharp ecstasy poked through my alcohol haze like a silver dagger, and I was awake, I was *alive*. I didn't care who was in the room, I didn't care what time it was, and if I had my way, I would never leave the room again. I would just keep on doing what I was doing, with her, and when I was done I would go back for more, and then go back again, and again, and again . . .

Sleeping six feet away from me, Crystal's breathing is a hurricane in my ears. Her facial soap is a meadow of fragrant wildflowers. My heart races as if I'm running, as if I'm chasing her across that fiery meadow, watching her run just fast enough to stay ahead of me, but not quite fast enough to get away. She looks back occasionally, through the swirling gale of her blond hair, beckoning me with that familiar spark in her eyes.

"Cameron," she calls to me. "Run faster."

My legs pump harder to close the distance between us.

"Cameron," she says again, and now I open my eyes.

The hotel room remains cloaked in shadows. The air conditioner hums a single-note melody.

Crystal is looking at me.

Or so it seems until my eyes clear and adjust to the darkness. Then I recognize the optical illusion: Her face is turned this way, but her eyes are closed.

Just wake me up, she'd said. *It's not too late to change your mind.*

I turn and listen to Cameron's breathing. It's rhythmic and heavy. He's asleep.

The alarm clock reads 1:52. A little more than three hours from now it'll be time to sneak out of here and begin preparing my case against NeuroStor. You'd think I'd be going over the plan in my head, checking for flaws, preparing for every conceivable obstacle I might encounter.

Instead I can't stop obsessing over the magnificent creature sleeping two yards away from me.

It's not too late to change your mind.

Cameron's breathing remains steady.

I slither out of the bed. Listen again to Cameron. Still sleeping.

On my knees, I cross the gulf between the two beds. Crystal faces me, her body an hourglass beneath the sheets. So still. So beautiful.

My voice a whisper. Too low for her to hear me. What the hell am I doing?

"Crystal."

Her eyelids pop open like window shades.

"Hi, Cameron."

She's not asleep. I swallow and search for an excuse, some reason why I came over here other than the real one.

She waits.

What difference does it make now? If she declines, we'll still go through with my plan tomorrow. I'll still invade the NeuroStor building. My cloned body will continue to betray me.

The risk is minimal, the reward immeasurable. Why can't I do it? Why can't I just say it?

Crystal opens her mouth to speak, but I decide to go first.

"I want you," I breathe, leaning now just inches from her face.

"Then come take me."

Crystal pulls aside the sheet and makes room for me beside her. The bed is warm and smells like the meadow in my dream. She pulls off her shirt, freeing those magnificent breasts, and I follow her lead. Our arms tangle, pulling each other close. I stiffen between us.

"What's this?" she asks, reaching for me.

Then our mouths together, devouring each other, eager tongues tasting someone new. My hands on her legs, her breasts.

"I love the way your skin feels," I tell her.

My mouth slides down her neck, tracing wet tongue circles. Velvet skin. Nipples erect.

"Honey," Crystal says, "don't stop doing that."

But my tongue has other intentions, and soon it begins tracing circles again, this time down the smooth plain of her stomach.

"Keep going," she tells me.

I do.

And we do.

Heavy breathing now. Loud in my ears.

The fleshy smell of sex.

Sweat nestled in the small of my back, in the cleft of my buttocks, where Crystal's hands cling for purchase.

Grunting. Sprinting toward climax. Pounding a feverish rhythm.

"Oh, *yes*," Crystal whispers.

A question occurs to me, distracting my attention from the task at hand.

"Inside," she says.

"Are you sure?"

"Goddammit, yes."

But for a moment I pause, suddenly aware that I am not alone in here, that my penis is traveling through real estate previously occupied by Rodrigo Batista. Uncountable seconds march by while my erection softens, while I struggle to find a pleasurable friction rhythm, while I try to coax back the suspension of consciousness required to conceal the physical absurdity of sexual congress. I picture Crystal's lips around the helmet of my penis. Imagine myself pushing gently into the dark netherworld of her anus. Call up entire libraries of pornographic interludes that do not include Batista's smug, greasy face. And finally, after endlessly thrusting into her, my erection returns and I begin again to run.

But now Misty's face, familiar and curious, appears to me in a splash of guilt, and I try to push it away, willing myself to believe that she is not my wife, that I have no claim to her and thus am not cheating on her, but my mind struggles to reconcile this information with the knowledge chiseled into my heart, and I begin to soften again, and . . .

And *no*! I will not! I am with *Crystal* now because the desire I feel for her blots out all logic, all reason, and now—

Now I sprint.

Climbing. Reaching. Clenching.

"Oh, Cameron!" Whispers still, but surely loud enough for Cameron to hear.

I explode inside her.

Meltdown.

"Do you think he heard us?" Crystal asks me.

We're lying there together, on top of the sheets, sweat cooling on our skin.

"I don't see how he could've missed it."

"It looks like he's sleeping."

"Like you were?"

"Touché."

I start to say more but don't.

Sometimes it's a crime to break the silence.

I think back to the cabin, to this motel room earlier in the day, and realize how much I've wanted her, how much I still want her.

"Can I ask you something personal?" she says.

"Sure."

"Did this make you feel guilty at all? Did you think you were cheating on your wife?"

"No," I lie.

"Did you think about her while we were having sex?"

"A little," I say. "Even though technically I've never even touched her, my brain tells me Misty is the only sexual partner I've had for sixteen years."

"Oh."

"Were you expecting me to be honest? Or was I supposed to lie and say you were my only conscious thought?"

"No, I was just thinking how weird it must be to have thirty-five years of memories but only be a week old."

"I don't really think of it like that. I can't distinguish between myself and Cameron. If he wasn't here now, if I hadn't seen him with my own eyes, I would have trouble believing this was even real."

"Do you know what that means?"

"What?"

"It means that you better hope this assault on NeuroStor is successful. Because otherwise less than a handful of people will ever know you were alive."

ten

⫶⫶⫶

Bravery was easy to come by when I dreamed up this preemptive strike yesterday, but as I stand here now, about to enter Clay's hotel room at 5:20 in the morning, I have lost that courage. In fact, I am so paralyzed by fear that I cannot imagine how I'm going to walk in there and take a suit, a gun, and a duffel bag full of C4 explosive without waking up everyone.

Clichéd as it might be, I close my eyes and draw in several deep, measured breaths. To my surprise, the smooth breathing stills my hands and slows my heart rate. Clear thoughts step forth to be recognized. The door between our hotel rooms is not locked. It should open quietly and does. I push it far enough forward to step through the opening.

Lee and Randy occupy one bed, while Clay lies by himself in the other one. All of them appear to be asleep.

I creep forward, wary of a creaky floorboard, until I stand above the table where the weapons lie. There are six machine guns and four duffel bags stuffed with C4. Beside the table stands a neat pile of the specially designed firefighter suits.

I am about to pick up a machine gun when Clay shifts in his sleep.

This is never going to work.

After a few seconds I look more closely at him, but Clay still seems to be sleeping. I wait another moment and then reach down again to pick up a machine gun, which is already fitted with a clip. Look back at Clay. His chest rises and falls. Rises and falls, like waves on the beach.

Now I reach for a duffel bag, and—

Clay blows out a dry, hacking cough. He shifts again and then opens his mouth.

"Don't forget the C4," he says thickly.

At this point, I'm afraid my bladder is going to fail me. My eyes dart to the other men in this room: Randy and especially Lee, who is sleeping closest to Clay. But none of them stir.

"Blow up his fuckin' blduuugg . . ."

He trails off. Talking in his sleep.

And after a moment, he starts breathing normally again.

I'm afraid to move, to do anything that might trigger Clay awake, but I can't just stand here either. From the corner of my eye I see a silhouette appear in the doorway to the other room.

It's Crystal. She's giving me the "hurry up" signal.

I pick up the bag of C4, which is much heavier than I thought, and carry it toward the door. Crystal pushes it open and then takes the gear from me.

"You need a suit," she tells me. "And get another weapon, too."

I look back into the room. Everyone is still sleeping, but we're really pushing our luck now. Still, I tiptoe back in and sling another machine gun over my shoulder. Then I reach for a suit. It rustles as I pick it up, but Clay doesn't stir. Nor does anyone else.

Crystal again beckons me to hurry. This is the home stretch. I head for the door, lucky as hell to have completed this first step without a hitch. I don't hear the voice until I reach the doorway.

Clay, from behind me.

"Where are you going?" he says.

But when I turn toward Clay, assuming he'll be propped on his hands watching us, I don't see anything like that at all.

He's still sleeping, of course. I guess I'm not the only one stressed out over the invasion.

"Let's get out of here," Crystal says.

She takes the suit from me as I step through the doorway. I watch

Clay as the door closes, but he never moves. The gap grows narrower and narrower, and finally I can't see him anymore. The latch clicks shut. If he wakes up now, we'll know it when the door flies open.

But that doesn't happen.

"Cameron is waiting for us outside," Crystal tells me. "Let's get the hell out of here."

We walk quickly to Lee's car. Sodium lamps cast pale reflections on its shiny hood. Cameron has the trunk open, and we dump the weapons inside. Then we climb into the car. Crystal will drive, Cameron shotgun, and me in the back.

"Where's the knife?" I ask.

Cameron reaches into the glove box and hands it to me. A utility knife with a stout six-inch blade.

While Crystal turns the ignition, I take the knife and get out. The engine roars into life, and I shoot a look toward the motel, sure that Clay is going to come running. But he doesn't, at least for now.

The van is just a few steps away. I make crisscross stabs in the two front tires—compressed air whistles through the slits, but not too loudly—and then do the same to the rear tires. When I get back into the car, we drive out of the parking lot. I watch the three hotel room doors. None of them open.

We drive for a while without saying much. Last night Clay made us study the route to NeuroStor until everyone could recite the streets and turns by heart, and Crystal drives about halfway there before veering off course. She's going to find an out-of-the-way place to park while I do my work on the computer.

We end up on a street populated by duplexes. Cars are parked against the curb in front of every other house, so Lee's car won't stand out if we have to sit here for a while. Cameron finds the laptop I bought yesterday and hands it to me. I hook it into the portable phone and go to work.

"So you're going to build a Web page with a link that will let people watch this movie we're going to make?" Crystal asks me. "How are they going to find it?"

I look up at her. "I thought you guys were computer experts."

"Lee is the technology guy. I'd be lost without him."

Suddenly it hits me: I'm in charge here. The success of the plan rests squarely on my shoulders.

Of course, this is what I want now. I'm going to derive closure by extracting vengeance from the man who put me here in the first place. And I'm going to do it exactly the way I want.

"In the old days you'd register with a search engine," I explain. "Yahoo, Excite, something like that. Send them information about your site, and they would add it to their database. These days, most search engines crawl the Web looking for new pages to list, using metatags or the content itself to classify them.

"But it takes weeks or months for crawlers to find you, so what we'll do instead is e-mail the URL to as many news agencies as we can think of and let them advertise for us."

"Okay, so let's say they find the site. How are you going to load the movie on there? And will it automatically start playing on their screen?"

"The camcorder we bought yesterday uses a hard drive instead of tape to store video information. It automatically encodes the picture using MPEG-2 compression algorithms, the same standard used by digital television satellites and DVD players. The camcorder will simultaneously record the footage onto its hard drive and broadcast it to this laptop with the FM transmitter. That way, if something happens to me or the camcorder and we can't get it back out of the building, the footage will be backed up on this laptop. Once the file is complete, Cameron will convert it to a couple of Web-friendly video formats and then upload them to the Web site. I'll include Media Player, QuickTime, and RealPlayer hyperlinks for people who don't already have the viewers, and then it'll be as easy as point and click. Streaming video, or download the file and watch it on your computer. Then he'll copy the high-quality, MPEG-2 footage to videotape and send it to a local television station. Once someone watches the tape, our story will be the hottest news in town. No one needs to hijack a satellite to get this on the air."

"We should e-mail the file to all the main news outlets, also," Cameron says. "In case NeuroStor somehow gets your Web site pulled."

"You're right," I say. "We could send it to every TV network.

Newspapers. Magazines. I didn't even think of that. There's no way Batista or King could stop them all."

I spend twenty minutes or so keying in the HTML and then pull up the FM software.

"I've used this kind of program before," I tell Cameron, "and it's easy. To make sure the connection signal is strong, all you have to—"

"Cameron," he says. "I know how to do it."

"Oh. Right. Of course you do."

I glance up at the dash clock. It's nearly 6:30. Someone at the hotel is probably already awake. What am I going to do between now and 8:00, when it will first become feasible to invade the NeuroStor building?

It will take Clay a few minutes to figure out what happened—I can hear him yelling already—and a little longer for them to agree on a course of action. The damaged tires will slow them even more. But if someone is already awake, can I reasonably hope to delay them for an hour and a half? Clay will know someone in town who can bring him a car. Or they could just hot-wire one. It's about twenty minutes from the hotel to the NeuroStor building, but the reality is that he'll be able to get there before I can go in.

I wonder what he'll do. If he'll try to stop me.

"What are you thinking about?" Crystal asks me.

"Problems. I knew this would be difficult, but now I'm starting to wonder if I can pull it off at all."

"Think positive, Cameron. Keep your chin up."

Easy for her to say. After all, this place where we sit is a five-minute drive to my death. Five minutes. Sure, I may have transmission sickness, and maybe I'm going to die anyway, and maybe I'm following through with a choice that will transform my death into something that will undoubtedly be remembered as something important and special. But the reality is that, as angry as I am, as much as the delicious vision of vengeance drives me, I am nothing short of terrified. I could die in approximately two hours. And even that statement, those words, what do they mean? What does it mean to die? Some people don't believe in God, in heaven or hell, in a soul to be placed in these planes of eternal bliss or suffering. Others can't imagine a world without spiritual afterlife. But where do I fit in? Regardless of your beliefs, what do they say about a clone like me who was created artificially less than a week ago?

I guess I can't fault Crystal for trying to improve my attitude. I didn't tell her, or Cameron, the entire story. They think I plan to get out of there alive.

A few minutes later we're standing outside Lee's car as the neighborhood comes alive around us. The people who populate these multiunit homes are a varied lot. A few minutes ago a clean-cut young man wearing a pressed white shirt and fashionable tie drove by in a sparkling Toyota Camry. He waved. A minute later some blue-collar fellow passed us in his dented blue Chevrolet pickup, a cigarette pinched between his angry fingers. Right now I'm watching a thin woman shuffle down the walk toward her morning paper. Something is wrong with her hip, and yellow hair hangs like a spent mop from her head. Her skin is paper white. She walks like she has a hangover. In the middle of the week.

Misty and I lived in a neighborhood like this once. Duplexes are transition living for some, a destination for others. They can be nicely kept or crumbling toward the ground. The benefit to Crystal, Cameron, and me is that with such diverse neighbors, no one is likely to glance at us twice, even if I am standing on the curb, talking to a miniature camcorder mounted on a tripod.

Right now, I'm the only person in frame. Crystal looks into the viewfinder and gives me a thumbs-up sign with her hand. Cameron is sitting on the curb with the computer balanced on his lap. We're taping some initial footage and testing the FM communication system.

"My name is Cameron Fisher," I say. "Six days ago I agreed to help test a machine for NeuroStor, the company I work for, which is based in Plano, Texas. This machine—"

Crystal steps away from the camera and waves me off. "You're not looking into the lens, and you sound like you're reciting something you memorized for school."

"I did memorize it. How else I am supposed to—"

"This thing has fucked you up, Cameron. You just spent the last five days running for your life for Christ's sake. Your best friend was murdered. Don't recite it for us. Make us *feel* what happened. Clay was right: It has to be big for TV."

"We don't have a lot of time for this," Cameron says from the curb. "Can we start again?"

The morning air is wet, and I'm beginning to perspire. Crystal signals for me to start again.

"My name is Cameron Fisher. I'm the victim of a sadistic experiment performed by a corporation you may know as NeuroStor. NeuroStor has invented a machine that can scan an object in one location, digitize it, and transmit that information via satellite to another location, where the digital data is used to reassimilate the object. I have worked for NeuroStor for six years, and its president, Rodrigo Batista, offered me a substantial amount of money to test the machine. I accepted this risk without realizing that he had deliberately misled me regarding the nature of the test.

"Five days ago I entered a transmission portal in Houston, where my body was scanned, and an hour later I woke up in Phoenix. Everything seemed fine at first, but after only a few hours, I began to feel weird. I lost my coordination, my balance. And I realized someone was following me.

"That 'someone' turned out to be a couple of armed security specialists from NeuroStor. Apparently they were watching me to find out if the transmission had altered my body in some way. I was afraid for my life, so I ran from these men. They chased me and killed my best friend, Tom Bishop. NeuroStor wants me dead as well because they plan to market this technology as viable, to use it on unsuspecting citizens. And the most important part of this is that their machine does not simply transmit a person from one place to another. A scan is performed, the digitized information is sent on its way, but *the original remains behind.* NeuroStor's technology amounts to nothing more than a human fax machine. Or nearly instant cloning, however you want to look at it."

I pause here and glance over at Cameron. He has put the laptop on the curb and is ready to join me. In order to prove our story is no hoax, we decided beforehand to do everything in one take. I nod, and he walks into frame.

"This is the original Cameron Fisher. Explain what happened to you, Cameron."

I watch as he relates the events from his point of view. The story NeuroStor told him, the confusion about his transmission, how he never made it to Arizona. The cash settlement.

"Our story may seem hard to believe, but together we are living proof that this machine exists," I say. "I do not have an identical twin, something that can be easily verified by government birth records.

"I will enter the building heavily armed. I will fire if fired upon. I may not leave the building alive. But if what we believe about NeuroStor is true, they must be stopped. At any cost."

I pause for a few seconds and try to remember anything I've left out. When you're not used to being in front of a camera, it's difficult to think clearly.

"This video will resume just before I enter the NeuroStor building. If I am attacked, portions of the program may become graphic. Thank you."

Crystal shuts off the camera.

"We ought to get moving," Cameron says. "By the time we drive over there and get everything set up, it'll be time to go in."

I put on the fire suit—for some reason, wearing it is a whole lot more tiring than carrying it—and away we go.

There has never been a reason for me, a Houston-based expense report auditor, to visit our headquarters. So ten minutes later, as we approach it from the south, I see the NeuroStor building in person for the first time.

The building's architecture is sort of boring, I guess; it's nearly cubic, and the facade is some kind of maroon stone with a lot of tinted windows. The blue-and-white logo, of course, is mounted near the top floor. The ninth floor. That is where I hope to make my stand.

Where I plan to die.

As grateful as I am to Rodrigo Batista for providing this opportunity, this platform on which I may enact my noble purpose, I shouldn't have to. My decision to transmit, to accept this life-threatening risk, was based on imperfect information, *even though better information was available*. In other words, Batista lied to me. Maybe, in some warped way, the jerk thought he was doing me a favor. Or maybe he was deliberately fucking with my life. I may never know why he chose me as a test subject, but I do know that he should not have misled me regarding the nature of the machine. Regardless of whatever else he does with this invention, whether he tries to market the technology for cloning purposes or sell it to a foreign government or whatever other perverted idea he can think of, he lied. He made decisions that should have been left to me. And while I am going through with this assault because it is the right thing to do, because this is the way I will finally do something truly meaningful, I cannot allow Batista's arrogance to go unpunished. Regardless of what his privileged upbringing and Harvard education has taught him, today I am going to introduce him to the idea that his life is no more important than anyone else's. Including mine. He is my symbol, my evil, and I am going to make sure he pays.

Fuck him. Fuck Rodrigo Batista.

Crystal drives us toward NeuroStor in a roundabout way. It sits among a cluster of similar office buildings owned mostly by telecom companies, and I see a large marble sign that tells us we've entered The Technology Center. Traffic is moderate as people head into work. Most of the cars are new and clean. I watch for any sign of Clay, but it will be difficult to spot him in an unfamiliar car. We, on the other hand, will be easy to identify in Lee's Buick.

The dash clock reads 7:49. T-minus eleven minutes and counting. Cameron has configured the laptop for the FM download, and as Crystal finds a place to park, I connect the cameras and the transmitter. The miniature, which is mounted in my fire suit and hidden from view, will do the actual filming. It will send its video feed to the digital camcorder, which will convert the footage into the proper format, and the FM transmitter will broadcast it all to Cameron's laptop.

The nearest building to NeuroStor is owned by a company called LMT Communications. Most of the LMT employees apparently park in an underground garage, but there is a small outdoor lot for overflow and visitor parking. Crystal finds a spot in the very back row. Behind us stands a line of trees, then a narrow asphalt road, then about a hundred yards to the NeuroStor property. Another fifty to the front doors, which are tinted glass like the windows and not locked, according to Clay.

NeuroStor, in spite of their true nature, must pretend to be a normal corporation, which means no armed guards, no bars on the doors, nothing but a normal office building where normal people work. At the very least, then, I'll be able to get inside. Everything will be uphill from there.

"You ready, Cameron?" Crystal asks me.

Fuck Rodrigo Batista. Of course I'm not ready.

"Cameron?"

"I'm ready as I'll ever be."

"Honey," she says. "You don't have to go through with this. I promise you we can accomplish the same thing as a group. Clay is—"

I open the car door and step outside. Pull on the yellow fire helmet, flip down the clear face shield. It's going to be hell running 150 yards wearing all this. I place the MP-5 in the specially sewn pocket, where its butt protrudes about an inch. Quick access but almost hidden. We can't have a fireman running into their building waving an automatic weapon.

Now the duffel bag. I reach and pull out blocks of C4, all strung together with insulated wire. Stuff my suit full of it. In the legs, in the arms, down my back, in front of my chest. The battery goes into another special pocket, the battery and the detonator. Press and let go. This is how I'll kill myself: press and let go.

The driver's side door opens and Crystal flies out.

"Cameron," she says.

I look away, ready to run. I can't stand here all day.

"Honey, you don't have to do this! Why don't you let us help? We can still do it the way Clay planned."

"Crystal, I can't. I have to do it this way."

Now Cameron gets out of the car.

"What's the problem? If he's going to do this, he needs to go now, before someone sees us and calls the police."

"But—"

"Thank you for being my friend, Crystal."

I reach forward to hug her as Cameron watches us.

"Good-bye," I tell her and turn away. Tears blur the NeuroStor building before me.

"Cameron!" she cries.

I take off running, afraid that if I wait any longer, I'll lose my nerve and never run at all.

One thought pushes me forward: Batista.

Heavy breathing. Loud in my ears. Some kind of weird smell. A car goes by on the road just after I cross it.

Now grass. A stone sculpture. Stitch in my side already. Sweat rushes down my forehead. Stings my eyes.

Now asphalt. These boots are heavy. Getting tired already. See the doors. Up ahead. And someone standing near the sidewalk, watching me.

My God, it's Clay.

My hand moves to the butt of the MP-5, but Clay never moves. He just stands there, arms closed over his chest, watching me. As if he knew I was going to be here.

As if this is what he wanted all along.

Did Crystal tell him? Or did he figure it out on his own? Was he awake when I took the weapons from his room?

I keep running. Clay is behind me now. What the hell is he doing?

No time to think about it unless I want to abort. Less than thirty yards to the doors now.

I can't abort. I'm in too deep. I hope this works.

Twenty yards.

Fuck.

Ten.

Rodrigo.

Five.

Batista.

Touchdown.

One set of doors and then another. Now a semicircular desk in front of me. A middle-aged woman with pale, wrinkled skin and long red hair sits behind it. Her eyes grow large like dinner plates, and I am seized by a sudden, uncontrollable urge to apprise her of the situation regarding Rodrigo Batista. That he, in fact, deserves to be fucked. Somehow, however, clear reason steps through the haze of my weary mind and convinces me this is a bad idea.

"Ma'am, the PPD bomb squad is currently trying to diffuse a large bomb at LMT, across the way there."

I point back the way I came. I'm using my deepest voice. Her alarm is obvious.

"We need to evacuate this building immediately. Do you have an evacuation alarm?"

She nods. Doesn't say anything.

"Sound it. And where is the nearest fire escape?"

She points to a set of glass doors.

"Through those doors. Go left. End of the hall."

"Are those doors locked?"

"Yes. You need an employee ID."

"Open them now."

"I can't."

"Why not?"

"I can't open them without leaving my desk, I mean."

"Then get up and open them!"

"Yes sir."

She jumps out of her chair and hurries to the sliding glass door. I follow her and run through as she opens it. Here the floor is carpeted. There are offices on both sides of the hall. Windows reveal desks in some and conference tables in others. I sprint, very tired now, toward the end of the hall. Toward the sign that reads EXIT in red letters.

Now the alarm sounds. A bright, white strobe flashes across the hall. An automated voice barks instructions, but somehow forgets to mention anything about Rodrigo Batista and how he is about to get fucked. Royally.

I reach a door marked STAIRS. Throw it open. Up the stairs. My hand is on the gun but I don't pull it out yet.

I've just reached the second floor when the door there is thrown open. Terror seizes me, and I almost jerk out the MP-5. Four people in professional clothing look at me and then take off down the stairs. Above, I hear another door open. My hand is on the gun again.

"What's happening?" someone screams. A fat, greasy man and a gorgeous woman jog by.

"Bomb," I say, and then, in a nearly inaudible whisper, I add this delicious morsel: "Fuck Rodrigo Batista."

Their legs take them faster.

Third floor. Getting very tired. Think I'm seeing double. Triple, even.

No more people now. This high up they take the elevator. Can't be bothered with physical exertion for a simple bomb scare. I wonder what the board is doing? Did Clay's contact lock the doors electronically even though the invasion is different from what he expected? I'm hoping he did, especially considering that Clay apparently knew about my plan already.

Fourth floor. Fuck. Fifth. Rodrigo. I'm nearly walking now. Batista.

Sixth. My heart is going to explode. I've got to stop. It's so hot. I've got to stop. Three more floors. Fuck. I'm never going to make it.

Gotta keep going. Stop now, never start again.

Rodrigo.

Seventh. Something is wrong. Gotta take a shit. Gotta shit bad. No bathroom here. What the hell?

Batista.

On my way to the eighth when someone opens a door above me. Loud footsteps.

"Hey!" someone yells.

"Bomb!" I yell back.

"There's no bomb! We called the police. There's no bomb at LMT!"

The ruse is up. Time to be honest. One hand goes to the MP-5.

"No. *I've* got a bomb."

Other hand goes into the bomb pocket. Grabs the detonator. This is it. I've got to press it now in case I get shot. Press and let go. They may kill me, but I'll kill Batista. All I have to do is press and let go.

I pull the MP-5 free as I reach the landing between the seventh and eighth floors. Flip the safety and point the gun upwards.

"Put the weapon down!" he screams at me. "Put it down or I'll blow your fucking brains out!"

My chest is heaving, my vision still doubled. God, I've never been so hot in all my life. The man stands above me on the eighth-floor landing. His gun is trained on me, and I have no doubt he's a quicker and more accurate shot than I am. But he's scared, his eyes betray him, and I have the secret, deadly weapon in my hand.

"Shoot me and die," I tell him. "This suit is packed with C4 plastic explosive. I've already depressed the detonator. If I let go now, it's all over."

He stares at me for what seems like an hour. Above him, another door opens.

"What the fuck is going on?" someone yells. I recognize this voice. Too tired to place it.

The guy in front of me doesn't know what to do. He's not sure if he should answer. I nod at him.

"The guy has a bomb!"

I wait for a response, something to break this stalemate. What I hear is so bizarre that, for a minute, I'm sure this is all a dream, that I'm really asleep somewhere, making it all up.

"Cameron Fisher," the familiar voice calls from above. "What do you want?"

My name! The guy knows my name!

I don't say anything. Shocked into silence.

"Cameron, tell us what you want."

"I want to talk to Batista."

"No way. Not gonna happen."

And then I realize who I'm talking to. It's Ivan. The man who chased me through the desert and left me to die at the river. I thought he was dead. But I guess in the NeuroStor world, death is not necessarily the end of the line.

"Fuck you!" I scream. "It's going to happen right now, or I'll blow this building apart! I don't have anything to lose!"

The guy in front of me, on the landing directly ahead, looks as if he just stumbled into the wrong life. His eyes are wide. I can tell he wants to let me by and then get the hell out. I'm willing to let him.

"Cameron—"

"Look," I yell. "I'm coming up now, and you can shoot me if you want. All I want to do is talk to Batista. You can let me talk to him, or you can die right here with me. Your choice."

And everything I just said is true. Now that I'm here, now that I'm hot and tired and seeing double, it's all true. I want to videotape King and Batista, want them to admit their crimes on camera, but at the very least they must die. Particularly Batista. Of course he is going to die. Like I am going to die.

My God. I'm going to die.

It's really going to happen. My body is going to be blown apart, incinerated, atomized, reduced to plasma among the ruins of this building in Plano, a suburb known to many in Texas but scarcely elsewhere, a place that will soon be on the front page of every newspaper in America, a headline on every evening news show, on every Internet news portal. *Terrorism in America! Tragedy in Texas! Science world shocked to learn of major new discovery!* It will all be so sensational, so scandalous. Incomparable watercooler discussion for weeks and months.

I won't be around for any of it. Because there is no story if I don't succeed today.

I begin to ascend the stairs with the MP-5 held out before me. The man on the steps above is not going to shoot, that much I know. In fact, he almost shrinks away as I pass him. Onward I continue, toward the ninth floor. Where the board of directors sit. Where Batista sits. Where Batista is going to be fucked. If he's still there at all.

Bullets. I'm waiting for bullets. Somehow I think Ivan's going to shoot me from above, having decided that my plastic explosive was only a bluff. That I, the weak, lowly accountant, couldn't possibly possess the nerve to commit suicide so violently. Each step forward is further ascension into terror, cringing as I do in anticipation of the agonizing blow to my head, my neck, my torso. The immediate, stinging pain as the bullets rip through me, and the final cathartic terror as my body loses control of itself and releases the detonator, the C4 evaporating me into limbo, into oblivion, into—

"Can't let you go any farther."

I look up, just now having reached the middle landing, and see Ivan standing at the door to the ninth floor. His military-style machine gun is pointed directly at me. My gun is more or less pointing in his direction as well.

"Get out of the way, Ivan."

"Cameron," he says, "we both know that—"

The MP-5 doesn't kick as much as I expect. Bullets tear through the air in short bursts as I finger the trigger. They clatter and bang and echo in the stairwell, detonating chunks of concrete block all around us. The sound is excruciatingly loud. Petals of blood form on Ivan's chest and arms and legs. He is hit everywhere, riddled with bullets, and topples down the stairs, forcing me to step aside as he somersaults toward the landing where I stand. He never even attempted to fire his own weapon.

"Fuck you," I say to Ivan as he lands in a heap beside me. "Fuck you and your boss. Fuck Rodrigo Batista."

Up I go. Toward the ninth. I can see the door from here. Step, step, step. The landing. The door. Throw it open.

Hallway. Empty.

What if he's running away? Leaving the building as I stand here, so that when my thumb grows tired and I decide to die, I will only be killing myself?

I begin to run, and that's when my legs fail me.

One step, I'm moving fine, but for the next one my left leg won't move. My body is positioned to run, angling forward, and without that next push off from my left foot, I careen toward the floor.

The detonator! My God! If my thumb is jarred loose—

I toss aside the MP-5 and hit the ground cringing. Wait for the explosion.

Still alive.

But time is wasting. I struggle to get up—keeping my thumb planted firmly on the detonator button—but something is drastically wrong with my left leg. It doesn't want to move. Somehow I manage to manipulate it with my free hand and use my right leg to push up. This gets me to my feet, and I lurch toward the wall. I inch down the hallway, using the wall for support, until finally enough feeling returns to my leg so that I can limp at a reasonable pace. But I have no idea how long I will be able to go on like this.

Glass walls reveal conference tables, desks, and chairs. Then I reach a set of heavy double doors on my left. The doorknobs are nickel and the plate on the door says BOARDROOM.

I reach for the MP-5 and realize I left it behind when I fell down. Now I have no gun. But I suppose it doesn't matter. Rodrigo Batista is in that room. I can feel him. He will pay and my life will be complete.

242 · RICHARD COX

The surveillance camera is just where Clay said it would be, mounted to the ceiling and pointed at the doors here. I nod my head in appreciation and reach for the doorknob. An audible click as the bolt is electronically released.

The door opens.

I am ready to die. I am ready to face Rodrigo Batista.

Only he's not who I face.

Standing before me, as the door swings open and bangs off a rubber bumper mounted to the wall, is, of all people, Crystal.

Her hair is darker, more brown than blond, and cut several inches shorter, but there is no mistaking the delicate nose, the perfectly contoured cheekbones, the beautiful planes of her face.

She isn't alone. Propped up against a long, oval meeting table is Batista, as much sitting as standing. The superficial grin on his face is nearly enough to make me let go of the detonator right now. Only my constant fear—and now, confusion—keeps my thumb pressed against the button.

I am stunned. My eyes search the room for more versions of Crystal, more clones, as if they might begin to crawl from beneath the meeting table, from behind the two desks at the far end of the room, or even smash through the plate windows nine stories above the Plano suburbs.

I step into the room and close the door behind me. Distantly I wonder if the camera's auto exposure mode will have a difficult time resolving the contrast between the bright sun and the ambient room lighting, but there is nothing to be done about that now.

I also realize that Crystal and Cameron are sitting in the car, staring at the laptop's LCD screen, watching and listening to this stunning turn of events from my point of view. What the hell are they thinking right now? What am I thinking?

What the hell is going on?

"Cameron," Batista says from the table. He shows no apparent interest in rising to greet me. "I have to admit you've impressed me. Very much so, as a matter of fact."

I want to ask questions, to understand what and why and how, but I reflexively answer him.

"I haven't been trying to impress anyone. I just wanted to stay alive."

"And that's why I'm so impressed," he says. "You eluded me for five days. I wouldn't have given you one."

My breath comes in desperate gasps. "I'm glad you underestimated me."

"Cameron," Crystal says, "don't flatter yourself. You didn't do it on your own. If it wasn't for that uncontrollable little *bitch*—"

Batista stands up.

"Honey," he says, moving toward her. "Don't get flustered. It really doesn't—"

Batista puts his hand on her shoulder, and she brushes it away.

"I'm *not*," she says. "I'm not getting flustered. I was simply pointing out—"

"What the hell is going on here?" I ask this loud enough for them to understand just how confused I am. Loud enough so even Crystal, my Crystal, who is watching everything from the car nine stories below, will understand. She must have known about this. *Had* to have known about it, and yet didn't tell me. Why?

Why?

"Well," Batista says. "Surely you must know the situation. She must have told you. Or her little brother. Don't just stand there and play dumb."

"Don't you tell me what the fuck to do, you prick!"

"Jesus," Batista says. "I think you should calm down."

Fuck him. Fuck Rodrigo Batista. I want to let go of this fucking button *right now* and kill him *right now,* but I don't understand what the *fuck* is going on here!

"Why the hell do you have a copy of Crystal? She isn't a soldier, for Christ's sake!"

But even as I ask the question, my answer emerges, clear and dark and hideous.

"Oh, Jesus," I say. "You were fucking her and she wanted to leave, so you copied her."

Batista's smile falters, and, for just the slightest moment, his eyes shift toward the ground. As if he might be guilty. As if he might realize— and this is the first time I have ever witnessed such a thing from him— that something he did is wrong.

"What the hell do you want? Your insurgent outfit figured out how to lock me in my own boardroom. Good for you. And I know that your suit is stuffed with explosive. So what is it that you want? What's it going to take for you to dismantle that detonator so no one has to die? Including you."

Dis*mantle* it? I didn't know that was an option. I didn't—

"Well," Batista asks again. "What's it going to be?"

I recognize this as an opportunity to fulfill one of my objectives, to make sure I get on record their admissions regarding the transmission machine.

"First, where are the other board members? Where is Stanley King? Wasn't there supposed to be a meeting today?"

"Don't bother with the charade, Cameron. I know how you got in here."

"I came in here to confront you and King and whichever board members were present. Where is everyone?"

"You are either a very good actor," he says, "or spectacularly naive."

"What the hell are you talking about?"

"The bolts on these boardroom doors don't spontaneously lock themselves, Cameron. And they don't just miraculously unlock when Captain America appears."

"You are ignoring my question. Where is King?"

"You'll have to ask your girlfriend's brother. The cowboy."

Clay. He means Clay, who stood watching as I ran into the NeuroStor building. Standing there as if he had expected me all along.

"Isn't it amazing how quickly people will betray their own flesh and blood if you wave enough money under their nose?"

The military-grade weapons, the metric ton of plastic explosive—these items weren't free. And perhaps it was more than a little convenient to find a "mole" in the building's security team who could lock Batista in his own boardroom. Does that mean I am a pawn even now? Was I somehow manipulated by Clay—or King, even—into taking on the assault myself?

"It's hard to accept when you're out of your league, isn't it?"

He's trying to distract me. Because it doesn't matter, in the end, whether I made it here on my own or was directed by some unknown entity. I came for Batista, and he now stands before me.

"Forget that. Who are you going to sell the transmission machine to?"

"With this preposterous move by King, apparently no one."

"I don't care about your internal power struggles. Tell me who you were going to sell the goddamn machine to."

"Pakistan is the leading candidate at the moment. Stanley is supposed to be in Islamabad right now. But who the hell knows now what—"

"Why are you selling it to a foreign country?"

"We are seeking foreign buyers, Cameron, because our frightened, puritanical government thinks tampering with genetics is the Devil's work. They'd rather people die than clone certain types of cells to help save them. What do you think they'd do if they learned of a machine that can duplicate an adult human in forty-five minutes?"

"But won't Pakistan or whoever use it to clone their best soldiers? Is that what you want? To help strengthen the military might of other countries?"

"Pakistan needs the machine because they want to replicate three or four of their elite soldiers to help root out terrorist cells in their country. It is very difficult, after all, to produce such well-trained warriors, but with this machine they can produce hundreds. And Israel sees a world of possibilities with multiple clones of their very best Mossad members. The Mossad is considered the word's most select unit of covert agents."

"But—"

"These tiny Middle Eastern countries can't destroy us because of the transmission machine, Cameron. But they are willing to pay a substantial amount of money for it. Billions, in fact."

I pause, uncertain if his words will be enough to seal the fate of NeuroStor. And the notion that King may be behind Crystal's entire operation is really beginning to disturb me, because if that is true, what exactly am I accomplishing here today?

"Is that what you wanted to know?" Batista says. "Can Crystal and I get the fuck out of here and go find that bastard?"

I search for an answer, not really sure what to do. I fully intended to come at Batista with all guns firing, admonishing his arrogance, but somehow that seems out of place now. My initial objective is complete, I have what I need, and anything negative from me will only serve to alienate my eventual television audience.

But there is something else here, something decidedly wrong with this situation. With the clone. How did they get her into the machine when they—

Wait a minute.

"When did Crystal go through the machine?" I ask him.

"Really, Cameron, why don't you—"

"Because if the machine is a cloning device, and if the scan doesn't disturb the original, why did you need me to test it? Why pay me five million dollars when you could have tested it on yourself? Sure, the clone may have come through fucked up, but why would you care about that? You could just destroy it and try again."

Seconds march by as I wait for his answer. I count the beats of time with my pounding heart. The Crystal clone stands at the plate window, trying to appear uninterested in our conversation.

"Congratulations, Cameron," Batista finally says. "It's great that you've finally figured this out. And that you've been maneuvered by Stanley to trap me in this boardroom with your detonator and martyrdom. But in the end, I have to wonder if you aren't still the underachieving loser who sucked my company dry for six years. Isn't this stand, this final hour you've created, isn't it really nothing more than a cry for help? 'I've got a bomb! I'll blow you to hell if you don't tell me why you did this to me!' Poor Cameron. Do you know why I picked you as my test subject? Because you always seemed like a leech to me, a leech stuck to the balls of NeuroStor, a company that thrives on the efforts of Go-Getters and Forward-Thinkers and teammates who can Walk the Talk. I chose you as our guinea pig because it was the only thing you had to offer me, because you were worth much more to me that way even if you died in the process."

"How am I a test subject? Aren't all the volunteers test subjects?"

"Cameron, *you* were the only 'volunteer.' "

"But you said—"

"Come on, you just figured it out. The scanning procedure doesn't disrupt the original, right? At least not until you run the scan wave at nine times normal speed. Did you know that our fastest supercomputer takes over fourteen hours to scan an original and reassemble him using the standard originally developed? That's much too long for interested buyers who might need to generate new clones on an emergency basis. So we developed a new scan procedure, a faster one, but one we feared might disrupt the original. And we couldn't very well risk valuable members of the team to test something that—"

Red. With Batista's admission I see only red. For not only did he lie to me about the nature of the machine, but apparently he transmitted me knowing that something would likely go wrong.

"—and what's funny, Cameron, is that it appears the new scanning procedure doesn't hurt the original after all. Just the copy. And that's because, on top of the increased scan speed, we also compressed the extracted data. Very complex algorithms were designed to perform this procedure, of course, but it appears our calculations need work. Because obviously you've developed significant compression artifacts."

My heart throttles. My eyes see red. I want to say something to him, make him understand the depth of my rage, the power of my vengeance—for singling me out, for picking me alone to suffer at the hands of his monstrous experiment—but just then my left leg begins to shudder. My free hand reaches for my thigh, trying to steady it, but of course this doesn't help. And I feel something wet in there.

"Come on, Cameron. You don't have the courage to commit suicide. Besides, what do you hope to gain by blowing up the building? Is killing me your only goal? I sure hope that isn't the case, because you have to know I've gone through the machine before. I can be reproduced as easily as Crystal was. And if you're looking for more than that, if you think you'll somehow put a stop to my plan, if you think I won't still be able to sell the machine, think again. This office is maintained purely for public appearance. Our nerve center is in Wyoming, far away from here and safe from renegade morality plays such as yours. So what do you say, Cameron? Why don't you give this up while you still have the chance?"

Am I bleeding? Has it begun already?

"Cameron?" someone says.

My hands begin to shake. Sweat spills out of my pores as if I've sprung a thousand leaks. My finger, pressed so firmly against the detonator button, nearly slips. Stops the heart. Starts it again. Can I go through with this?

"I have your wife, Cameron."

Batista again. Red and red. What the hell is he saying now?

"If you blow up this building, if you kill us, I have given instructions to have her terminated."

"Liar," I manage. "I know she's safe. The other Cameron told me so."

"He's going to do it!" a female voice says. A blur as the Crystal clone dashes toward the doors. But they are locked again.

Oh, God.

"Don't be stupid, Cameron. They've been lying to you. Crystal used you to get to us, and her brother sold out to King. This has nothing, really, to do with you. Don't—"

But his shaking hands betray him. His voice, normally rugged and intelligent and confident, has begun to crack. He knows this has everything to do with me. He lied to me and created me and cursed me with terminal compression artifacts. I can't know if he's being truthful about the complex in Wyoming or if he has really been through the machine, but I do not care. The video I have shot, that he apparently knows nothing about, will take care of everything after today. But right now, in this moment, Batista is about to pay, finally, for his transgressions against me, against humanity, against . . . against . . .

Nausea begins to creep into my belly, up my throat, lodging the Ping-Pong ball there once more. Continued sweat in my eyes. Blurred vision.

"She will die, Cameron. Misty will die, do you hear me, do you . . ."

His voice, still going, fades away from me. Rushing air or water or rushing *something* fills my ears. I can't do this. I can't kill myself. My God, Misty, Crystal, what have I done? My hand is on the button, and maybe I could dismantle this, maybe I could rip this detonator from the C4 so the electrical current never enters the explosive, but—

—but this . . . this is death. No hope for survival. And though I knew mine was a one-way ticket, knew that my sprint into this building and climb up the stairs would be the last race I would ever run, I can't seem to let go of the button. And Batista continues to preach to me, his voice rising with each sentence, imploring me to give myself up, to lie down in defeat.

There is enough C4 in my suit to blow the top off this building and kill me instantly, but he doesn't believe I can do it. Batista doesn't believe in me.

Do I believe in me?

Can I go through with this?

God, I loved Misty with all my heart. I still love her, but she is not mine, and I could have loved another, I could have loved Crystal, I don't want to lose her, not when she just came into my life, and I . . .

and

Oh, God, Luke, I could have had a reason to live if you just hadn't died, if you hadn't died as a baby, just a tiny, innocent baby who we loved so much, Luke

Luke! I—

—have this recurring dream. It involves my own death. My funeral, really. The service is held at Hemingford Unity Cemetery, where every so often a body is hidden in the red clay north of Wichita Falls, Texas—

—and I raise the detonator out again, up again, in front of me, in front of Batista, in front of the Crystal clone, in front of the minuscule turnout at my funeral, so they can see what I am about to do, so he can see, Batista, so *he* can see, it's in his eyes, fear, because he is *scared,* he is *afraid,* because he brought this upon himself, arrogance overshadowing reason, his drive to succeed running roughshod over moral principles, and in this moment—

fuck you Rodrigo Batista

—in this moment I know he is just as frightened and unsure about death and afterlife as I am, and I feel pity for the Crystal clone because she did nothing to bring this on herself, she is a copy of the woman I could have loved—

—and much closer now I hear sirens I hear I hear I feel—

—I feel pity for the beautiful clone as I do for myself because death is a mystery to us, because none of us really knows God, and maybe I *do* believe, maybe I *need* Him now, but where is He, where is He, anywhere but here, oh God why am I here, what has become of me, what am I, who am I, no longer Cameron, the division complete, two separate entities, a rift, Misty gone, our relationship disintegrated, the pieces no longer fit, they didn't fit and this is who I am, a corrupted human, the cracks are showing they don't fit together they don't fit the pieces don't fit I love you Misty I love you Crystal I don't want to die but the pieces don't fit and I can't help it I see red I see red I . . . no, I can't do it I cannot self-terminate . . . I see redredred . . . I redredredredred I . . . don't forget my eulogy . . . I see redredred I release the—

epilogue

▐ ▐ ▐

I gasp and Crystal screams as Cameron thrusts the detonator before him. We see everything as he sees it—the camera is mounted just to the right of his forehead after all—and then Crystal grabs me, and I grab the laptop, and together we turn away from the NeuroStor building. One hundred and fifty yards and a row of trees separate us from Cameron and his C4, and still the explosion rocks the ground beneath us and throws the Buick forward. Chunks of concrete and rebar missiles rain down around us. The car is hit once, twice, and the second one nearly punches a hole in the roof.

Then the world around us, already wise to the tension inside the NeuroStor building, roars and screams as engines and sirens converge on this business park in Plano, Texas.

I look down at the laptop and am relieved to find it still running. The transfer is complete. Now all I have to do is end the recording, perform the MPEG conversions, and then begin the e-mails.

"Let's get out of here," Crystal says, her voice wavering.

Slowly, she maneuvers the car through the parking lot. She's crying fiercely, and there is nothing I can say to comfort her, so I don't say anything.

It seems likely that a patrol car might pull us over to ask questions, but the pandemonium has drawn all attention to NeuroStor. Soon we are out of the business park, and in another few minutes we have made it to the freeway.

"Where to?" she asks, now somewhat composed.

"Wait a minute," I say to her. "What the hell just happened in there? What was that business about Clay? And what the hell did Batista mean when he said the scan wave was run at nine times speed?"

"We need to get somewhere safe," Crystal says. "You'll have time to ask all the questions you want later."

"No way. Cameron just went in there and sacrificed himself. I think I deserve answers now, and I want you to give them to me."

Crystal just looks at me.

"Well? Am I in danger now, too?"

"I don't know."

"What do you mean, you don't know?"

"I mean that Rodrigo's scientists weren't sure what effect the altered scanning process would have on the original. So he devised a 'volunteer' program that was nothing more than forcing you to go through the machine."

"One test subject? Me?"

She doesn't answer.

"That's not exactly a statistically valid sample, one person."

"He planned others later. You weren't going to be the only one. But the Israelis and Pakistanis were really after him. He needed something to show them, so he picked you first."

"I don't understand how he thought he was going to pull this off. I mean, what was he going to do with me? Before Cameron ran?"

"To be honest, I don't think he expected Cameron to come through alive," Crystal says. "I'm sure the whole time he just planned to tell you that it didn't work. But when Cameron came through okay, Rodrigo probably decided to watch him for the two days and then kill him."

"*Kill* him?"

"Kill him and then do everything else the same. Feed you the story about how you were okay at first and then showed up at the Phoenix portal with amnesia."

"But if Batista was just going to kill Cameron anyway, why even let him leave at all? Why not keep him in lockdown and run tests on him?"

"Well, if they're going to keep him for two days, they'd have to make it look to Misty and Tom that everything was okay."

"But they still could have kept him locked up and just told me that it didn't work. Since they didn't expect it to work anyway."

"I suppose. But that doesn't sound like Rodrigo, does it? When his experiment actually worked, he probably couldn't resist seeing his precious clone interact with the real world."

I consider this and realize that maybe it's not the easiest thing to guess why a madman like Batista would do anything.

But I still have more questions. "What about that woman? What the hell was she doing there? Obviously you've been through the machine."

Crystal nods.

"She was your clone."

"Obviously she was a clone."

"And you're the original?"

"We're coming up on 635. We need to make a decision on where to go, Cameron. Let's figure that out, and then I'll answer more questions."

"Fine. You have any suggestions?"

"We should obviously turn ourselves in," she says. "But not to the police. The FBI is better for something like this. We'll tell them everything. What do you think?"

"Sounds good to me. But first let's get to a motel room or somewhere I can hook up this computer and get the video onto the Internet."

We spot an Embassy Suites about a half mile ahead. Crystal navigates the car in that direction.

"So now tell me," I say to her. "How is it that you went through the machine?"

"It was an early test. An early human one, I mean. We all knew the original wasn't disturbed by the scanning process, so it wasn't really a risk. This was after I left Stanley, when I was just beginning to see Rodrigo. I wanted to make him happy. He was really persuasive. He made up some kind of crap like the machine would only be successful if it could flawlessly transmit real beauty. Some kind of shit like that. And since there wasn't a risk, I didn't see the problem."

"And when you saw what he did, how he made a copy of you, that's what turned you against him?"

"Sort of."

"Sort of?"

"Stanley found out about Rodrigo and me."

She pauses for a moment. I think I know where she's going with this.

"He killed her. Stanley did. At least that's what Rodrigo told me. Hunted them down one night, followed them to Rodrigo's house in Lewisville, and then broke in when everything was quiet. Caught them in the act, if you know what I mean. Stanley pulled her off the bed and gutshot her. Made Rodrigo watch her bleed to death."

"My God."

"Yeah. And the next day Stanley showed up at the office in Plano with a copy of her."

It hits me then—finally now, in sharp, bright Technicolor—just what the transmission machine can do. All the talk about outfits of super-soldiers seemed so abstract to me, so unabashedly sci-fi, but here is a real-world application that leaves no doubt about the nature of their invention. King and Batista are monsters.

"So that copy was you."

"Actually, no. He assembled me, but I figured out what happened and ran from him. So he had to make another one."

"What . . . I mean, how did you know? When did you realize you weren't you?"

"I was confused at first. When I woke up in the research facility, I thought I had just finished the initial test. My last memory was Rodrigo and Stanley, a bunch of NeuroStor officers, and a few technicians watching me step into the machine. In other words, a whole lot of people were there. But when I woke up, just Stanley was waiting for me. Not Rodrigo, not the technicians, no one. Only a few lights were on. I was frightened. I asked Stanley what had happened, and that's when he told me there had been a terrible accident. He said my original had been killed in another test, and that they had reproduced me from memory. From when I had tested the machine earlier. They had saved me electronically, after all."

We have arrived at the Embassy Suites and now sit in the parking lot as she tells me the rest of the story.

"But I knew he was lying, and I told him that. He asked why the hell I was having an affair with Rodrigo. He wanted to know why I had betrayed him, so I knew right then something was up. I decided to cool off and treat him nicely. Actually, you could say I seduced him. Got him into a sort of compromising position and then just ran. Out the door. Out of Dallas. Lee was an old friend and wanted to help me. My brother, Clay, went ballistic when he found out what had happened, so he offered to help. After a while we had a nice little group who wanted to get back at Stanley, and in the process do the right thing by exposing NeuroStor."

"What about Batista? Didn't you still have feelings for him?"

"I did. Until I found out he had made another copy of me. A copy of me for himself." She closes her eyes for a moment, seemingly overcome by rage. "That's why Rodrigo had to go manage the office in Houston, because he couldn't very well live in Dallas when he and Stanley had the same goddamn girlfriend."

"What about your brother? Why was he standing there?"

"I told him Cameron was going in alone."

"You what?"

"I had to. We could never have taken those supplies without waking him up, and even if we did, he would have intercepted us at the building."

"And he was willing to ditch his whole plan?"

"I'm the one who got him into this. He did it because I wanted him to. And because it would keep me out of harm's way."

"So how did you get King involved in this?"

"I didn't," she says.

"But Batista said your brother—"

"I know," she says, and the resurgent tears signal that she is telling the truth. "I know."

Crystal leaps out of the car then and slams the door shut. She comes back a few moments later with a plastic entry key. In the room I type out a brief description of today's events and the MPEG file's place within them. Then I begin sending the message and attached file to every news agency I can think of: NBC, ABC, CBS, FOX, CNN, AP, et cetera. I even send it to myself in case this laptop is damaged later. Each message goes separately, as Cameron requested. An hour or so later we reach a Dallas FBI field office.

And begin two weeks like none I've ever lived.

The FBI is not as understanding as I'd hoped, at least not at first. It is difficult to make them understand that we are not here to take responsibility for the blast. Finally, we convince them to watch the camcorder footage, first the back story we shot in the duplex neighborhood and then the entire broadcast Cameron made after he left us at the car.

Sympathy from the FBI is not readily forthcoming. The NeuroStor building is a smoldering ruin. The seventh, eighth, and ninth floors are scattered around the building in a three-hundred-yard radius. The northern wall is a pile of rubble on the ground below. Nearby buildings suffered significant damage.

But our video footage intrigues them greatly. They can easily verify that I do not have a twin brother—or any brother, for that matter—and the admissions made by Batista, including his intention to sell the machine to a foreign government, light up the agents' eyes like a winning slot machine.

The FBI is not thrilled that newsrooms across the country already have access to the footage—public broadcast of the video will likely drive other NeuroStor leaders into seclusion—but they are glad to have it, nonetheless.

The MPEG file is first shown by CNN, which plays the footage unedited the same day they receive it. Other networks quickly follow suit, editing various portions of the video for content, and the story quickly becomes the nation's biggest.

Within twenty-four hours all NeuroStor branch offices are shut down. Searches are conducted, producing enough proof to back up our story and Batista's video-recorded assertion.

The following day, at the e-mail address from which I sent the infamous video clip, this message appears:

> My dear sister,
>
> I am sorry. When you asked for my help I knew I needed money, but I didn't know where to get it from. I figured I could play those two against each other. So I decided to go to King. He offered to pay for the operation if I took out Batista, so that's what I did.
>
> Now I'm going after King.
>
> I love you,
> Clay

I pass the message on to Crystal, who takes the news better than I expect. At least she knows her brother made his decision for a noble reason.

Clay and King remain at large.

Misty comes to me in shock, almost unable to believe that for five days a clone of her husband walked the earth. The video footage fascinates her. She asks me about Cameron, but I can tell her little because I really didn't know very much about him. At least not much more than I know about myself.

Crystal is shattered by what happened—by her brother's disappearance and the loss of Cameron—but for a long time she refuses to talk about it. I heard them that night, of course. I heard them make love. They tried not to make a lot of noise, but good sex is never quiet. More than anything it pleased me that Cameron could enjoy himself the night before his assault. I was even a little jealous, if I allow myself to admit such a thing.

When the FBI finally absolves us of any wrongdoing—promising immunity in exchange for testimony against NeuroStor in future trials— the requests for interviews are constant and frequent. Crystal and I sign exclusivity agreements with NBC and are interviewed by them on several different occasions. The news personalities treat us like heroes, especially me, and when I am asked how it feels to have exposed such a huge and dirty secret, I always answer the same way: I didn't do it. *He* did it. My friend, Cameron Fisher.

Concerns about my own health arose after the revelations about the altered scanning procedure, of course, and the media is quick to play up this angle for added suspense. But so far I've experienced no side effects. It worries me that something could arise later, neurological defects like what Cameron experienced, but with no concrete evidence I see no point in worrying about this.

There are also many questions regarding how it "felt" to have a clone. I never really figure out how to answer this one. It was strange, that much is certain, but sometimes I'm a little jealous of him. Because during his brief life, Cameron experienced what I have spent my entire life looking for: purpose. His was a doomed existence, but he knew what he wanted to do—what he *needed* to do, really—and accomplished it. For that I will be forever proud of him.

Luke's death closed my eyes a long time ago. By my own choice, and my own admission, I have ignored life since then. I have taken for granted Misty's love and my own existence in this world. But Cameron's death has convinced me that life is something to be cherished. Perhaps this concept seems simple, a clichéd axiom any intelligent person should understand without question. Perhaps. But a quick examination of our volatile global community reveals that not everyone has reached the same conclusion. I guess all any of us can do is get the most out of every day, treat others with respect, and make sure we teach the same thing to our children.

The last thing I should mention is that Crystal is pregnant.

With Cameron's child.

She was worried at first that her condition as a clone, combined with Cameron's rapid deterioration, might jeopardize the baby's future. But so far, six months into the pregnancy, everything has proven to be perfectly routine. Crystal is healthy, the baby is healthy, and she has decided, after much soul-searching, to allow my wife and me to adopt him. Misty was a little hesitant, of course, to accept into our family a child conceived (in a roundabout way) by her husband's infidelity, but in the end she decided there was no better outcome from this terrible situation than a child for us to love.

A child.

My son.

I'm going to be a father.

It's a strange feeling to have been given such a miraculous blessing. Already I find myself worrying that I will never be the father he deserves. But the best way I can celebrate Cameron's brief existence is to devote myself to making the most of his wonderful gift.

So I will celebrate him.

Celebrate life.

Celebrate his extraordinary life.

author's note

While the science of the transmission machine ultimately goes unexplained, quantum teleportation is, in fact, real. Lee's explanation of EPR correlation is based on actual experiments—which only work, however, if the original is destroyed. The idea of using entanglement to transmit something as complex as a human being (or even a single-celled organism, for that matter) is wildly speculative. A more likely near-future application of quantum teleportation is in the field of computing.

I would also like to acknowledge that Lee's mathematical assessment of scanning a human being—the amount of data such an examination would generate and the resulting problem with bandwidth and transmission technology—was paraphrased from an informal discussion of quantum teleportation by Samuel Braunstein.

Readers in Arizona and Texas may also notice that some geographic locations have been fictionalized. It is all intentionally done.

More information about *Rift* and the author can be found at www.richardcox.net.

about the author

RICHARD COX was born in Texas and currently lives in Tulsa, Oklahoma, where he is at work on his next novel.

Anderson County Library
300 North McDuffie Street
Anderson, South Carolina 29621
(864) 260-4500

elton, Honea Path, Iva,
nder Regional, Pendleton,
iedmont, Powdersville,
Westside, Bookmobile